THE PIT

The Bugging Out Series: Book Four

NOAH MANN

© 2015 Noah Mann

ISBN-10: 1517548721
ISBN-13: 978-1517548728

*Leave in concealment
what has long been concealed.*

Lucius Annaeus Seneca

Part One

Beacon

One

The ocean burned.

"Neil!"

I shouted to my friend before I was even on my feet. He slept below in one of the cramped crew cabins, shut off from the world above. The world Elaine and I had woken to as acrid smoke and an orange glow invaded the *Sandy*'s wheelhouse.

"I'll untie us," Elaine said, loud and quick, but not frantic.

Before I could offer a yea or nay she was heading out, thick blackness rolling in as she opened and closed the door. Neil bounded up the steeply inclined stairs from below a few seconds later. He coughed and covered his mouth,

"What the hell..."

"Yeah," I said, concurring with my friend's reaction.

He came forward in the wheelhouse, standing next to me at the helm as I tried to get the big diesel fired up, the both of us staring out the forward windows at the lake of fire roiling atop the almost glassy sea.

"It's coming at us," Neil said.

He was right. We'd stopped for the night, tying the boat to a channel buoy a few miles off the coast where the Columbia cleaved a border between Oregon and Washington. On the bow, through momentary breaks in the sooty clouds washing past, I saw Elaine, leaning over the forward rail, trying to untie us. Struggling with the vaguely nautical knot I'd made the night before.

"We've gotta get out of here, Fletch."

I looked to the east, to where the coast should stand out clear beneath the full moon. Now I saw only that horrid black smoke and a creeping wave of flame closing in.

"I know," I told my friend.

Thirty six hours it had been since we left. Since we cruised slowly out of Bandon's small harbor and began our journey north. Through night, then day, then into our second night on the water, to the point where we now bobbed on the blazing sea.

"Got it!" Elaine shouted outside, her words ending in a choking cough.

I worked the controls again, pressing the button that would, that should, start the big diesel and get us moving. But still it did not.

"Fletch..."

Neil's gentle urging brought my gaze up as Elaine stumbled back into the wheelhouse, dropping to her knees and gasping for clean air. I glanced to her, worried, but she looked up to me and nodded, her face smudged sooty black.

Then I looked outside. To the water. Huge bolts of orange flame leapt through the smoke, the improbable inferno groping its way toward us as the *Sandy* bobbed now, free of its mooring. Fire closing in. A dozen yards away. Then ten. Then five.

And still the engine chugged uselessly.

"What am I doing wrong?" I asked.

The question was meant for no one in particular. None of us had any experience in a boat of this type or size. We'd fumbled our way through manuals we were able to find before setting out, logs and maintenance reports. We knew the capacity of the fuel tanks—a lot—and the distance we could travel before refueling from the barrels of diesel in the hold—a long way. But we didn't understand the intricacies, the finicky tendencies, of a machine like the one that was about to become our tomb.

"Eric!"

Elaine's scream made me turn. The sight past her, out the rear windows and beyond the stern, *just* beyond the stern, dragged my heart down even further than it had already fallen. Fire billowed there, rolling over the wooden rail at the rear of the vessel.

We were on fire.

"Damn!" Neil cursed, grabbing the fire extinguisher, an act more of desperation than hope.

I held the starter button down hard as my friend scooted past me toward the stairs. He was going out into the maelstrom. Out to fight the unfightable. The world of roiling orange surrounding us left no mistake in the outcome of what he was about to do.

Then, when I wasn't even thinking of it, of surviving, the engine coughed to life, rumbling low and steady in the hull beneath. I felt it in my feet, that wonderful vibration. That incessant noise that had been maddening until we'd shut the engine down for the night after a constant run, taking shifts over the day and a half we'd traveled to this point. Sleeping with the hammering pistons transmitting their captured violence through the structure of the *Sandy* had been impossible. I'd begun to hate the ten cylinder beast.

Now it was the most beautiful thing I could imagine.

"Hang on," I said, with a sudden and certain calm.

I put the *Sandy* in reverse and throttled up, backing us away from the massive wall of fire, but into the smaller inferno bubbling at our stern. Flaming seawater rolled over the transom and onto the deck, sloshing forward toward the wheelhouse as Neil stood in the open door, extinguisher in hand. He yanked the pin from the handle and aimed it into the leaping flames below. A bloom of misty white filled the space behind the wheelhouse as I took us out of reverse and jammed the throttle forward. The diesel spun up, fast, screaming, the bow rising as the propeller chopped at the burning water aft and pushed us forward.

"We're not gonna miss it," Elaine said, staring out the windshield from where she stood next to me.

"I know," I told her, and kept my hand on the throttle.

We only had one chance, I thought. One roll of the dice. Either the wall of flame ahead was thin enough to punch through, or I'd be driving us into a vast sea of flame that would consume us.

"Neil, it's going to get hot," I told my friend.

Behind, he emptied the last of the wheelhouse fire extinguisher onto the aft deck and then tossed it out, closing the door just as the bow sliced into the leaping flames. The run up we'd made, short as it was, had given us speed, if only a bit, and as the *Sandy* drove fully into the inferno I began to count.

One...

The night outside became day. An orange day, swirling and spitting fire at us.

Two...

More fire, thick now, as if we were swimming through it. Waves of it leapt at the wheelhouse. A window to my right cracked, then shattered. Smoke, choking and foul, poured through the jagged opening, stinging my eyes, our eyes.

Three...

It had to end soon. Or we would. But all I could see ahead through the blazing sea outside and the acrid smoke within was more of the hell that enveloped us.

Four...

"Fletch..."

Neil groped at the wall to my left as he spat the words out, coughing. He'd swallowed too much smoke fighting the fire on the aft deck and now was drowning in the black nightmare filling the wheelhouse.

Five...

Black. Not smoke. A different kind of darkness. That was what I glimpsed, what I saw, through the tangle of flames ahead.

"Eric..."

Elaine saw it, too. Open ocean. Dark and flat. No fire.

"We're through!" I shouted, and the boat emerged from the far edge of the inferno, driving into the clear, just water spraying up from her hull as it cut through the nearly still ocean.

Neil gasped and vomited on the wheelhouse floor, retching on all fours. Elaine went to him and helped him up. He dragged a sleeve across his mouth and took in the sight ahead. The wonderful sight of the cold black ocean.

"We've got some fire on deck," Elaine said, calm and driven as she made her way out of the wheelhouse.

"There's another extinguisher below," Neil said.

I shook my head after a brief look aft. We wouldn't need it. Just small residual flames licked up from oily pools spotting the deck and the flat rail. Elaine was already dousing the spot fires with buckets of seawater she was hauling over the rail. I leaned over the dashboard, wondering for an instant if it was even called that on a boat, and surveyed the bow. The spray of clear water had smothered any flames that might have lingered there.

We were okay. We'd made it through. But through what?

I brought the throttles back and slowed the *Sandy* until she sat nearly motionless on the water, then left the wheelhouse with Neil to join Elaine on deck, the last of the fires aboard out.

"What the hell was that?" Neil asked, still catching his breath.

"Over there," Elaine said, pointing past the lake of fire behind us, to the shore beyond.

Smoke rose in the east, a column seeming as wide as the horizon, black and boiling, like a storm cloud spat skyward from an angry earth.

"The river's on fire," Neil said.

He was right. The whole of the Columbia, spilling into the sea from the dead lands beyond, churned orange and yellow, flames swirling against the dawn.

"Are there any refineries upriver?" Elaine asked. "Anything that could spill that much?"

I doubted that there was, but I didn't know.

Neil darted back into the wheelhouse and emerged a moment later, binoculars in hand. He scanned the shore and, a moment later, made plain to us the source of the inferno.

"Oil tanker," he said, then passed the binoculars to Elaine.

"Jesus..."

I looked next, offering no reaction other than the coldly descriptive.

"It's split in half," I said, lowering the binoculars. "It looks like it went broadside into a rock jetty."

Elaine looked again through the optics, focusing in, the pulsing light of raging fires illuminating the destruction spreading from land to sea.

"It could have been aground on that jetty for months," she said. "Or longer."

How many boats, large and small, drifted upon the waters of the earth's oceans, lakes, and rivers? Their mooring lines rotted. Crew dead. Thousands, it had to be. Just riding the currents until a hunk of land ended their journey.

But what were the odds that what we'd just survived would happen after we tied up for the night? The beached and battered vessel had been ripped open, its metal hull grinding against stone. A spark rose. Then a flame. All it took then was the rushing current of the Columbia to spread the blazing waters out to sea. Out to us.

Was it a thousand to one? A million to one? That such an event would occur not in the days before, nor in the days after, but precisely when *we* were in the path of the fire...

I did not believe in such things, but a small part of me did wonder, if only in passing, if it might be an omen. Yes, we'd come through the fire. Through *this* fire. But was it only a harbinger of more tests, more travails, which lay ahead?

"Let's get out of here," Elaine said, passing the binoculars to Neil as she climbed back into the wheelhouse.

A few seconds later the engine rose from its chugging idle as she advanced the throttles. Neil took a step toward the wheelhouse, then stopped, looking back to me.

"You coming?"

I said nothing for a moment, still staring toward the origin of the blaze.

"Fletch?"

"Yeah. I'll be there in a minute."

I needed that minute, my friend sensed. He didn't push the question, or wait for me to follow, joining Elaine by himself and leaving me alone on deck.

Alone...

That was how I'd begun this new phase of life. As the world spun toward its blighted oblivion I'd hidden myself away at my Montana refuge. Others had come into my life since then. Del. Neil. Grace and Krista. Then we'd moved on to Bandon where Martin and Micah entered the picture. And Burke. And many more in that seaside town.

Including Elaine.

For months now the world that I had come to know on a solitary basis had been boiled down to just her, and Neil, and me. We'd set out on a mission fueled by hope. A mission to find whether there was truly a way to overcome the blight. And we'd found that there was.

But finding that was no end. We were on the move again.

Alone...

I'd thought for a while that I would spend the remainder of my life in that state of singularity. My friends gone. No special person to journey with me through this new and bleak wilderness. But looking to the wheelhouse I could just make out the silhouettes of those who were proving that early fear wrong.

My friend stood there. My love, as well. Both looking forward. To the way ahead. To the way we all had to go.

Together.

Two

"White. White. White."

Neil turned the boat's radio off and settled into a seat at the rear of the wheelhouse, a few feet from where Elaine stood at the controls. There would be no more tying off and bedding down for the night below deck. Not after what had snuck up on us while we rested. One of us would be at the wheel at all times with the others resting nearby until we reached our destination.

Ketchikan.

That was the point on the map we were aiming for. The first major port one would reach in Alaska heading north from the lower forty-eight. If those we knew, and loved, had been spirited off to the great white north, Ketchikan, a lumber town turned tourist trap for cruise ship passengers, was a logical place to think they'd been, or passed through.

Or passed by.

I had to remind myself of that. There were hundreds of points along the vast Alaskan coast where those traveling by sea could stop. Maybe thousands. We were sailing in the blind, even more so than when we'd left Bandon in search of salvation in the form of a tomato plant glimpsed over the airwaves. Micah had at least given us a general destination then, Cheyenne, but here all we had were two letters scrawled hastily on a wall—*AK*.

"Sorry," Neil said.

I shook off his apology. He hadn't woken me. I'd been trying to catch some sleep as we cruised north in the dark, twisting my body awkwardly into another of the wheelhouse chairs, but drifting off had been an elusive desire. The sound of the boat pushing through the light chop, which might have soothed, did not. I was not a creature of open waters. Land, terra firma, was what I knew, and where I belonged.

"I just have to listen once in a while," he explained.

We'd been gone less than two days, and in that short span I'd caught him hovering over the radio at least a dozen times. Listening for a few minutes, then letting the reality of the situation inform his decision to abandon any monitoring. That he kept turning it back on belied that most precious resource, one which he had preached to me in the earliest stages of the blight's march across the planet—hope.

There might be some transmission breaking through, as had come from the Denver television station whose satellite feed I watched from my refuge. The White Signal could simply cease overwhelming the airwaves and stop broadcasting, just as the Red Signal had abruptly ended. There was always those possibilities. Or something we couldn't yet imagine.

"What do you think happened, Fletch?"

My friend looked at me, not pained, and not overwhelmed by the separation from Grace and Krista, but confused. That they, and a whole town, could up and disappear, to God knows where, with no time or opportunity to leave anything other than the most cryptic of messages behind, was hard to fathom.

"I wish I had some solid guess," I said. "But I don't."

"Martin wouldn't have left," Neil said. "Not voluntarily."

"No," I agreed. "He wouldn't."

He would not have left the son he'd only recently buried. Not in a thousand years. Not at the point of a legion of bayonets. Which made me fear that the bloodstain we'd found in the meeting hall could easily have come from him. Because of his resistance to some command to leave. At the hands of whoever might have been behind such a directive.

"It had to be military," Neil suggested. "Taking the whole town, the sentries, everyone. It had to be overwhelming force."

"Or surprise," I countered. "Or both."

The question beyond that which clearly nagged at my friend was *which* military? From *what* nation? Or was the force aligned with some self-styled ruling entity?

"Neil, we'll know for sure when we find them. Everything else is just guesswork."

He nodded, knowing I was right. But my assurance did not erase his worry or his wondering. It only forced it into the quiet place within, where it gnawed at him as the ocean rustled around us.

"Fletch," he said, hesitating as he looked across the space to where Elaine stood at the controls of the *Sandy*, keeping us moving.

"Yeah?"

He stared at her, then looked to me again. In the dim mix of moon and starlight drizzling through the wheelhouse windows I saw his expression. And I saw it change, shifting fast, almost too fast, from a mask of uncertainty to a quick, oversure smile. Like a camera flash going off. There and gone.

"Nothing," Neil said.

Whatever thought it was that had compelled him to seek some conversation with me, it was gone. Forgotten or buried.

I suspected the latter.

Neil pulled his body into the seat and turned half away from me, closing his eyes and seeking that slumber which eluded me. I wondered while I watched him what it was he'd wanted to say. Something about Elaine, I imagined, considering his brief focus on her at that moment. Was he about to express some doubt to me about her? About the bond, the love, that had developed between us?

No. He wouldn't. He'd expressed the exact opposite of that to me on several occasions since Elaine and I had breached whatever barrier had kept us apart. His opinion would not have shifted a hundred and eighty degrees. Not this soon, and not without reason.

It was something else.

If it was important, he would tell me when the time was right. If it was not, it wouldn't matter. That's what I told myself.

But still I wondered. For a while. The thought, the curiosity, faded as we pressed north, and by the second day after Neil had sparked that wondering, it was gone. Out of my mind as we kept moving. Slowing not a bit.

Until we saw the graveyard.

Three

The hulking ship lay upside down on the water, capsized fully, rust red belly swamped each time a wind wave rolled in past the islands. Its rudder and the tip of one propeller blade rose a few feet above the surface of the gently curling sea. Stern high was how she had come to rest, deck planted solidly on the sloping shallows below. A good storm might shift the dead vessel further down that submerged incline, burying her forever, surviving microorganisms in the briny ocean attacking every bit of exposed metal. Consuming what remained over the millennia to come.

"There's more ahead," Neil said. "A lot more."

I slowed the *Sandy* and brought us alongside the capsized ship, creeping forward. I looked ahead, to what Neil was seeing through the binoculars. Even unaided I could make out what he was seeing in the day's waning light—lines of ships, large and small, sunk and scattered along the shore to either side of the Hecate Strait. Freighters and fishing boats and bulk carriers abandoned upon the unforgiving shores of Graham Island to the west, and those splits of land to the east.

"Does this look random to you?" Neil asked.

"No," I answered.

"That hull's been breached," Elaine said, pointing through the wheelhouse windows.

She was right. The capsized ship we were cruising slowly past had a pair of jagged holes in her bottom. Folds of thick steel were peeled outward, like the blooming petals of some rusty flower.

"From inside," I said.

Neil lowered the binoculars and looked to the ship we'd pulled alongside. Just one in a massive nautical boneyard. Where craft after craft had been sent to their final resting places with intentional violence.

"She was scuttled," he said. "They all were."

Intentionally sunk. But not just that. They'd all had their seaworthy lives ended along the shores of the strait, out of any lanes that ships might still pass through. Keeping the way ahead clear.

But the way ahead to what?

"I think we're on the right track," Neil said.

I nodded and steered us away from the capsized freighter. Back into the strait. None of us said anything about the most obvious part of what we'd just come upon. Obvious and welcome. Something good because of its absence.

Bodies.

Neither beached and bloating, nor floating upon the water. There was no sign of death. No equivalent to the bleached bones we'd tread upon on our trek across the wastelands to Cheyenne. Whatever souls had been upon the sunken ships, they were not here. They had gone on.

That gave us hope.

Night came. The water ahead sloshed black in the darkness. To either side, land rose as shadows that blotted out stars low in the sky. My shift at the wheel was nearly up. Fifteen minutes more and it would be my turn to make an attempt at sleep. But that was not to be.

Two minutes after I turned the wheel over to my friend we saw the light.

Four

We should have only seen night. Instead, we saw a speck of white, off to our left, sweeping across the water and land in the distance. A spoke of bright, almost blinding white that revealed features along the shore. Low, craggy hills. Shallow, jagged cliffs.

And a short jetty reaching out into the sea.

"A lighthouse?" Elaine wondered aloud, more disbelief than doubt in the question she posed.

I looked to Neil. He brought the throttles back and turned us toward the origin of the beam. Toward land.

"A lot of these were automated," he said. "Almost all."

"And it would still be operating?"

The doubt in my question was clear. No, it wouldn't. It couldn't. Even the most automated machinery, save the satellites that hung invisibly above in orbit, required maintenance. Care. Repair. Gears needed lubrication. Wires corroded from the salt air. Bulbs burned out.

What shone in the darkness before us shouldn't be.

"I see someone," Elaine said, binoculars zeroing in on something. "Just a shadow, but they're there."

I lifted my smaller pair of binoculars and focused in through the windshield, scanning the looming structure as its light swept across my field of vision, drizzling a glow to the ground at its base. That was where I saw what Elaine did. A figure in silhouette. A man. Standing there. Waving his hands back and forth above his head.

Beckoning us.

"Mary Island," Neil said, glancing away from the ship's controls to a map we'd taped to the wall above the side window. "There's a lighthouse marked on here."

Elaine looked to me, uncertain.

"Why would anyone be set up on an island?" she asked.

"Same reason Bandon kept its food on a ship offshore," I suggested. "Isolation and protection."

"Announcing your presence with a big ass light isn't exactly hunkering down," Neil countered.

He was right. But so was I. Both of our estimations were made in the blind, however. The truth, I suspected, would only come from the man in the shadows waving us toward shore.

* * *

We tied the *Sandy* off to posts rising from the makeshift dock in a cove out of view of the lighthouse and looked toward land.

"I don't see him," I said.

"I don't see anyone," Elaine added.

"I see something," Neil said, gesturing toward the rocky shore to our right.

We looked, the high sweep of the unseen light spinning beyond the terrain drizzling enough from above to reveal a boat wrecked on the rocks. It was small, with an outboard motor swinging free against the gentle waves washing in from the channel. The same waves that had swamped it, submerging its left side, the opposite still visible above the water's edge.

"That thing took some fire," Elaine observed.

Its wooden hull, dirty white, was marred by darker splotches. Bullet holes.

Neil stepped past us, his AK at the ready, even more so than a moment before. We'd come off the boat with our weapons and packs. Circumstances had taught us to always be prepared to leave at a moment's notice, with everything necessary to survive on our person. If the *Sandy* should blow up as we transitioned from dock to solid ground, we could still survive. For how long wasn't entirely up to us.

"I have movement," Neil said.

Looking past him we saw the same. Motion. A certain frenetic quality to it. An urgency. That could accurately be said about the slim man running toward us down a rocky path that ended at the dock.

"Hold it right there," Neil told the individual, bringing his AK up to punctuate the command.

The man slowed, then stopped, the light spinning above beyond the terrain scarred with dead woods and toppled trees. His sunken gaze regarded us with utter surprise.

"What the hell are you doing?" the man asked us, breathing fast. "Are you crazy?"

I gripped my AR just a bit tighter and stepped past Neil. His gaze, I could see, was sweeping the darkened shore to either side of the dock. Elaine, too, would be doing the same, scanning for threats. This could be nothing more than an ambush. A performance to lure us to a place of vulnerability, not unlike the sirens of mythology beckoning ships to their demise on jagged shores.

"You turned on the light," I said, my own gaze drifting on and off the man, fearing a nasty surprise that might emerge from the shadows.

But all there was was him. This scrawny stranger in something that had once vaguely looked like a military uniform. Now it hung threadbare from his frame, shirt and pants mismatched, boots nearly worn through and stained with something dark.

I activated the weapon light attached to my AR and shone it at his feet, his soiled boots shining with splotches of wet red.

Blood.

My AR came up again, harsh light aimed right between his eyes.

"Can you ease off, pal?" the man requested.

But I didn't. I kept the light where it would nearly blind him. Where it would keep him off balance. At a disadvantage.

"Who are you and why did you turn on the light?" I pressed him.

"I'm Jeremy."

I glanced to Neil. He nodded and moved past Jeremy, off the dock, to the path the man had come down, moving a dozen yards or so up the rocky trail, to a position of better cover.

"Are you military?" I asked Jeremy.

He nodded lightly. A half confirmation at best.

"I was," he said. "I might still be. Who the hell knows anymore?"

That answer didn't suffice. The look on my face spoke plainly to that.

"Private Jeremy Ebersol," he said. "Okay? Now what the hell are you doing here?"

Again I waited. Another question hadn't yet been answered.

"I saw you on radar, okay? I turned on the light because I thought you were stragglers."

Elaine stepped close. Standing next to me, her MP5 aimed at the dock beneath our feet.

"Stragglers?" she asked.

Jeremy reached up and combed his fingers through his wispy hair, shaking his head at the mild interrogation he was being subjected to.

"Everyone's already come through," Jeremy tried to explain. "At least I thought they had. When I saw you..."

"People have come through here?" I pressed him. "People from down south?"

He puzzled at that question, as if the answer would have been self-evident to even the least intelligent of our species.

"You got the signal, right?" he asked.

"The White Signal," Elaine said.

He nodded, still confused that we were failing to grasp what he was trying to get across.

"You got the signal," he repeated. "You had your directions to here, so..."

I shook my head at the young enlisted man. He'd probably joined up just before the blight took hold, planning on four years, some G.I. benefits, and maybe a free beer or two over the years to thank him for his service. Instead he got this, whatever *this* was.

"We don't have any directions," I told him. "No one sent us here."

His gaze narrowed down, then began to swell, worry rising. His gaze shifted to our weapons and he took a step back.

"Look, I'm just supposed to log the channel transits," Jeremy explained, a pleading in his tone and manner. "I'm a nobody."

"No," I said, reaching out with one hand and grabbing him by the collar. "You're the somebody who's going to give us answers."

I spun him around and began walking him off the dock, Elaine just behind. We only made it to the transition from rickety wood to solid land. That was where Neil stopped us as he jogged down the path he'd moved up.

"There are bodies up there," my friend said.

I glanced to Jeremy's stained boots, then looked to my friends.

"We have our first answer," I said.

Elaine grabbed the young soldier's arm and pulled him from my hold, shoving him past Neil with the butt of her weapon.

"Get moving," she said.

Jeremy turned toward us, hands held in front, palms open in some sign of surrender.

"Move," Elaine repeated.

Finally the young man nodded and led us up the path.

Five

They lay in a neat row outside the blockish base of the old lighthouse. Five of them, in full camouflage, the pattern vaguely familiar without allowing me to know, with any specificity, from where it originated.

Neil was not so limited.

"Russians," my friend said, staring down at the bodies, each mangled by bullet holes and signs of explosive trauma. "Elite troops."

Elite, possibly, if my friend was correct. But the wasting frames beneath their uniforms belied the harsh truth that, wherever they'd come from, they were poorly supplied.

"I saw a demonstration they put on while I was on assignment in St. Petersburg," Neil said. "A lot of door blowing and dummy shooting. House clearing stuff."

It was easy to forget sometimes what we'd all done and experienced in the old world. Working for the State Department, my friend had trotted the globe, sampling local fare, experiencing whatever his hosts decided to present. Things such as what he described were not out of the ordinary, I imagined. Blowing things up with some precision gunfire added for good measure was an easy, and impressive, show to put on.

But here, it appeared, they'd met their match.

In this guy?

I wondered that to myself as I focused on the young private.

"They hit us just before first light yesterday," Jeremy said, looking over the fallen soldiers with a mix of sadness and dread. "They got inside before we got the upper hand."

Conical impact craters from bullet strikes and scorch marks from explosions marred the thick walls of the base structure, evidence of the fight he'd described. Or some fight.

"Who's we?" Neil asked.

Jeremy tipped his head toward the lighthouse door. Elaine stepped that way, careful, and nudged the door open with the muzzle of her MP5. A quick flick of her flashlight revealed the interior for an instant. Just long enough to see what she then reported to us.

"Bodies in here," she said. "Crappy uniforms like his."

"We hit some of them from the tower," Jeremy said. "The rest my buddies nailed with grenades as they got through the door. Some of them caught the blast, too."

Elaine glanced back into the interior of the lighthouse, then looked to me. *Really* looked to me. Trying to share some understanding with her eyes. A warning maybe.

"Private Ebersol," Elaine said, joining us again around the young soldier. "Where did the Russians come from?"

He shrugged and shook his head, just a kid beaten down by circumstance and what the new world served up to every survivor each and every day they still drew breath.

"We heard rumors from command that they'd hit the Aleutians a while back and were working their way down the coast," Jeremy told us. "Someone said they were trying to get to the lower forty-eight."

Elaine soaked in what the young man was sharing. Eyeing him with some practiced analysis. Drawing on the requirements of her old self. The one where the FBI credentials she still hung onto put her in situations just like this. Questioning someone.

As she would a suspect.

That she was doing so registered quietly with me. I made no overt moves, simply letting my finger slide closer to the trigger of my AR. At the ready. For what I didn't know. At the moment, she was in control.

To my left, Neil hadn't yet picked up on what Elaine was doing. On the doubt she was expressing with subtle shifts in her manner. He was focused very intently on the mangled bodies at our feet.

"Your buddies in there saved your ass," Elaine said.

Jeremy nodded, grateful, almost teary.

Elaine, too, nodded. An understanding rising. I saw her fingers flex tight around the MP5's grip.

"They meant a lot to you," Elaine continued. "You were stationed here together. You get to know people pretty good when you're isolated like this."

"Yeah," Jeremy confirmed, emotion ready to well.

"You guys were all close," Elaine said. "You were friends."

"We were."

Jeremy's gaze settled toward the ground. Elaine glanced to me, just a quick look, some intensity in the brief connection. Some wariness.

Then she fixed hard on the soldier trying to sell the tale.

"Jeremy..."

He looked up from the ground to Elaine.

"If they were such good friends, why are they lying inside in a bloody heap while these invaders are arranged out here like heroes?"

For an instant he puzzled at the question. An instant in which Neil finally caught the gist of Elaine's doubt and brought his AK slowly up.

It was in the next instant when all hell broke loose.

Jeremy, whose real name was most likely something akin to Yevgeny or Igor or Vladimir, reached fast behind his back and drew a long, dark knife from beneath his shirt. A combat blade meant to be as intimidating as it was deadly. Elaine stepped back first, Neil and I following suit, putting a few yards distance between us and the now obvious imposter. He swiveled his body, tracking each of our movements, shifting the blade between us, keeping us at bay.

"You're outgunned," Neil said, stating more than the obvious. "Put it down."

'Jeremy' made no move to acquiesce, his gaze sampling the three muzzles directed squarely at him.

"It's over," I said.

"All we want to do is talk," Elaine said.

Our journey north was mostly in the blind. We'd stopped at Mary Island hoping that the light which had called us to shore might mark a place where answers would be found. Guidance. Now more than ever I believed that to be a distinct probability. That belief was borne of the concocted tale Jeremy had told. A lie sprinkled with truths.

He'd spoken of people 'from down south'. And of logging 'channel transits'. Whether the remainder of his story, including the Russians advancing down the coast, held any basis in fact, I didn't know. It might. But what he'd shared about people from south of here heading north fit almost perfectly with what we'd believed had happened to those who'd disappeared from Bandon. The symmetry was undeniable. And Jeremy's knowing that, particularly if he was some part of this unit of Russians who'd assaulted the island, made perfect sense. For one simple reason.

Intelligence.

You wanted to know as much about a target before attacking it. That was a concept easy to grasp even for one without extensive knowledge of military operations. If possible, you'd want to infiltrate it. Learn its weaknesses. Its strengths.

"Drop the knife," Neil commanded the young man again.

He did nothing. He said nothing.

But he *had* said things. In perfect English. Just how an infiltrator would be expected to speak. To not draw suspicions.

"You snuck in here," I said to him, my AR slightly lowered. "You got inside the perimeter. Probed the defenses."

It was all metaphorical, what I was suggesting. There was no perimeter but the meeting of land and sea. No obvious defenses other than the sheer bulk of the lighthouse and its base structure. But he knew what I meant. He knew that I knew. That *we* knew. And, in a way, what I'd just said to him was the impetus for what happened next.

For what he chose to do next.

With a swift, clean motion he brought the knife up. None of us fired because the blade did not shift toward us. It moved toward *him.* Its sharp, stained edge came to the far left side of his neck and carved deep into the flesh as the committed young soldier drew it quickly around his neck, slicing a bloody smile a few inches beneath the real one.

"Christ!"

Elaine's exclamation sounded at almost exactly the same instant that the young soldier crumpled before us, the sudden, rapid loss of blood sapping his consciousness. His ability to control any motor function whatsoever ceased as the wet red tide spilled out of him through the hideous wound.

"Why the hell would he do that?" Elaine asked, almost shaken by the grotesque end unfolding before us.

Neil stared down at Jeremy's still body. A slowing flow of blood bubbled from his severed jugular. His heart was barely going through the motions now, no longer able to sustain the gush that had erupted in the first seconds after the blade sliced into and through the vein.

"He didn't want to talk," Neil said, confused as he looked to us. "Why?"

"Training?" I half suggested. "Not supposed to be taken alive?"

It was a thin possibility. I knew that.

"It doesn't make sense," Neil said.

"That and more," Elaine added.

We focused on her now.

"He turns on the light and draws us to shore," she recounted. "Then he meets us at the dock with nothing but a knife tucked in his belt? There are Kalashnikovs scattered all over here."

She was right. Next to the carefully arranged row of bodies were two distinct piles of weapons. AK-47s that had seen battle, here and elsewhere by the look of them. Yet 'Jeremy' hadn't armed himself with any of them. Where he could have met our approach with devastating gunfire from cover along the shore, he instead welcomed us. As if he'd been expecting us.

Or someone else.

My heartbeat quickened at that realization.

"He was expecting friendlies," I said. "His friendlies."

Neil understood now, too.

"A follow on force," he said.

I nodded.

"To occupy after the assault force has neutralized the enemy," I said.

"That's why he turned on the light," Neil said. "And why he offed himself. He couldn't take the chance that we'd get that out of him."

Elaine, too, was coming up to speed on the situation we were now facing.

"If that's true," she began, "then they're still coming."

They...

How many that represented we had no idea. In the world as it was, certainly no large units existed to maraud the coast of Alaska and its myriad of islands. Then again, it wouldn't take mass numbers of troops to do so. They'd taken this hunk of rock and its lighthouse at the cost of a half dozen dead. A price had been paid, to be certain, but they'd captured their objective. For a while.

It now belonged to us. And that scared the hell out of me.

"We've gotta get back to the boat," I said.

"And far away from this place," Elaine added.

Elaine and I were turning away from the collection of bodies and toward the path to the dock when we noticed that Neil was not. He looked to us and slowly shook his head.

"We can't," he said.

"This is not the place to make a stand," I told my friend.

He didn't try to counter my statement of logic. Instead, he gestured toward the doorway Elaine had peered through just moments ago.

"We need information," Neil reminded us. "If there were transits past this island, it might be them."

Them...

Grace. Krista. Martin. And hundreds more. If they'd cruised past Mary Island on whatever craft had taken them from Bandon, that movement could very well have been recorded here, as 'Jeremy' had mentioned. Because *this place* had to have been maintained as an operational station for a reason.

"He's right," I said, looking to Elaine.

She wasn't going to fight the choice we were making. But it was plain on her face that she wasn't happy about it.

"We'd better do it fast," she said.

I glanced upward, to the light spinning slowly atop the tower, its beam less brilliant than when we'd first spotted it from a distance.

"Find a way to shut that off," I told Elaine. "Then see if you can get to the top."

"Observation post," Elaine said, understanding. "I'm on it."

We moved toward the door together. Then through, weapons ready. We didn't expect any firefight. That action seemed certain to have preceded our arrival. But we'd faced our share of surprises on our journeys together, and being prepared to face any of them had never served us poorly.

And now, once again, we were ready to fight, but hoped that we could get done what needed to be done, and depart this treacherous rock, before that fight came to us.

Six

A single light, its enclosure shattered but bulb miraculously still burning, shone in the large room at the base of the lighthouse tower. Just enough to reveal the blackened and bloody mess left from the battle for Mary Island.

The sight slowed us for just an instant. One couldn't look upon fallen soldiers, young and brave, crumpled near windows, limbs severed, charred from blasts in the confined space, without pausing, if only to take a breath and say a silent prayer.

"I'm heading up," Elaine said, aiming herself for the stairs off to the right.

Above, a motor groaned, struggling, the mechanism that turned the light at the top of the tower sounding as though it was on its last legs. Or drawing some final surge of power from whatever source fed it.

"Over there," Neil said as Elaine disappeared up the stairs.

I looked to where my friend was pointing, our weapons now slung. A pair of old metal file cabinets on the far side of the room, toppled and dented, had caught his attention. And now mine. Particularly with several drawers open, the contents of each spilled, pages and pages of forms and documents mounded close and scattered by the blasts which had decimated the space.

Neil hurried to the cabinets, stepping around and over the remains strewn about.

"We're back in the age of paper," he said, crouching near the literal data dump.

I joined him, the both of us sifting through the documents. Some were pristine, as if they'd just been dropped by a clumsy courier. Most were not. Splatters of blood dotted many of the handwritten sheets. Some were perforated by shrapnel.

"Here," Neil said, holding a single sheet out to me. "Look at the date."

I did. At the top of the page a date was noted in pen.

"That's six days ago," he said. "And look below."

Again, I followed his direction. There was a name. The name of a ship.

"The *Vensterdam*," I read aloud.

Neil pointed to the description and notations further down the page.

"A cruise ship," he said.

I struggled to read what came next. The skim of crimson spray had mostly obliterated the words.

"Hey!"

The shout came from above.

"The tower light is on a battery bank!" Elaine reported, her voice ping-ponging down the switchback staircase. "When I pull this I think you're gonna lose lights, too!"

Neil and I both took our flashlights out.

"Go for it!" I shouted toward the stairs.

A few seconds later the already dim light went black, and the grinding sound from above spun quickly down to silence.

"We're dark!" Neil told her. "You see anything from up there?"

"Nothing!"

It was the only reply we wanted to hear. And we hoped the situation it represented wouldn't change.

"Put your light on here, too," I told my friend.

Neil shifted the beam of his flashlight to join mine on the obscured portion on the page, the angle and convergence of illumination revealing enough detail that I was able to make what I believed was a fairly precise guess at what it said. I looked up to my friend before I gave voice to what I'd seen.

"One hundred and fifty from Yuma colony," I said.

Neil processed that for a moment.

"Yuma?"

That he was perplexed was clear. So was I.

"A hundred and fifty miles from the west coast," I said.

"Colony," my friend parroted. "That sounds a lot like—"

"Like Bandon," I finished for him.

That was exactly what our seaside Oregon village had become. A colony of survivors. Now, apparently, we had confirmation that there were others.

We weren't alone.

"If they came through here…"

Neil had barely finished the statement when he was, again, digging through the papers. Looking almost madly for the same kind of document that would tell him, that would tell us all that our friends and loved ones had actually passed by here.

The 'where' of the larger question still lingered. A place of destination. But only until I scanned the rest of the page and saw a final notation near the bottom.

"Neil…"

My friend looked as I pointed to a single word prominent in the narrow beam of my flashlight.

"Skagway," he said, reading it, some fast mental math following. "That's three or four hundred miles north of here. Way past Ketchikan."

Probably closer to three hundred and fifty miles, I knew. Hours and hours studying the maps of our planned route along the Alaskan coast allowed me to narrow down his estimate. Still, whatever it said, that was where the

Yuma group had been headed. Not necessarily where our friends had been taken.

Taken...

That word, that term, and its inherent nefariousness, rang sour in my thoughts. None of this had been voluntary. I didn't want to let my mind conjure what might have awaited them there.

"Got it," Neil said, something below a shout, but not by much.

He showed me the page, energized by what he'd found. It was ripped in half, torn and shredded by an impact almost perfectly down the middle, just a small sliver of paper at the bottom keeping the halves together.

"Four hundred and six from..."

I could read no more. The rest was gone. Obliterated by whatever hunk of metal had gouged its way through the file cabinet and the documents it once held.

"There were four hundred and twelve before we left for Cheyenne," Neil said, and I knew where his train of thought was going.

"Four hundred and eleven," I corrected him, adding a single name to identify his mistake. "Micah."

The child had died shortly before our departure. One soul erased before salvation could be found.

"Right," Neil said. "Minus four."

Neil. Elaine. Me. And Burke.

Burke...

Another who would never know a better world. The hope of a world turned green again. He'd fallen so soon in our quest that any hint of what we had ultimately found dwarfed what he, or any of us, might have expected. He was caustic and distant. He drank. He reeked of superiority at times. But he was a good man. A damaged man. And, whether he knew it or not, at the end he was my friend.

"Four hundred and seven," Neil said, narrowing our math down to a confirmation we'd rather have been wrong about. "Minus the blood stain."

A dried pool of dark crimson staining the floor of Bandon's meeting hall. That was the mark which had convinced us that violence had erupted as our friends and neighbors were taken away. One had fallen there. Another who would had no chance of witnessing new and better days.

"Four hundred and six," I said, matching the number that had likely disappeared from Bandon with the number marked on the crude and battered form my friend had found.

"What are the odds, Fletch?" he wondered aloud, no answer necessary to confirm what we both knew.

This document was proof that the town's population had been taken along this route. To where we still did not know.

"I can't make anything else out on here," Neil said, frustrated. "It's torn all to pieces."

He dropped the document and began pulling small pieces from what remained piled where he crouched.

"It could be Skagway," I said.

"We don't know that for sure," Neil countered. "Just because it said that on one piece of—"

"I see something!"

Elaine's report from above stopped us both cold. For an instant. Then Neil was back digging through the pages scattered about.

"Go see," he said. "We've gotta know where they went."

I could have pressed the issue with him. I could have reminded him that we were likely in the crosshairs of some Russian excursion upon American soil. But I doubted any prodding would work to penetrate his focus. Instead I rose and moved quickly to the stairwell.

"What is it?" I asked Elaine.

Fifty feet above her face appeared over a railing in the dim glow of starlight bleeding through the tower's glass enclosure.

"I don't know. Maybe nothing."

"Maybe isn't reassuring," I told her.

"There was something in the strait," she said. "Like something solid blocking reflections on the water."

Just like a boat would, I knew. She did as well.

"How far out?" I asked.

"Close to shore," she said.

Nothing of what she was reporting was comforting. But that paled in comparison to the reality which hit like a thunderbolt as the wall of the lighthouse tower above exploded inward.

Seven

In an instant Elaine was gone. Gone from my sight. And, I feared, gone from this world, as the west facing wall of the lighthouse tower burst inward with a shower of jagged stone and orange flame.

"Elaine!"

I screamed her name upward, then ducked back against the wall as debris from the obvious impact of some explosive weapon rained down. Blocks of stone bounced off the stairs and tore the old steel railings from their mounts. Twisted lengths of metal snapped and rocketed across the narrow width of the tower staircase, ricocheting like shrapnel spears, one missing my head by inches as it planted itself in the concrete wall behind.

"Elaine!" I shouted again.

But she didn't respond. Either she was dead, or hurt. Or, quite possibly, my words had been drowned out by the sudden and ear shattering chorus of gunfire rising from outside.

"We've got company!"

Neil's warning from the main room was followed immediately by the sound of his own weapon opening up, quick bursts, ejected shell casings tinging off the solid walls and floor that surrounded him. I looked back up the stairs, the smoke and dust clearing just enough that I could see all the way to the top between the switchbacking stairs.

"Elaine!"

"I'm here!" she finally replied, coughing. "Two groups! One from the west and another from the south!"

Then I heard glass break, and her own weapon open up, the crack of her MP5 almost dainty compared to the sound of what was incoming. For an instant I debated whether I should head up, to provide cover from above with Elaine, or move to where Neil was to repel the obvious attack at ground level.

The sound my friend let out next made the decision for me.

It was a piercing cry, followed by a brief spurt of invectives.

"I'm hit!"

I ran back into the main room and caught a glimpse of Neil across the darkened space, muzzle flashes from outside illuminating his writhing form in harsh, agonizing pulses of hot light. He leaned against the wall near the window he'd been using as a gun port, AK slung, hanging loose, one hand grabbing at the opposite shoulder.

"Neil!"

I started toward him, but never made it. The main door blowing in with a cloud of fire and smoke stopped my progress and threw me to the floor.

"Fletch!"

It was a warning cry my friend let out, the words stretched out, almost distant, my stunned brain processing what was happening in some weird slow motion. There was his shout, and there was movement, from both Neil and near the door. My friend lifted his AK with one hand and brought it to bear. Fast splashes of flame leapt from its muzzle. Dark shapes near the door dove and ducked, their own weapons firing. But only for an instant.

Then, at least in the immediate space that surrounded us, it fell quiet, just gunfire from beyond the walls drifting in. Neil ran across the room, firing at the mangled entryway, bursts meant to deter any entry.

"Fletch! Can you get up?!"

The foggy world I'd tumbled into began to clear. Maybe it was just the momentary effects clearing on their own. Or the presence of my friend and the urgency about him. Whichever it was, my wits returned as though I'd been doused with icy water and I pushed myself up from the ground, AR that dangled from its harness coming quickly to bear in my grip.

"I'm good," I said.

A stream of rounds poured through the doorway, chewing at the toppled file cabinets. Neil and I retreated to the stairwell, my friend almost tripping over the rubble mounded at the bottom. I could still hear fire from above, Elaine firing quick, controlled bursts, the sound seeming to shift after each time she fired. That told me she was moving positions at the top of the tower as she tried to cover both advances she'd seen.

"Elaine needs help up there," I told Neil just before something small and solid and metal sailed through the door and *thunked* across the concrete floor.

A grenade.

I grabbed my friend and pulled him behind the concrete wall between the main room and the staircase. The instant we were both behind that solid cover a deafening *CRACK* shook the space around us. Smoke and flame and debris blew past us from the main room and rose up the tower stairwell as if it were a chimney.

"They're gonna come," Neil told me.

Before I could agree he was clearing himself around the corner and firing across the main room toward the door, trying to deter the attackers. The shoulder of his jacket was soaked dark, blood seeping through from the wound he'd just suffered. It was the same shoulder in which he'd been stabbed by a desperate father in a desolate Utah town.

"Watch that shoulder," I told my friend.

"What shoulder?" he shot back, expressing the inner toughness and resolve I knew him to possess.

"I'm going up," I told him.

Between a fast magazine change he gave me an even faster thumbs up, acknowledging my plan. I turned and looked up through the rising smoke as my friend continued trading fire with the attackers trying to fight their way in.

Eight

I never made it to the top.

Halfway up, after climbing over knots of curled steel and chunks of mangled concrete, I reached the hole that had been blasted in the wall of the lighthouse tower. I paused just before the scorched opening and glanced out. Fifty yards to the west I saw movement and muzzle flashes at the same instant that Elaine's fire from above paused, the sound of an empty magazine from her MP5 hitting the tower floor indicating why. That momentary halt in fire was, apparently, what the group of attackers near a small outbuilding had been waiting for as one of them stepped into the clear around the corner and brought a slender tubed weapon to his shoulder, conical projectile at its tip silhouetted by muzzle flashes from his comrades' covering fire. Anyone who'd paid any attention to news from war-torn areas of the globe in the decade before the blight would have recognized it immediately.

"RPG!" I shouted.

The words had no sooner passed my lips when a gout of flame pulsed from the weapon, its operator firing before I could bring my AR to bear. The projectile rocketed from the tube launcher and dragged a tail of hot white smoke behind as it flew directly toward a spot twenty feet above me. The top of the tower.

"Elaine!"

Another explosion rocked the structure, more debris falling, a rain of steel framework and broken glass chasing

Elaine as she dove into the stairwell. Her body tumbled down the steps, bouncing off the outer wall, one leg catching on part of the railing that hadn't been blasted to bits. If not for one simple visual cue I might have thought her dead or badly injured—both hands still held her MP5, the weapon tucked tight against her chest.

"Are you all right?!" I shouted, more fire coming now, rounds bouncing off the tower and whizzing past through the hole next to me.

"I'm okay!" Elaine screamed back, rolling to a sitting position on the opposite side of the hole. "Where's Neil?"

I didn't have to answer. From below we could both hear him firing and ducking, rounds coming his way angling through the door and ricocheting in the base of the tower.

"Another RPG in the right place and we won't have a building to defend," Elaine said.

I couldn't disagree. All we could do, though, was fight from the position we had. With the weapons we had. Against the enemy that was presenting itself.

Elaine leaned toward the hole and fired bursts to the south. Then I leaned in and fired toward the west, trying to keep the group pinned at the outbuilding. A trio of them stepped into the open and began returning fire, pinning us against the inside wall for cover.

"Neil!" I called out. "We lost the top!"

"We're about to lose the bottom!" he shouted back.

I looked to Elaine. Both of us knew what had to be done. Staying put was a death sentence.

"We have to go on offense," she said.

We had no impenetrable bunker to retreat to here, as we'd had outside of Cheyenne. Our choice right here, right now, was to fight and win. Or die.

"I'll cover," I said.

I leaned into the opening and fired bursts at the two groups advancing from the west and east, Elaine darting across the hole in the tower to join me on the lower side. Immediate fire came back at me, tearing at the scorched hole in the concrete. Below, Neil was still holding off part of the southern advance which had reached the building.

"How many do you think there are?" Elaine asked.

"Ten or twelve."

I figured two trying to breach the main door. I'd seen four near the outbuilding and glimpsed the same number to the south. Which didn't account for any who'd slipped around the sides of the structure we couldn't see. We were blind in here.

BOOM!

A huge explosion shook the building from below. Smoke jetted up the tower past Elaine and me. I clambered down through the acrid haze, climbing over the debris from multiple explosions, just in time to see my friend. He wasn't dead. And he wasn't holding his position near the wall anymore.

He was running *into* the main room.

"Neil!"

I jumped the last few yards to reach the spot where my friend had been, Elaine coming up right behind. Neil was firing at the door as he moved across the battered space. I swung my AR around the corner toward the door and saw that the opening which had been there was now larger by a factor of three, the last blast we'd heard having ripped a hole large enough to drive a small car through. Through that gaping wound in the structure I saw shapes. And movement. And staccato flashes from muzzles spraying rounds into the building.

"Neil, what are you doing?!"

My question was almost absurd. Knowing why my friend had left cover would do nothing to change the situation we now faced. But, as I dropped to one knee and began laying down what fire I could to cover his dash into danger, an understanding of what he was trying to do came together piece by piece.

The bodies we'd seen upon entry were still there, but they'd been tossed about by the subsequent explosions.

The bodies were those of soldiers.

Armed soldiers.

Soldiers with guns.

And grenades.

If we were going to fight back, on a more level playing field, we needed to at least give as good as we were getting. And that was what Neil was attempting to do as he reached with his wounded arm, snatching up grenades which had fallen loose from the soldiers who'd carried them into their last battle. He did this while firing his AK one handed, stopping only when he reached meager cover on the far side of the room behind a battered pillar, the rebar within its structure exposed by the most recent blast.

"They're closing on the door!"

I yelled the warning to my friend as I tried to fire, but a steady stream from some heavier automatic weapon kept forcing me back to cover. Just behind, Elaine tried to move past, to a stubby wall at the very base of the stairs, but the same fire kept her planted against the tower wall.

"Take cover!"

Neil gave the warning just before I heard a series of metallic clicks. Three, I thought, distinct amidst the cacophony of gunfire. He'd pulled the pins on a trio of grenades and, from the sharp *thuds* that came next, also three in number, he'd hurled them through the widened entrance where they'd landed and skidded across the concrete pad outside.

BOOM!

BOOM! BOOM!

The explosions popped off like giant cherry bombs, sharp and quick, one, then two more in quick succession.

Just a fast pulse of air from the blasts washed into the space, the majority of their force spent outside.

Outside where someone screamed.

"Move!" Neil shouted.

From his position he could see directly outside, and had made the decision that making some move was the best course of action. I had no place, nor any inclination, to disagree, and I moved quickly around the corner of the wall, Elaine right behind, the three of us heading for what the main door had become.

More screaming pierced the sudden quiet, followed by gunfire aimed at the tower we'd abandoned. And there was shouting. In a language that sounded almost certainly Russian. Neil took a position to the right of the opening, Elaine and I to the left. I brought my AR up and scanned the dim exterior, tracking the sounds of the voices and the obvious cries of pain. One man was down, and it sounded as though there were two of his fellow soldiers trying to help him.

"We've gotta get to the boat," I said.

"If it's still there," Elaine said. "And afloat."

Right then, Neil tucked his AK in tight against his cheek and began firing bursts into his slice of the tactical pie. The return fire was immediate, along with more screams in Russian. More than had been there just seconds before.

"They're reinforcing," my friend said across the space that separated us.

That was the worst of all worlds. The groups that had been moving in from the west and south were, if Neil was right, now converging on this one point. The way in. And our way out.

"There's no back door," Elaine said.

I'd seen what she had. The stairwell was the only way out of this main room. If we wanted another way out, we'd have to make it ourselves. And we had no way to breach the thick stone walls.

Brrrrrrr-brrrrrrrrrrrrrrr-brrrrrrrrrrr.

A controlled stream of full auto fire poured into the main room through the blown entrance. The machinegun the attackers had brought with them was now positioned to pin us.

"We've gotta move!" Neil yelled above the sound from outside, and the constant timpani of ricochets threatening to cut us down at any moment.

I stuck my AR around the corner and fired a series of bursts. Elaine went low and did the same, shooting past my knees. Neil, too, was adding to the attempt at suppressing fire. But all our resistance did was draw more of the hellish rain of lead upon us. Chunks of stone peeled away from the wall that protected us. Bits of the ceiling cracked and fell at our feet. The structure, which had withstood a series of blasts both high and low, was signaling that it could take no more.

"One more RPG and this thing comes down on us!" Elaine shouted.

She was right. They didn't have to shoot us down or blow us up. Even a miss with an explosive weapon would bury us alive. I looked across to Neil, his gaze meeting mine.

"We don't have a choice!"

I wondered if those were the last words my friend would ever speak to me. Then I nodded and dropped the magazine from my AR, loading a full replacement. We were going to need every round of ammunition we had. And that might still not be enough.

"I'm going first," Elaine said just behind me.

I chanced a quick, disapproving look back at her.

"I'm faster than both of you," she said.

That she was right pissed me off.

"Go left," I told her.

She nodded and checked her MP5 as Neil fired a series of aimed shots toward muzzle flashes coming from the dead woods.

"We'll get to the trees, then down to the water," Elaine said, a fatalistic smile softening her determined expression. "Then to the boat and outta here."

"Yeah," I said, playing along with what we both knew was likely a last ditch, and futile, chance at survival. "That should work."

She snickered lightly and I looked across to Neil.

"Elaine's got the lead," I told my friend, and he nodded as he continued to squeeze off rounds.

"Okay," Elaine said. "Try to keep up."

She shifted to my side, weapon up and ready. Just a few steps would put her beyond my position of cover. Out into the line of fire. I hated that this was happening. And I hated even more that I was powerless to change the situation.

"One," she said, beginning her countdown.

Our countdown.

"Two."

She rose up beside me. Ready to move as incoming rounds ticked off the floor and splintered the walls behind us.

"Thr—"

I stopped her mid word as she started past me, hand coming off my AR's grip to block her. Something had caught my eye. Just a glimpse. Like stars suddenly brightening in the distance over the trees against the night sky. Dozens of fiery orange spots appeared in close proximity to each other and grew larger. And larger. And larger.

"Get down!"

I screamed the warning to Neil as I grabbed Elaine and pulled her back, dragging her as far behind the wall as I could. From the corner of my eye I saw my friend hesitate, then leap away from the opening as an awful shriek rose. Like screaming fireworks raining down upon us.

Right after that the earth shook from a series of rippling impacts that seemed to surround the lighthouse. Explosions rocked the structure. Cracks appeared in the walls, and those that had already been created by the ongoing fight widened. Smoke poured in. Flame, too, licked in from the penetrations opened on the west side of the main room.

Hell had been brought to this small slice of Mary Island. And we were right in the middle of it.

Part Two

The Unit

Nine

The silence was jarring. But it was not total.

Where seconds before there had been gunfire and screaming and urgent commands shouted in Russian, then a final volley of detonations that seemed to pepper the landscape surrounding the lighthouse, now there was just a hushed crackle of smoldering debris and a rhythmic thrumming drawing closer by the second.

I turned toward the gaping hole in the building's front and slipped to my right, past Elaine, chancing a look outside.

"Eric," she said. "Be careful."

Across the opening from me, Neil had recovered from the earth shaking blasts and was also creeping forward to survey the situation outside.

"Neil."

My friend looked to me and gave a thumbs up. He was okay, his wounded shoulder and arm still usable. In battle terms, he'd gotten a scratch. Something that would have sent him to the hospital in ordinary times.

These, most definitely, were not ordinary times.

"You hear that?" I asked him.

He stilled and listened for a moment.

"Helicopter," he said.

"It has to be one of ours," Elaine said. "They laid down that fire."

She was at least half right. It was the 'ours' identifier that concerned me. Something that could have been 'one of ours' had tried to slaughter Neil and me at my Montana refuge. Being certain of allegiances was no longer a slam dunk. The blight had turned more than the landscape to shades of grey.

"It's closing in," Neil said, gauging the sound from the unseen aircraft. "That's no Blackhawk."

No, it wasn't. There was a deeper, harder resonance to the timbre of the chopper. For lack of any better description, it sounded *big*.

"Here it comes," I said.

The bass *whop whop whop* of the big craft's rotors grew louder, the thing passing directly over, a single weapon aboard it opening up as it flew above. A weapon whose sound was frighteningly familiar to Neil and me.

"Minigun," my friend said.

I nodded. It was the same type of weapon, a Gatling gun on steroids, that had nearly chewed the both of us to bits back in Montana. The major difference here was that it was not firing at us.

"It's spraying the tree line," Neil said, watching from just inside the blasted door, low on his belly, AK ready to fire from his prone position.

"No one is shooting back," Elaine said.

"After that rocket barrage, who'd be dumb enough to," Neil said. "If they're even alive."

It had been a volley of rockets, fired expertly to carpet the compound outside with deadly shrapnel. Sparing us while saving us.

"It has to be friendlies," Elaine said.

I wanted to believe that. I truly did. Because we sure as hell could use some friends right then.

"It's coming back," Neil reported.

The helicopter had flown over, fired briefly, and was now swinging around. Maybe for another pass.

It turned out not to be that at all.

From the darkness above a brilliant, burning object fell as the aircraft passed over and continued over the barren forest. It landed in the clearing and bounced, the hot white light it gave off almost blinding.

"It's a flare," I said.

Outside, night turned to day in a hundred yard bubble around the blazing flare, revealing the carnage that had been visited upon the isolated island. Dark objects lay upon the ground. Half a dozen, I counted. Bodies. There would be more, I knew, beyond the reach of the light. Lost in shadow or hidden near the edge of the dead woods.

"I think they want us to show ourselves," Elaine said.

"We're easy targets if we walk out into that," Neil reminded us.

"If they wanted us dead," I said, "we'd already be dead."

Neil knew I was right. He wasn't really protesting Elaine's suggestion. All that we'd been through had simply ingrained a layer of distrust in all things except those with which we were intimately familiar. And a hovering helicopter in the night, armed to the teeth, was not that.

"Let's go," I said.

We rose from where we'd taken cover and lowered our weapons. Then, with me in the lead, we walked out into the sizzling light.

Ten

We stopped twenty feet from the flare, in the full wash of its illumination, and waited, listening to the helicopter hover in the distance. And hover. Making no move to approach.

"I don't like this," Neil said.

His wariness was well founded. Aside from the aircraft continuing to stand off, as a hunter might with prey in their sights, we were completely exposed where we stood. Easy pickings for any Russian who might have survived the aerial attack and was lurking in the darkened woods.

"I'm with Neil," Elaine agreed.

"We don't have a lot of options here," I reminded them.

Then, slowly, the sound of the helicopter changed. It grew louder. And louder. Soon we began to feel the wash of its rotor. Smoke from the flare swirled in the brightening glow as the rush of air fed its flame.

I looked up and saw the stars blotted out. Something dark and solid between us and the heavens. The wind it generated blasted us and pushed the flare a dozen yards from where it had landed. Soon we were leaning into the raging wash as the craft settled toward the earth, its shape plunging into the glow of the nearby flare. Gaining definition. Revealing a massive helicopter, single main rotor spinning atop a wide fuselage with weapon pods mounted on stubby outriggers protruding from each side. Ganged rocket launchers and missile racks I could make out, along with forward facing single barrel weapons. Fifty-calibers by the appearance. And from openings on each side just aft of the cockpit, multi-barrel weapons were swiveling, masked and helmeted operators manning each. These were the miniguns we'd heard firing.

"Sea Stallion," Neil said as the craft came to rest on the flat earth, wheels supporting it as a ramp at the rear slowly lowered.

"What?"

My friend looked to me.

"It's a Marine Sea Stallion," he said, identifying the aircraft, then looking back to it. "This one is tricked out."

That it was, I had to agree, even though I knew little about the specific craft. Besides the almost comical array of weaponry it carried, two elongated fuel tanks hung beneath each outrigger. The thing had been outfitted to go into battle at some distance from its base.

Still, its grey body bore no markings. Or those which it had carried had been painted over. For what reason, I had no clue.

"We've got company," Elaine said.

Figures spilled from the back of the Sea Stallion, coming down the loading ramp. There were four, all uniformed identically, grey and black pattern of camouflage from neck to boots. They wore no helmets, but they were all armed, with what appeared to be M4s, the military cousin to my AR.

And each and every one was pointed at us.

"Just keep your weapons down for now."

The words seemed more suggestion than order as the group stopped just short of where we stood, and the soldier who spoke them, a woman, bore no aggressiveness in her stance as she stepped past the three who'd approached with her, lowering her weapon. A name was sewn onto the right breast of her uniform, but she identified herself before there was any need to read it.

"I'm Lieutenant Angela Schiavo," she said, offering each of us a look. "United States Army."

We looked amongst ourselves, then to the lieutenant again. She nodded to the soldiers just behind and they brought their rifles down to a low ready position. Not aimed at us anymore, but easily returned to that state.

"You're civilians," Schiavo said, eyeing us. "Where is the garrison assigned here?"

"If you mean the Americans, they're dead," I told her.

She let that register for a moment.

"Where?"

"Inside," I said.

She made a couple hand motions and the three soldiers behind split up and moved off, one heading into the building and the other two toward the woods, weapon lights switching on as they began to search the perimeter.

"Can you tell me what happened here?" Schiavo asked.

"Besides you blowing the hell out of the place?" Neil responded, rolling his wounded shoulder.

Schiavo motioned toward the helicopter as its rotor spun down. The door gunner facing us disappeared from his position, and a moment later he and another soldier appeared on the loading ramp and approached quickly.

"I have someone who can look at the shoulder for you," Schiavo said. "Now, do you actually know what happened here?"

I explained to her about our arrival after seeing the light, and about the Russians, including their infiltrator. As I did so, one of the newly arrived soldiers, whose name patch identified him as Hart, had Neil sit on the ground as he began checking his wound.

"So this was the second attack," she said.

"Is there going to be a third?" Elaine asked.

Schiavo surveyed the identifiable body count and shook her head.

"If they lost this many after two goes, they can't afford a third."

"Chunk of stone," Hart said, looking up from where he was tending to Neil. "Secondary shrapnel. He's lucky."

"Hear that, Neil?" I said. "You're lucky."

My friend shot me a look and winced as Hart began to clean the penetration in his shoulder.

"I feel so, so lucky," he said.

"Specialist Hart is a fine medic," Schiavo said. "Finest I've ever served with."

The soldier who'd entered the building returned, his M4 slung and his expression grim. Enderson was stitched on his right breast, and a pair of stripes on his upper sleeve put his rank at corporal.

"The garrison is KIA," Enderson reported to Schiavo.

Killed In Action. Truer words had never been spoken. The unlucky few soldiers who'd been assigned to this hunk of rock had given their best, and then their all, trying to hold onto it.

"Thank you, corporal," Schiavo said.

Her attention shifted for a moment, from the three of us and her troops to the bodies scattered about outside. What had been a neat arrangement of fallen Russians when we'd arrived had been violently disturbed by explosions used in the second attack. Now those corpses, and that of the infiltrator, were strewn about, some whole, most blasted to pieces.

"They're Russians," I said.

"They were," Schiavo corrected me.

The two soldiers who'd headed off to check the perimeter, a Sergeant named Lorenzen and a Private named Westin, returned, the latter lowering himself onto a fallen log nearby.

"We swept the tree line and the back side of the lighthouse," Lorenzen told his commander. "Just bodies."

"Okay, sergeant."

"If we're going to spend any time here, I suggest a sweep all the way to the shore," Lorenzen said.

"We're not setting up shop," Schiavo assured him. "Acosta."

The other soldier who'd come off the helicopter with Hart stepped forward. He was a wide eyed private, eager and ripped. The young man had found time in the blighted world to pump iron.

"Lieutenant," Acosta said.

"Tell the pilots we'll be wheels up in forty minutes," Schiavo said.

"Yes, ma'am," Acosta acknowledged, then he hustled off back to the helicopter and disappeared up the loading ramp.

"What do they want with this place?" I asked, and Schiavo looked to me. "The Russians."

"What does anyone want?" Schiavo asked, answering herself an instant later. "Food."

People would kill for food. I'd seen it. Elaine and Neil, too, had witnessed what human beings had been driven to in the pursuit of sustenance. Why would armies be any different?

"There's a small cellar with a few months' provisions," Schiavo explained. "That was their objective."

"Like the Army of Northern Virginia foraging their way across the union," Sergeant Lorenzen said.

"Have we been invaded by Russia?" Elaine asked.

Westin, bald and somewhere between twenty years old and dead, snickered from where he'd taken a seat on the log.

"Did I make a joke?" Elaine asked the soldier sharply.

"Invade?" Westin asked. "Russians?"

Lorenzen eyed his subordinate.

"Easy, private," the sergeant cautioned the man.

Westin stood and faced Elaine, but moved no closer.

"You think they want to plant a flag here?" Westin challenged Elaine.

"I think that might have been one of their intentions," Corporal Enderson said as he stood from where he'd been searching through an attacker's gear, unfurling a small banner he'd retrieved, its white, blue, and red horizontal stripes crisp and clean.

Westin gave the flag a dismissive glance and focused on Elaine again.

"They're scavengers," he said. "Just like us. Just like anybody left on this Godforsake—"

"I believe your sergeant suggested you stand down," Schiavo interrupted. "Private."

Westin eyed her, his commander, a hint of the same dismissiveness he'd shown the Russian flag in his gaze as he regarded her. I couldn't tell if there was a lack of respect, or if the man was just beaten down by what we'd all been through. Whatever it was, he took the reiteration of Lorenzen's subdued order and turned away, striding off past the pair of Russian bodies to a position where he stood alone.

"It was just a question," Elaine said to Schiavo.

"He's on edge," the lieutenant explained. "We all are. This is just our first area to clear. There are garrisons up and down the coast."

"Why here?" Neil asked, standing, his shoulder now bandaged. "Why were ships with people coming by here?"

"It was for processing," Schiavo answered.

"Processing," Neil repeated, his disdain plain for the word. "Processing."

Schiavo nodded, puzzled.

"You do know how terrible that sounds," I said.

"Like Nazi terrible," Elaine added.

"They just get 'processed' and then they're taken away," Neil said.

Schiavo eyed each of us and shook her head.

"No," she said. "Not like that. I promise."

Neil stepped toward her and shifted his AK so that it hung solidly across his front.

"Processing for what?" my friend pressed her.

"For Repop," Schiavo said, the truncated term holding enough possible innocence in what it implied that the worry was momentarily dialed back for the three of us.

"Repopulation?" Elaine asked.

Schiavo nodded and ran a hand over her head. Elaine looked to me.

"It makes sense," she said. "If you're trying to stabilize things, you gather everyone in one place so it's easier to supply."

"Transports with survivors would transit this route and be logged," Schiavo said. "Mary Island was the southernmost point of that route."

"Is that what this is all about?" I pressed her. "Herding everyone together?"

"That's my understanding," she confirmed. "A repopulation center was established in Skagway. Identified communities with a sufficient number of survivors were evacuated there."

"Forcibly evacuated," I said.

"I don't know anything about the parameters of the specific evacuations," Schiavo said.

"We do," Neil told her. "The parameters include blood stains and four hundred of the people we care about disappearing."

Schiavo considered what Neil had just told her. What we'd all told her. But there was something we hadn't shared.

"Why weren't you three among those?"

Neil said nothing. Neither did Elaine. I suspected that my friends were making the same decision that I was—that offering up information on where we'd traveled, and what we'd found, was not completely prudent. Not yet. We knew nothing of the lieutenant and her unit. Only what they had shared. None of which we could verify. So, for the time being, we would hold close what we knew. And what we possessed.

Information, even in this new age, could be power.

"Don't want to talk about it," Schiavo said. "I see."

"Why Skagway?" Elaine asked.

Schiavo shrugged and slung her M4, some coolness rising. A chill about the subject I'd sensed in her as each morsel about where our friends had been taken was drawn out.

"That information was not part of my briefing."

"You don't sound enthused about any of this," I said.

Schiavo thought for a moment. Maybe weighing the propriety of any reply. Of making any statement of discord to an outsider.

"In my world, you don't group your assets," she said. "You spread out as a matter of defense."

So she spoke her mind. Somewhat. Without being insubordinate or belaboring the issue. She was a thinking soldier. An honest leader. That shouldn't have surprised me, but it did.

"Are you going there?" Elaine asked. "To Skagway?"

Schiavo didn't answer this time. Maybe doing some withholding of her own.

"Is that your boat tied off at the east dock?" the lieutenant asked.

"It is," I confirmed.

Schiavo thought for a moment. Studying us. Maybe appraising our wherewithal. Our grit.

"You look like you've been through some hard times," the lieutenant said.

"Do you know anybody who's had it easy since the blight?" I asked.

She smiled and shook her head.

"Lieutenant..."

It was Enderson. He'd retrieved something else from one of the dead Russians. A small round of metal, a bit larger than a quarter, a dull, rusty sheen upon its surface. He held it up and Schiavo stared at it, her expression darkening.

"Kuratov," Enderson said.

Schiavo took the small medallion and rolled it over again and again in her fingers like a foul talisman.

"Yeah," she said, agreeing with the corporal.

"Is that his name?" Elaine asked.

"Him?" Schiavo asked, gesturing to the Russian the medallion had been retrieved from before shaking her head. "No. This little hunk of metal here identifies this soldier as belonging to Forty Fifth Spetsnaz."

"The same unit that went into Ukraine without insignia," Enderson added.

Ukraine. It was difficult to remember the time when that dominated the news. It all seemed so small now. So insignificant compared to what had followed. And what was still unfolding.

"Their commander was...is a man named Aleksy Kuratov," Schiavo said. "There were some reports that he'd gone rogue with his unit after the blight spread across Asia and Europe. When we had later reports of possible Russian incursions in the Aleutians, command just figured it was isolated instances of starving units acting out of desperation."

"Kuratov doesn't act out of desperation," Sergeant Lorenzen said. "He always has a plan."

"Right," Schiavo said, that reality seeming to spark some concern in her. "Right."

Enderson found a second red medallion in another Russian's pocket and stood, handing it to me. I wiped a splotch of blood from it with the thumb of my glove and examined both sides. There were no markings. None at all. Just a smooth reddish patina upon the circle of metal.

"Kuratov gives every one of his troopers those," Enderson said. "They treasure it more than any medal they could be given. Now, it's yours."

I wondered if what I'd just been given could be considered a war trophy. Something akin to a Samurai sword taken from a Japanese officer during World War Two. Or a Luger off a dead German soldier in the same conflict. Was this to be my memento of this battle?

"Go ahead," Enderson said, smiling. "Might be worth something someday."

The thought of just tossing it back amongst the dead Russians was there, but so was the odd desire to retain it, so I slipped the small trinket into my shirt pocket, an uncertain keepsake at best.

"If you're going to Skagway, I'd recommend against the boat," Schiavo said. "If Kuratov is in the area, that craft will not absorb much fire. And he will fire at anything that moves."

"Movement means life," Enderson said.

"Life means food," Lorenzen added, completing the train of logic.

I thought on the warning she was giving us. We all did. Neil, though, was the first to utilize it to try and push through the lieutenant's reluctance to offer certain information.

"So maybe we'll ask again," Neil said. "Are you going to Skagway? Because whether we get there by boat or by chopper, I don't much care. None of us do. We just want to get there ASAP. And by air is sure as hell going to be quicker than by boat, especially since you're telling us our choice of transport could be very unhealthy."

Schiavo considered what Neil was asking, and what he was suggesting.

"We have to check on garrisons in Ketchikan and Juneau before we continue on to Skagway," Schiavo said. "And I can't get authorization to let you tag along for..."

She looked beyond those gathered close to the one who'd separated himself.

"Westin..."

The private looked her way, then, after seeming to take a breath, he jogged back and joined the group.

"How long until our next com opportunity?"

Westin took a small device from his pocket. It was compact and electronic and rugged. I could just make out bits of information on the display—latitude, longitude, altitude, and a timer. Counting down.

"About two hours," Westin reported.

"Com," Elaine said. "You have communications?"

Schiavo didn't answer. A look to Westin suggested he get past the minor conflict and answer the lady's question.

"We can relay burst transmissions off a satellite that passes over different locations at varying times," he explained. "And we listen at the same time for any messages from our HQ."

"Basically a line of sight communication with one bounce," Neil said, impressed. "And that gets through the White Signal?"

"With the right equipment, yeah," Westin confirmed.

I thought for a moment then fixed on the lieutenant.

"Look, our people are in Skagway. Everything we found here, and everything you've said, points to that as fact. We'd be with them if we'd been in town when this evacuation happened. You're going to Skagway, and that's where we're supposed to be. Wouldn't you just be transporting civilians to safety? Isn't that something you'd do in other circumstances?"

She considered the scenario I was laying out, but wasn't buying it yet.

"The circumstances here are the two stops we have to make before heading to Skagway could very well be hot. Hotter than this. I'm talking combat situations. Ketchikan is twenty miles up the coast from here. Twenty miles. If these Russians came from anywhere, Ketchikan is a logical spot."

"Which means the garrison there could have suffered the same fate as this one," Lorenzen said.

"Ma'am," Westin said, and Schiavo looked to him. "If we transmit a request in two hours, there's a six hour wait for the next opportunity to receive a reply."

"Eight hours," Lorenzen said, clearly not relishing that much time on Mary Island.

Neither, I could see quite plainly, was the lieutenant.

"We're not going to get in your way," Neil assured her. "And, just so you know, we know how to fight. We've had to fight to stay alive."

Schiavo considered the three of us for a moment, some decision rising.

"Okay," she said. "You need anything from your boat?"

I shook my head. We'd left the *Sandy* with all we needed. The supplies in her hold wouldn't be necessary anymore. What would have been a week or more journey through Alaska's inside passage might now be completed in eight hours.

Might.

"Do you really think the Russians are in Ketchikan and Juneau?" Elaine asked.

"I don't know," Schiavo said, maybe doubting the suggestion she'd made before. "Kuratov had a regiment. But what's a regiment in this new reality? Fifty men? Sixty? I should have a platoon of thirty, but I've got a weakened squad of five. If he's stretched as thin as we are, he could have lost half his force trying to take this island. The rest could be heading back to Kamchatka for all I know. Or dead."

She quieted then. Something about her hardening.

"But I know that however low the probability of contact is, I have to be ready to kill every living thing that's not on our side."

"Ooo-rah," Lorenzen said with fierce calm, his concurrence almost timid compared to the sentiment it validated.

"Sergeant," Schiavo said, looking to her number two. "Police up any food from the cellar. And anything from the boat. Get it aboard the chopper and let's get out of here. We'll transmit a status report from Ketchikan."

Her troops moved quickly on her orders. We assisted lugging cases of MREs up the trail from the dock. In twenty minutes everything was aboard the Sea Stallion.

But there was something still to do. A matter of honor to attend to.

Westin, Hart, and Enderson broke out shovels and began digging. In just ten minutes they had a communal grave dug. A few minutes more and they'd transferred the remains of the fallen Americans from inside the building to their final resting place. The bodies, whole and mangled alike, were covered with ponchos, then with dirt. Schiavo said a few words. Lorenzen recited the Lord's Prayer.

There was no marker left. The only record that they had fought and died were the dog tags collected from each. Schiavo slipped those into a pocket and that was that.

"Time to go," she said.

The rotors began to turn as we followed Schiavo and her unit to the Sea Stallion and climbed into the cabin. Hart and Acosta were already on the side miniguns. The loading ramp folded upward and Enderson helped secure us in the simple seats folded out from the fuselage, Elaine and Neil across the cabin from me.

Schiavo stepped past us, slipping into a headset and settling into a seat closest to Acosta on the right side minigun.

"Here we go!" Schiavo shouted, signaling with a twirl of her upraised finger that we were taking off.

The Sea Stallion shook and rumbled, then half of that noise and shuddering seemed to drain away as the craft was enveloped by air. Floating. I felt the sudden lightness as it was transmitted through me. It was a slightly unsettling sensation, different from that one experiences in a plane. For lack of a better description, it was as though I wasn't being thrust into the sky, but pulled toward the heavens.

A moment later, someone tried to send each and every one of us to that very place.

Eleven

I happened to be looking past Hart on the left door gun
when a flash bloomed in the dead woods beyond the
smoldering lighthouse.

"RPG!"

Someone screamed the warning. I don't know who it
was. Hart let out a burst from his miniguns as the pilots
reacted, the modified Sea Stallion jerking hard to the left,
turbines screaming overhead as they tried to shift the
aircraft clear of the unguided missile streaking toward it.

They were unsuccessful.

The warhead impacted at the extreme front of the
helicopter when it was barely thirty feet off the ground,
exploding through the cockpit. A shower of flame and
shrapnel and body parts sprayed into the cabin, engines
suddenly spinning down, controls destroyed, both pilots
obviously dead. I grabbed for a handhold as the aircraft
rolled to the right, away from the direction it had been
turning, nose coming up. I saw Elaine steadying herself
across from me as the Sea Stallion tipped slowly forward.

"We're going down!" Schiavo yelled.

"Brace!" Lorenzen shouted.

I looked away from Elaine for a moment, toward the
front of the bird. Most of what had existed forward of the
side gunners was gone, just shredded metal and sparking
wires remaining.

And the earth. I saw that, too. It was what we were
heading for, open ground near the edge of the tree line, not

far from where the RPG had been fired. Once more I turned to Elaine. She was fixed on me, forcing a smile. Some gallows humor version of joy on her face. Maybe an acknowledgment that, after all we'd come through, we were going to die in, of all things, an aircraft that had been shot down in battle.

Then, something odd happened. As the engines continued to slow down, rotors above chopping through the air at a reduced rate, the helicopter began to right itself, the nose coming up, as if we'd reached the bottom of some arc and were about to head up again.

"Autorotation!" Hart shouted, his death grip still on the controls of the left side minigun.

Autorotation. I knew vaguely what that was. It was, for helicopters, the equivalent of an airplane's dead stick landing. A distant cousin of a gliding touch down. The Sea Stallion's rotor, as I recalled, while without power, was still spinning enough to provide some lift, and as the chopper neared the ground, pulling back on the stick and flaring the bird could, sometimes, allow something approximating a survivable landing. In our case, physics had taken over where the pilots, now gone, would have initiated the maneuver. The balance of the helicopter, heavier aft now with the cockpit and its structure blasted away, equalized, with the nose coming up as we neared the ground.

Which is precisely what happened just before we hit. Hard.

There was no explosion. Not any like we'd experienced recently, in any case. But gears and engines and metal stiffeners in the fuselage came apart with showers of smoke and sparks. The rear of the Sea Stallion buckled, a great gash opening across the top of the fuselage just above the loading ramp.

Then, everything began to tremble. I'd never been in an earthquake larger than a small shaker, but what I felt then was more than I could imagine even tectonic plates unleashing. The rotor spinning above, which had sheared partially as we hit and its blades flexed, was instantly unbalanced, the wobbling motion tearing it apart transmitted to everything within. Like a child's toy being tossed by an unruly toddler, the Sea Stallion was whipped onto its side by the torqueing test between whipping blades and hulking fuselage, bodies within tumbling, shattered rotors chewing into the earth, spinning slower. And slower. And slower.

Until the mechanical violence ended, just the fading whine of the turbines spinning down left.

"We've gotta cover that tree line!" Lorenzen shouted, unstrapping himself from the canvas bucket seat affixed to what was now the floor of the space.

I hung above him, still buckled in, still dazed by the horrific end to our short flight.

"Eric!"

It was Elaine. She stood below me, a trickle of blood on the side of her face. Other than that minor injury she seemed unhurt.

"I'm okay," I said, convinced of that a few seconds later as I caught my breath and shook off the impact. "I'm good."

I undid my belt and lowered myself down. Neil had recovered and was already gearing up. Everyone was, it seemed, no serious injuries or, thank God, fatalities, other than the cockpit crew. To call it a miracle might not be far from accurate, I thought.

"Westin, Enderson, on me," Lorenzen shouted, his M4 ready as he led his men through the gaping rip in the fuselage. "Hart, give a check on everyone then bring up the rear."

"You okay?" Hart asked, looking to me and Elaine and Neil.

We all gave him an assuring nod and he headed for the opening, Schiavo and Acosta approaching next.

"You smell that?" Schiavo asked.

We all did. A stark and pungent wave was scenting the air within what was left of the Sea Stallion.

"We have to get some supplies out," I said, and Schiavo nodded.

"Fast," Acosta suggested. "Before we all become crispy critters."

That the helicopter hadn't been engulfed in flames by the spilled fuel igniting was maybe another miracle. Or a testament to its toughness. In either case, the luck we were having might very well not last. We needed to get as much of what we'd brought onto the Sea Stallion back off, lest starvation be the next obstacle we'd be facing instead of Russians.

"Acosta and I will cover," Schiavo said. "You three mule everything you can grab away from the chopper. Clear?"

It was. Schiavo and Acosta stepped through the opening and took up positions a few yards away from the capsized helicopter. I carried the first cases out with my pack on and AR slung at my side. Neil and Elaine matched my load. The three of us had almost all of the MREs and water bottles off when we heard a few quick bursts of gunfire from the woods to the west.

"Cover!" Schiavo ordered.

Acosta moved to the Sea Stallion's shattered cockpit and crouched low there, focusing his attention to the west and south. Schiavo sprinted to the half demolished outbuilding near the lighthouse and covered the west and north. The actions were practiced and precise. We had no such connection with how Schiavo had drilled her troops, but we knew enough that to be useful we should be adding eyes and weaponry to where they were not.

"Lighthouse," I said.

Neil nodded and took the lead, running to the side of the building with Elaine and me behind. When we reached the battle scarred south wall we positioned ourselves to cover the eastern side of the clearing. Then we waited.

It was likely a minute or two that passed, but the silence was palpable. The not knowing made the time drag.

"Quick boat trip and bring them home," Neil said quietly, injecting what relief he could into the tense moment.

"What's this, an added bonus?" Elaine wondered, joining in.

"Go to Alaska and fight Russians," I said. "New state tourism slogan."

The brief interlude of humor ended then, not with further violence, but with calm voices and familiar faces emerging from the woods behind us.

"One down," Lorenzen reported.

Westin, Enderson, and Hart followed him as we all regrouped with Schiavo and Acosta near the stacks of supplies.

"That last burst of minigun fire was dead on," Enderson said. "We just made sure he was down."

"I think he was already wounded when he fired at the chopper," Lorenzen said. "There was a blood trail."

"He was alone?" Schiavo asked.

Lorenzen nodded.

"Where's the radio?" Westin asked, eyeing what we'd salvaged.

Schiavo's gaze widened.

"Get it," she said, and Westin hurried back into the crashed chopper.

"If it's..." Lorenzen began, apparently not needing to complete the worry.

"Yeah," Schiavo said, nodding sharply, some self-directed anger working on her.

A moment later Westin emerged from the Sea Stallion with his rifle slung and his hands empty. He shook his head.

"Wonderful," Schiavo said, turning away for a moment.

"What is it?" Elaine asked.

"Without the radio we're deaf," Lorenzen said. "If something's happening where we're heading, the garrison there might have reported it. But we'll never hear that."

"We could head right into an ambush," Enderson said.

"We're not really heading anywhere," Neil said, gesturing to the Sea Stallion.

Schiavo turned to face us right then, looking very purposely at me, and Neil, and Elaine.

"Yes we are," the lieutenant said.

Twelve

The *Sandy* would carry us north. All of us. That decision was not agreed upon. It was imposed.

"I'm not saying we'd resist," Neil told Schiavo. "I'm just saying you don't have to use the terms you are."

Requisitioning. That was what Schiavo had said. That she and her men were 'requisitioning' the fishing boat we'd brought north from Bandon. There was no asking. In essence, they were taking it.

"This isn't a negotiation," Schiavo said. "I have the authority to—"

"Don't," I interrupted her. "Don't."

"What?" she pressed me.

"You're going to take the boat, fine," I said. "But please don't claim authority over it, or us."

She stared at me for a moment, then that look turned to a glare.

"I let you on the chopper," she said, her tone verging on anger. "I was going to get you to your people. Was that some kind of authority you were opposed to? Because if it was, and if what I'm doing now is, I also have the authority to leave you right here on this rock with a three day supply of food and water. That authority has been given to me as well when I encounter civilians who may impede my mission. So, if you are dissatisfied with me requisitioning your transport and *still* allowing you to come along, let's decide real fast who's on the boat, and who's making Mary Island their new home."

It was a calculated rant. And I suspected Schiavo regretted the tenacity with which she'd given it as soon as she'd finished.

But I had sparked the response from her. And I wanted her to understand the why and where of what might have seemed like defiance on my part.

"You don't need to exert authority over us, Lieutenant Schiavo," I said. "You didn't come off that chopper and prone us out when you landed. You gave us consideration as civilians. As human beings. All I'm saying is you don't need to revert to whatever position some bureaucrat with stars on their collar has given you. I've seen authority exerted since the blight, and it's not pretty when all those on the receiving end of it want is that same kind of consideration we already know you're capable of."

I didn't know if my words would stoke the sudden fire that had ignited her response, but I doubted they would, and I was right. She breathed, slow and shallow, absorbing what I'd said to her, and, if anything, a measure of calm seemed to come to her.

"Sergeant, have the men start getting these supplies onto the boat," Schiavo said while looking directly at me.

Lorenzen knew what she wanted. Shifting the cases of water and MREs was a convenient necessity allowing the lieutenant to get all of her troops clear of the place where she stood with us. A few minutes later that was precisely what happened as her five subordinates carried the first load away from the lighthouse.

"Do you know what I did before this?" Schiavo asked. "Before the damn blight, do you know where I was stationed? What my job was?"

We waited, silent, no need to prompt the answer we knew was coming.

"I was a musician," Schiavo said, a hint of a grin flashing. "I played piano in DC for get-togethers where

Army brass and political types would dress up and dance and eat food I could only dream of where I grew up."

I hadn't seen that coming. I doubted Neil or Elaine had, either.

"Musician," I said.

"Did my time before that in a logistics unit," Schiavo said. "Before that I had two years of infantry. But somehow I sat down at a piano one day at an off base club, just to fool around, and some colonel heard me. And recognized me. And told his superiors I was being misused in logistics. Next thing I knew I was sitting at the ivories."

She waited for commentary from us, but, to be honest, I had no idea what to say. Nor did I have any idea why she'd chosen this moment, after what had just transpired, to share this bit of her past. It certainly didn't seem germane to what had just transpired.

"So you have a piano player issuing commands," Schiavo said. "I wanted you to know that. I wanted you to know I'm not some born to kill Army lifer out to piss vinegar in your direction for the hell of it. I'm a piano player who happened to be one of the few who stuck around to keep taking orders when everything went to hell. Eventually I was told to step away from the keys and grab my M4, so that's what I did. Then I was on an Air Force transport that left me and others like me in Hawaii. And you know what we did there?"

"I'm guessing it wasn't surf," Neil said.

"We waited," she said. "And were split up into units. Every lowly lieutenant was given their own command. Five hell raisers and a louie that played piano. That's what my unit was. Then we trained. It was back to basic infantry. We didn't even know what for, but I made a promise to myself right then that the person leading my men anywhere was not going to be the piano player—it was going to be the warrior."

"That's one hell of a personal narrative," I said.

"I hoped you'd think so," Schiavo said. "Because if I revert to the rulebook at times and seem like an a-hole, it's because sometimes I'm afraid that I should still be playing piano. Okay?"

She'd used a term I hadn't expected—afraid. Fear was a common emotion, even in those who wore the uniform and served their country. Cops felt it. Boxers in the ring knew it. Crabbers on a boat in stormy seas, as well. But rarely did they admit to it to virtual strangers.

Lieutenant Angela Schiavo, in her own way, was offering up an explanation as apology. And hoping that we would take it to heart.

"Fair enough," I said.

Schiavo nodded.

"And I'll try to remember that you haven't been riding out this hell in some cushy civilian nirvana," she said.

She needed to offer no more explanation. No more apology.

"We won't share any of this with your men," Elaine said.

Schiavo smiled lightly at the assurance.

"They know," she said, then looked to the crashed Sea Stallion, worry and hope sharing the space in her gaze. "There'll be a radio in Ketchikan. Every garrison has one."

She looked back to us, those eyes filled only with certainty now.

"And we'll get you to Skagway," she added, pure promise about her as she spoke. "It's still your boat, still your destination. We're just borrowing it for a while along the way."

And that was it. Some understanding had settled in between the lieutenant and us. As for myself, I fully appreciated what it was she was charged with accomplishing, and, along with that, the pressures to perform that weighed upon her. Despite any societal changes, she was a woman in a man's army, evidenced by the makeup of the unit she led. I didn't know if that disparity pushed her to work harder, or be harder, but, so far, it hadn't exposed any deep flaw in her ability to lead.

And I hoped, for all our sakes, that it would not.

For the next hour we all pitched in, carrying what had been salvaged from the Sea Stallion down to the dock and loading it on the *Sandy*. She was heavier now, with both more supplies and more live bodies aboard, which, we discovered, wasn't necessarily a bad thing for a craft designed to operate with its tanks filled with caught fish. She rode more solid, I felt, as we pulled away from the dock and out into the channel.

Ketchikan was just twenty miles away.

Thirteen

It was good to have others to pilot the *Sandy*. And especially good to have someone, in Acosta, who actually had experience on similar craft. He steered us expertly along the eastern shore, islands to our west. He'd commented after taking the wheel that it felt little different from his uncle's cod boat in his birth state of Massachusetts. That was the home he'd left behind when joining the Army shortly before the blight made its first appearance in a Polish potato field. Now, like the rest of us, it was the home he'd likely never know again.

There was another reason to appreciate having Acosta at the wheel, and the others to back him up. It gave us time. Elaine, Neil, and me. Time to sit on deck near the stern of the vessel and have a moment to talk. Away from any who might hear.

"What if there is a radio they can use in Ketchikan?"

Neil wondered that aloud, glancing toward the wheelhouse. Acosta was there, Lorenzen and Hart with him on watch. Schiavo, Westin, and Enderson were bunked out below, catching what rest they could before the sun rose.

"If they can make contact with some higher authority, what about what we found?" my friend asked. "And the notebook?"

"They could pass on what we learned," Elaine said. "On how to beat the blight."

"Yeah," I agreed. "They could."

Neil and Elaine both puzzled at my wariness.

"But you don't want them to," Elaine said.

"We may have the holy grail here," I said. "What if we get to Skagway and this evacuation isn't as innocuous as the good lieutenant makes it sound?"

"Bargaining chip," Neil said, understanding.

"If our people want out, and someone doesn't want to allow that, then we have something to give them," I said. "Or something to withhold."

Elaine looked toward the wheelhouse, then back to us. "You don't trust them?"

"I don't know them," I said. "None of us do. I'm just not in the mood to blindly put my faith in someone because they wear a uniform."

"Ben wore a uniform," Neil said.

My friend's gaze bore hard into me. I did remember that. And I remembered what Colonel Ben Michaels had done. What he'd sacrificed so that my friend could live. Neil knew I would never speak of that. I hadn't with Elaine, and I wouldn't even hint of what I'd seen. That was a secret I would take to my grave.

"We were with him for a long time," I reminded Neil. "We've been acquainted with these people for a few hours."

"I'm not disagreeing with you," Neil said. "I'm just suggesting there may come a time when we need to trust them."

"They did save us," Elaine said. "But I agree with you. We keep it—"

She never had a chance to finish. The boat tipped severely to port as Acosta steered hard right, taking us into a small cove, the motion tossing us against the side rail, the low rise of its wooded structure all that kept us from tumbling into the black water.

"What the hell..." Elaine cursed, getting to her knees as the boat straightened out and slowed, engines reversing to bring us to a stop.

Neil and I got to our feet just as the door to the wheelhouse swung outward, Hart leaning out, weapon in hand and a single finger to his lips. Behind him I could see Schiavo, Enderson, and Westin coming up from below, M4s at the ready. The lieutenant conversed with Acosta for a moment, then came out onto deck.

"They saw a light ahead," Schiavo told us. "On a small island."

"Not a reflection?" I asked. "The water plays tricks on you."

She shook her head, complete confidence in her men.

"It's there," she said. "We're out of sight in this cove. I'm sending a patrol to shore to scout ahead overland. That point that's shielding us will give a decent vantage to scan the way ahead and see what that light is."

"Who's going?" Neil asked.

"I'm about to decide that," Schiavo answered, then turned to head back into the wheelhouse.

My suggestion stopped her before that could happen.

"Let us scout it."

Schiavo looked to me, partly puzzled, partly amused.

"This is actually what we train for," she said.

"I know," I told her. "But this is actually what we've been doing for months. Out where threats exists among the completely innocuous."

It was weighing the man walking along a deserted highway holding a dead cell phone to his ear against the little girl on a tricycle who was a distraction that allowed her father to almost impale my best friend. We'd seen and felt and dealt with unexpected oddities of all sorts. And we'd learned that, sometimes, just giving these things a wide berth was the best course of action. My suggestion to Schiavo was based only on that understanding. And on the reality that she, and her men, were warriors, each and every one ready for a fight.

And maybe too willing to seek one.

The lieutenant considered my suggestion for a moment, eyeing each of us, up and down, in some silent appraisal. What she spent the most time on, though, were our eyes. How they remained fixed on her gaze. Locked on. Confident.

Even haunted.

"You've seen things," Schiavo said.

"All of us," I confirmed.

She weighed what I'd offered, then nodded.

"Sergeant..."

Lorenzen came out of the wheelhouse at his lieutenant's call.

"Yes, ma'am."

Schiavo gestured to us with a nod.

"Set them up with the night sight."

* * *

We took the small dinghy lashed to the deck near the stern and paddled the short distance to shore.

"How far off is this light we're scouting?" Elaine asked.

Acosta had given me an estimation before we shoved off from the *Sandy*.

"A mile when first spotted," I said. "Make it half that by the time we reach the point."

The point was just a stubby peninsula jutting out into the channel. As Schiavo had thought, it would provide a perfect vantage point to observe whatever it was her men had seen from the wheelhouse.

"Feet dry," Neil said, his last stroke with the paddle beaching the dinghy's bow on the flat and rocky shore.

We climbed out, boots splashing through a few inches of surf before we tied off the dinghy and began working our way up the shore. It couldn't have been more than ten minutes before we reached the point and crept low along its ridge to a spot where a pair of leaning boulders formed a near perfect V which we could peer through.

"Go ahead, eagle eye," I told Elaine.

Neil passed her the thermal binoculars and she took a position at the base of the boulders, turning the device on as Sergeant Lorenzen had shown her. The barest glow escaped past the cups shrouding the eyepieces, a muted grey white light splashed upon her cheeks. She made adjustments to the focus and the zoom, studying the distant view for a moment before easing her face away from the binoculars and turning them off.

"We can sail right past," she said, handing the hunk of advanced optics back to Neil and standing.

Her desire to depart abruptly stood stark against her usual sober and methodical approach to almost any situation.

"What is it?" Neil asked.

She glanced quickly to him, but gave no answer, nor any hint of explanation.

"Let's get back to the boat," she said.

Neil looked to me, then turned the thermal binoculars back on once more, about to bring them to his face when Elaine seized his arm.

"Let's just get back to the boat," she reiterated.

Her grip remained on his arm until he turned the device off once again and stowed it in its case.

"Come on," Elaine said, then started back along the point's sloping southern face on her way to the shore.

"What the hell did she see?"

I thought on my friend's question, but I had no specific answer. No real guess, either. What Elaine must have focused in on across the water had to have disturbed her without raising any real fear. We'd all seen so much already that I wondered what might have affected her the way it had.

"Are you coming?" she asked, pausing to look back when Neil and I hadn't yet moved from our position on the point.

"Yeah," I said.

I looked to my friend, and he started off, following Elaine. A moment after him, I did, as well. Back at the dinghy we pushed off and paddled back to the *Sandy*.

"What is it?" Schiavo asked as we climbed back aboard.

Enderson and Hart stowed the dinghy and listened for an answer to their leader's question. None actually came.

"We can go on," Elaine said.

Schiavo puzzled briefly at the oblique reply.

"It's safe," Elaine assured her, offering everyone on deck a quick look, her gaze finally settling on me. "I'm sure."

She walked away then, heading into the wheelhouse and below deck.

"That's not what I was expecting," Schiavo said, looking to me.

It wasn't what I'd anticipated, either, but I didn't share that with the lieutenant. Instead, I added my assurance to that of Elaine.

"If she says it's all right, then it is."

My own promise, offered in the blind, was enough to move Schiavo, if not convince her entirely.

"Acosta, get us moving."

"Yes, ma'am."

"Sergeant, I want shooters on the bow."

"Westin, Enderson, warm up your trigger fingers," Lorenzen said, carrying out his lieutenant's order.

"Elaine wouldn't say it was safe if it wasn't," I told Schiavo.

"I had friends who were told the same thing before they were blown up while meeting with tribal elders in Afghanistan," Schiavo said. "So it's a good idea to be ready to kill anything you see."

She said no more, simply taking the thermal binoculars back from Neil and joining Acosta in the wheelhouse.

"I hope this doesn't go south," Neil told me.

"Yeah," I said, then joined the others in the wheelhouse as the *Sandy* started to move.

* * *

We pulled around the point and into the channel. Immediately we all could see the light ahead, flickering small in the darkness.

"Keep us at a distance," Schiavo ordered.

"Yes, ma'am," Acosta acknowledged.

He steered the *Sandy* right, hugging the eastern shore as close as he could without grounding her on the bottom displayed on the boat's instruments. Just forward, through the windows, I could see Westin and Enderson kneeling behind the low, solid rail that surrounded the bow. They had their M4s up and ready, eyes to the compact scopes mounted atop each. They would see only minimal definition at this distance. Schiavo, though, would take in a much clearer picture as she brought the thermal binoculars to her eyes and activated them.

Just a few seconds later she lowered them and looked to me. Just a dim glow from the instruments filled the wheelhouse. Hardly enough to see by. But in that wash of muted light I could tell that some of the color had drained from the lieutenant's face.

"She was right," Schiavo said.

The lieutenant handed the binoculars to Lorenzen and went below decks. He scanned the scene she'd just appraised and leaned out the wheelhouse window and told his shooters to stand down.

"What did she see?" Neil asked.

The sergeant turned and thought for a moment, then handed the binoculars over. My friend stepped close to the wheelhouse front window and focused in on the scene. He let his gaze linger on what was out there for just a moment before he, too, wanted to look no more.

"Neil..."

He looked to me. More a glance, actually, furtive and grim. I reached out and took the binoculars from him and took my own turn surveying the scene, stepping to the window, Acosta at the wheel to my right, the island with the small fire at its southernmost point close now off the port side of the boat. It took just a moment to do what others had done before me and dial the focus and zoom so that what lay out there in the night became clear.

I wished it hadn't.

A gauzy mist hovering just above the water softened some of what I saw in the grey and white hues imparted by the thermal sensors. They registered heat, and cold, and the reflectivity of the former on pooled liquid. Liquid like blood.

That, I knew, was what shimmered on the ground near the fire. A wide pool with sparkles of heat twinkling upon its glassy surface. Next to it a saw lay. A bow saw, what someone might use to remove limbs from a tree. Or other limbs.

Near that cutting instrument a man lay. Even in the digitally enhanced interpretation of his form I could see that he was near wasted away. Skin and bones in monochrome. I could also see that one arm below the elbow was missing, and from that point of amputation a clear path of shining liquid could be traced to the larger pool.

That was horror enough, I thought. But there was more.

Over the fire the man had constructed a simple cooking apparatus. A stick leaned over the low blaze, propped up at an angle by a mound of flat stones, its base held in place by still more rocks. At its end, impaled on the sharpened point, the man's severed arm, charred and shriveled, was suspended above the licking flames.

Desperation...

That was the only term I could manage upon seeing what I was. It was the worst combination of what I'd experienced over the previous months. Man turned to cannibal, and the mind twisted to bring that horror upon one's self. Here the crazed individual had considered his action with some logic, it appeared, preparing a fire, and a manner of cooking a meal, before taking the blade to his flesh and bleeding out before he could find sustenance in his own sacrifice.

I lowered the binoculars. Lorenzen was looking at me. No, it was more than that. He was *watching* me. Maybe expecting some reaction. Some overt expression of horror. I don't know what he saw upon my face as I handed the binoculars back, but the manner about him softened. For that moment, in that exchange between us, he was not a soldier. He was just a member of the human race.

"Hell of a world," the sergeant said, his voice cracking slightly.

I nodded and headed for the stairs.

Fourteen

I found Elaine in the boat's cramped dining area, Schiavo in the attached galley, pouring steaming water from a kettle into two cups with teabag strings hanging over their lips.

"Care for some?" the lieutenant asked when she saw me at the bottom of the steep stairs.

"No. Thanks."

Schiavo took the two cups to the dining area and sat across the table from Elaine, sliding a cup toward her. She eased her hands around the warm mug and stared into the brownish liquid.

"Why are tea leaves not affected by the blight?" Schiavo asked. "Shouldn't these be dried and grey like every other thing that came from a plant?"

It was an interesting question asked for lack of a desire to probe Elaine's darkened mood.

"Already dead," I said, slipping to a place closer to the table, but still standing in the belly of the gently rocking boat. "Picked and dried."

Schiavo accepted that with a nod and sipped her tea as she looked between Elaine and me, her expression begging the question as to whether I knew why Elaine had been affected so much by what we'd seen on the island. I didn't, but I was also wondering the same thing. It was terrible, to be sure, a sight no person should ever have to imagine, much less see. But was it the worst thing we'd witnessed?

No. In Cheyenne I'd seen things that would haunt me. A woman, her legs and arms removed in some attempt by

Moto to sustain a population of human cattle. She'd spoken to me in the dark, and I couldn't help her. That, to me, was far worse than seeing a man driven to see his own wasting body as something that could sustain him.

To Elaine, though, that sight had found some deep nerve, and was still twisting it. She was hurting, and I didn't know why.

Then, without prompting, she asked a question that, for me, began to explain her distress.

"Lieutenant, have you heard anything about our troops overseas?"

"No," Schiavo answered.

Elaine looked up from her tea, hands still embracing the cup, liquid within sloshing with the roll of the boat.

"My little brother is in Germany," Elaine explained. "Albert. He's in the army."

Schiavo nodded, some sense of understanding rising now.

"You haven't heard from him in a while," Schiavo said.

"Not since the initial rioting over there," Elaine told her. "I just..."

I went to the dining table and slid onto the bench seat next to her. She took one hand from the cup and let it rest atop mine on the tabletop.

"I just worry that he's...that he's having to do things to survive that he shouldn't have to."

It was a terrible fear to harbor. One clearly brought to the forefront of her thoughts by what she'd spotted near the fire. How irrational it might be to transfer such a horror to a sibling unseen for years I didn't know, and it really didn't matter. She was feeling what she was feeling. I had no real relationship to equate it to. My parents were both passed, and I'd not had brothers or sisters. There was just me.

But, now, with Elaine in my life, I could imagine loss, true loss, for the first time. Not the death of a friend or acquaintance, but of one I felt bound to by the truest love I'd ever known. And I never wanted to feel what Elaine was.

"I wish I had a way to find out for you," Schiavo said. "But everything broke down. Communications. Reporting. Order. We've lost so many people that we'll never know about."

Elaine nodded. She understood. It was grasping at straws, but grasp she had to.

"If there comes a time when I can pass along a request for status," Schiavo said, "I will."

By just a degree, Elaine brightened. But that slimmest glimmer of hope mattered. She and I both knew that.

"Thank you."

Schiavo took a long sip of tea and stood, stepping back into the kitchen to rinse her cup.

"We'll reach Ketchikan in a couple hours," Schiavo said. "You might want to rest. I don't know how lively things will be when we get there."

Lively...

That was a disarming way to describe what might mirror the sounds and sights and resultant death that we'd left behind on Mary Island. Another battle. More risk.

And more delay. More time spent getting to our friends.

If things were to get 'lively', as the lieutenant put it, I wanted to do my part to bring it to a satisfactory end as quickly as possible. The same would apply to Elaine, I knew. And Neil.

Without being asked, we'd drafted ourselves into any fight that might come between us and Skagway.

Fifteen

We neared Ketchikan as the first wisps of daylight glowed blue upon the mountains towering to the east.

"Stop us here."

Westin followed his lieutenant's order and throttled back all the way, putting the *Sandy* in reverse for a moment to fully stop her forward motion. He'd taken over for Acosta at the wheel an hour before, the Massachusetts native giving his relief some quick instruction on the controls and what to watch for on the instruments. Since passing the small fire on the remote island, nothing had appeared out of the ordinary. And looking ahead now at the town nestled close to the Pacific, all looked quiet. All sounded quiet. Peaceful.

Deserted.

"Something's wrong," Schiavo said.

"What?" I asked.

She passed over the standard binoculars, enough light to make its thermal imaging cousin unnecessary.

"Do you see the stars and stripes anywhere?" the lieutenant asked.

I didn't. Scanning the waterfront along the shore that stretched out to the north on our starboard side, I could make out buildings, and docks. Even a boat swamped at its mooring, just the top of its wheelhouse and radio mast visible above the water. But no hint of our national flag. Not even a tattered semblance of one left flapping atop a pole after years of neglect and weathering.

"Straight ahead, large installation," Schiavo directed. "Docks but no boats. You see that."

I did. Exactly as she described. I even noted a flagpole, no banner at its top. Just bare metal.

"US Coast Guard Station Ketchikan," Schiavo said. "That's where the garrison is supposed to be."

"The flag would be flying if they were in control," Lorenzen added.

The sergeant's statement wasn't delivered with any ominous tone, but it arrived with that very effect.

Schiavo looked to her troops and to us.

"Gear up," she said. "And stay sharp."

* * *

We moored the *Sandy* alongside a small pier at an industrial area a mile and a half south of the Coast Guard Station. Hart and Westin stayed with the boat while the remaining seven of us moved north along Tongass Avenue, the coastal road, in a single line hugging the left shoulder, Acosta on point fifty yards ahead of our main group.

"It had to be beautiful here once," Enderson said.

Green. That was what he was letting his mind's eye conjure. Trees that weren't grey and crumbling. Slopes that weren't ashen and bare. Every hundred yards or so a house was planted along the mountainside to the right of the road. Only signs of wear and weathering made them appear anything but normal.

"People up and left," I said.

"Why?" Enderson asked. "This would seem perfect. Easily defensible."

"And where do you scrounge for supplies?" Neil asked him.

"Everything comes in by sea," Elaine said. "Once the canned goods run out, there's no nearby town to raid for food."

Enderson eyed the water just a stone's throw from the road.

"Helluva a view," the corporal commented.

"It was," I said.

We walked on in silence. An unnerving silence. That absence of the hush and rush of life still bothered me. The breeze whispered hollow and cold, absent any cry of gulls or laughter of children. Still, the quiet that surrounded us was preferable to any deafening eruption of automatic weapons and exploding rockets.

And that stillness lasted. All along the route to the Coast Guard station. Schiavo halted us at the curving drive that sloped gently down from the highway to the station's buildings. A rolling gate that had once secured it was pushed open, not blasted or torn from its mounts.

"Sergeant, take Acosta up the road and approach from the other entrance," Schiavo said. "Enderson, you're with me. You three stay out here."

You three...

We weren't professional soldiers. But we hadn't come along for the exercise, either.

"You brought us along to wait?" Neil pressed the lieutenant.

"No, I brought you to cover our six," Schiavo said. "Now grab some cover and make sure nothing comes down that mountain or up the road to surprise us."

She offered no more guidance, then turned and led Enderson through the gate as Lorenzen and Acosta jogged up the road to the far entrance.

"I'll take the right," Elaine said, almost drowsily, the assignment as exciting as it sounded.

"I'll stay right here," Neil said, wandering a few feet to the chain link fence that ran along the inland perimeter of the facility.

I shifted my position, to a point where I could see a good distance past the far entrance. Every minute or so I glanced back to my friend, one boot digging at the hard earth where he stood. He was impatient. Waiting was not anything he'd seen himself doing on this journey. The whole point was to get to our friends and loved ones as quickly as possible. How long 'quickly' turned out to be depended on more external factors than we'd expected when we set out from Bandon.

"We'll get there," I told my friend, just loud enough to carry the dozen yards that separated us.

He looked to me, a hard worry about him.

"We will," I reiterated.

Finally he nodded, accepting my assurance. Whether he believed it was another question.

"Hey."

I turned toward the newly familiar voice. It was Corporal Enderson, Private Acosta trailing just behind.

"You can head on down to the building," Enderson said as he and his fellow trooper moved past, back onto the road in the direction we'd come from. "We're going to get back to the boat and have them bring it up here."

"What did you find inside?" I asked.

"Is the garrison there?" Elaine added her own question before Enderson or Acosta could offer any reply to mine.

Enderson paused for just a brief second and looked to us, confused.

"We didn't find a damn thing," he said, then continued back along the road with Acosta.

"What does that even mean?" Elaine asked.

Neil moved past Elaine, and then me, glancing back as he headed down the driveway toward the building.

"It means they have no idea what the hell's going on," my friend said.

I thought on that for a moment as Elaine began walking, following Neil. We'd come here with Schiavo and her unit for a specific purpose, because the garrison, and their radio, was supposed to be here. If that was not the case, then Neil was right.

But we'd found the same when returning from our trek to Cheyenne. The residents of Bandon gone. My friend, I guessed, wasn't factoring that into what was stoking his frustration. This was no different. The world wasn't providing us, or anyone, with an easy path to what we wanted. To what we needed.

And I feared that wasn't about to change anytime soon.

* * *

Not a damn thing...

By that they'd clearly meant not a living soul, because that was what awaited us. There was no garrison where the garrison should be. No sign of life, or of death, either. The place was empty, main and support buildings deserted, bunkhouse space the same, recreation room filled with chairs and couches and a pool table, with no one to enjoy the amenities.

"Any bodies?" I asked.

Lieutenant Schiavo, standing at a window looking out to the waters of the Tongass Narrows and Pennock Island beyond, shook her head. Clouds swept in low and fast, erasing the fat sliver of land across the channel, sheets of rain descending. Weather was moving in.

"No bodies, no troops, no radio," she said, then turned and looked to us as Sergeant Lorenzen entered the spacious room from a hallway. "Anything?"

"No," Lorenzen answered. "Boat sheds are empty. They could have left by sea."

"If they had transport," Schiavo said. "We don't know if they did. And even if they did..."

Lorenzen nodded, seizing on the incongruity of what they'd found.

"Why not leave a note," he said. "Some communication."

Schiavo nodded.

"So five soldiers are missing," Neil said. "Just gone? Just like that?"

"No," Schiavo said. "Not just like that. We haven't checked the town yet."

Roughly a mile up the road was the center of Ketchikan. Its business district. Shops and eateries to serve the masses of humanity cruise ships would deposit when calling on the port. It was small by lower forty-eight standards, but, one would imagine, held enough out of the way places where someone, or five someones, could hide.

"Why would they leave this and head into town?" Elaine asked.

"Don't know," Schiavo said. "But we have to make sure they aren't holed up somewhere else nearby. With that radio."

She was concerned for the absent garrison, I knew. But the radio, some link to higher authority, was at the forefront of her focus. Almost an obsession, I sensed.

"When they get back with the boat, we'll scout the town," Schiavo said.

"I'm going," Neil said.

Schiavo eyed him.

"I decide who goes," she said.

"Then decide that I'm going," Neil challenged her. "I'm not sitting around here waiting for you to do your job. We need to get moving. We need to get to Skagway. So I'm going into town to find your lost garrison, or not find them, so we can get back on the water."

The moment was charged. Lorenzen glared at Neil. Schiavo, though, showed nothing beyond a determined stare. No animus in it. No raised chin superiority.

"You're going," she said. "I need two of my men to stay here with the boat and the station. The sergeant will take two with him, and you three will be with me."

She took a few steps toward Neil, facing him, but not facing off with him.

"That was going to be my decision before you *volunteered*," Schiavo told him. "Understood?"

Neil sensed he had come close to a line Schiavo couldn't let him cross. Couldn't let anyone cross while she was tasked with completing a mission. I'd never seen my friend retreat from a fight, but this wasn't that. This was him being eaten alive inside from worry over Grace and Krista. He wasn't thinking with one hundred percent clarity. But in that moment between himself and the lieutenant, I saw that he realized he needed to at least make an attempt at rationalizing the reality of our situation.

"Yes," Neil said. "Clearly."

Schiavo stepped back and let the moment settle before looking to her sergeant.

"Leave Acosta and Hart here," she said. "We'll head out now. You follow when they get here with the boat. Take the northern end of town. We'll cover the south."

"Will do," Lorenzen said.

Schiavo said no more to him. She just looked to us and gestured to the door.

"Gear up."

Sixteen

Ketchikan was a ghost town. Like any other of the tens of thousands of places waiting to be haunted in the new world.

If they weren't already.

"Neil, you and Elaine check the right side," Schiavo directed.

I followed Schiavo up the left side of the street. The rain had come, steady and cool, long torrents of it spilling from rooftops and awnings along the avenue. We stepped around the drainage but kept close to the buildings on this block. The seventh we'd checked. Switching off our pairings each time. Putting fresh eyes and perspectives together, Schiavo had explained it. That was our purpose on this foray into town—looking. And searching. And, hopefully, finding. Someone or something that would shed some light on the missing garrison.

As we passed every shop or store or eatery or business of any kind we'd pause and check briefly within, one member of each pair waiting just inside the door, covering while the other made a cursory search of the inside. So far we'd found nothing.

That changed at the real estate office two doors from the corner.

"Stop," I said from my position just inside, watching as Schiavo moved through the interior. "Don't move."

She froze calmly, her weapon coming up with an easy motion, eyes sweeping the space around her.

"What is it?"

I didn't answer her. Instead I leaned back through the open front door and spotted Neil and Elaine across the street, about to enter a pizza restaurant.

"Stop!" I shouted. "Don't go in. Hold right there."

Neil and Elaine read the urgency in my voice. They spread out, each taking positions across the street to cover approaches from either direction.

"Eric..."

I looked back to Schiavo and pointed to the desk on her right. Its drawers had been ransacked, papers spilled, a small mound of the documents spread across the top, covering something. But not completely.

"Tripwire," I said.

Schiavo leaned her head to look over the papers and saw a thin blue cord beneath. It ran along the far edge of the desk and dove down to the opposite, unseen side. From there it disappeared from my view, but I suspected that it was running under another mass of strategically placed papers on the floor.

Right where Schiavo would have taken her next, and possibly last, step.

"Just don't move," I said.

I shifted to the right and looked to the side of the desk where it nearly butted up against the wall. There was a space there between the piece of furniture and the drywall. Not much. About as wide as my fist. Just large enough to conceal the three grenades duct taped to the hidden side of the desk.

"Grenades," I said.

"You've gotta guide me," Schiavo said.

"Give me a minute."

I looked closely, taking out my flashlight to examine the improvised trap. The pins on each grenade were connected to the blue line with an elaborate series of knots, the string already taut. Any further pressure on it, such as Schiavo stepping on the concealed trigger wire, would cause the pins to be pulled. With the safety lever not depressed, a detonation would be imminent. Would we have noticed the sound? And if we had, would we have recognized it in time to avoid being blown to pieces in the confined space?

"Take one step back, on the carpet only," I directed the lieutenant.

She followed my instructions. A couple more steps had her fully in the clear. She joined me in examining the grenades.

"Those are ours," she said. "M Sixty Seven frags."

Her knowledge on the subject was greater than mine by far. I knew only that the small green globes were fragmentation grenades, potentially lethal out to nearly fifty feet. Where we stood they would have shredded us to bits.

"What do we do?" I asked.

"I don't have a demo guy," she said. "So we leave it."

I didn't full agree. I'd disarmed traps that major Layton's people had set around my refuge in Montana. But that had been TNT. Cutting simple wired fuses was different than making safe a tensioned tripwire. That much I was certain of.

"Let's back out and do visuals from the sidewalk from now on," Schiavo said.

A few minutes later we were outside in the rain. We briefed Neil and Elaine on what we'd found. An hour later, simply peering through still intact windows and broken front entrance doors, we'd identified five more booby traps inside differing establishments. All set the same. Three grenades connected to a tensioned tripwire. We marked each on our map and started back to the Coast Guard Station.

"I wish we had com," Schiavo said.

I knew why she was expressing that particular concern. Up the road, in the north of the town, her sergeant and his team could very well be facing the same improvised traps we'd come across. Having a regularly working radio would allow her to inform him of the hazards we'd encountered. Before his team did with possibly tragic results.

"Your sergeant seems sharp," I said. "He'll spot anything not right."

"I didn't," Schiavo said.

The rain began to pound, drenching us and the town as we left it behind.

* * *

Sergeant Lorenzen made it back to the station with Westin and Enderson an hour after we'd returned. He reported that they'd found no sign of the garrison, and, after hearing what we'd come across, that no traps had impeded their search.

"Who would lay traps with our own gear?" Enderson wondered.

"The garrison," Westin said. "They got spooked, boogied out of here, and rigged the town."

"Then they up and vanish?" Enderson challenged him, shaking his head. "I don't buy that."

"They are not here," Westin said. "But some of their munitions are in town. Add it up."

Westin left the discussion, heading across the rec room to dry off and tear open an MRE. He sneered at the contents.

"Sarge, you gotta make us up something palatable again soon," Westin said.

"Damn straight," Hart agreed.

Lorenzen nodded. But he wasn't thinking about food.

"What do you think about the traps?" I asked him.

Lorenzen thought for a moment.

"Fox in the henhouse, you set traps for the fox," he said. "I'm not so sure Private Westin isn't onto something."

"You think they were overrun?" Schiavo asked, doubtful. "Look at this place. There was no fight here. There wasn't any fight in town."

"There was a fight somewhere," Lorenzen told his commander. "If we had a weekend pass, I'd bet mine on that."

The conversation was turning as gloomy as the weather. Everyone was either soaked or drying out. Rain was drumming on the station roof. Through the window I could see waves leaping white in the channel.

I could also see Acosta. Standing in the downpour near the edge of the dock, the top of the *Sandy*'s wheelhouse bobbing just beyond. He was staring alternately at the water and up to the clouds.

"I'll be back in a minute," I said, taking my coat from where I'd hung it to dry and slipping into it again.

"Where are you going?" Elaine asked.

"Outside for a sec," I said, leaning in to plant a quick kiss on her forehead. "I'll be right back."

Seventeen

"This isn't looking all that promising," Private Acosta said

He stood at the dock where the *Sandy* was tied off, wind and wave pushing the boat against the wood and concrete mooring structure as rain hammered everything. Just north of the Coast Guard Station cruise ships had docked when the world was still whole. They would dump their passengers, the town's population swelling temporarily while wallets were emptied to pay for souvenirs and lumberjack shows. Then they'd board their floating hotels and be off to the next destination along the inside passage.

In this weather, though, some would have been losing their lunch.

"Lieutenant wants to move at night," he said.

That made sense. The less chance we faced of being seen made it more likely that we'd reach our ultimate destination. Sailing at night was risky in itself. Doing so in this weather, and especially in the seas as they were, made far less sense.

"Coastal Alaska is basically a rainforest," Acosta said.

That it was. To our sudden detriment.

"Are we stuck?" I asked.

Acosta nodded. He'd come out of the station's main building to check on our transport and now the both of us stood in rain that had begun to fall vertical, but had shifted to near horizontal.

"It could blow through quick," Acosta said, looking to me, water gushing off the brim of his hat. "Or..."

"Yeah," I agreed, annoyed at Mother Nature's sudden appearance. "Or..."

*   *   *

"How long?" Neil pressed once the lieutenant finished. "Exactly."

Schiavo, to her credit, didn't take my friend's bait. He was beyond frustrated now.

"I don't have any access to weather reports," she said. "I know what you know the same way you know—by looking outside."

Neil turned away and paced across the rec room, which we'd appropriated as our communal bunk house. After discussing the situation with Acosta, Schiavo had informed her men, and us, that continuing on before the weather broke was out of the question. While my friend reacted with predictable harshness at the delay, the lieutenant's troops continued drying their gear and found couches and overstuffed chairs in the space, letting their bodies fall into the cushions.

"I'm not sure everyone knows everyone still," Schiavo said, looking to me.

She waited, signaling that the formal introductions should begin with those of us her unit had risked their lives to save. We'd only had the most basic sharing of information since leaving Mary Island. Hearing another use a name. Reading last names on uniforms. We were mostly unknowns to Schiavo and her men, and they to us.

"Eric Fletcher," I said, pointing to those who'd come so far with me. "Elaine Morales. Neil Moore."

Schiavo nodded, then offered the particulars of those she commanded.

"Sergeant Paul Lorenzen," she said. "Does wonders with MREs."

"Chef du cuisine of meals rarely edible," the sergeant said.

"Private Ed Westin," Schiavo continued.

The trooper she'd just named, who we'd gotten off to a rocky start with on Mary Island, offered half a wave and let his head loll back against the back of a pillowy lounge chair he'd claimed, eyes closed.

"Specialist Trey Hart, our medic," she said, looking very deliberately to Neil next. "How's that shoulder?"

Neil let the question hang for a moment, then nodded to both Schiavo and Hart.

"It's good," he answered. "Thank you for what you did."

"He does chin lifts on the side," Schiavo joked, reaching up to stretch her own neck skin.

Hart smiled at the ribbing and brought his feet up to rest on a coffee table, boots on cheap government issue wood.

"My two on watch are Corporal Morris Enderson..."

"Just stick with Enderson," Lorenzen interjected, sharing that bit of advice with us. "Or Mo."

Schiavo nodded, chuckling lightly.

"For such a sweet young warrior he sure hates that name," she said, moving quickly on. "Mr. Universe is Fernando Acosta. Makes me wish we had a SAW or an M60 every time I see those pythons covered with sleeves."

Both weapons she'd mentioned, the Squad Automatic Weapon and the Vietnam vintage M60, were machineguns that increased a small unit's firepower almost immeasurably. That she would want one was not a surprise. That they did not have one actually was.

"Why don't you have one?" I asked.

"I suspect Acosta found one back in Hawaii and threw it into the ocean so he wouldn't have to carry it," Lorenzen said.

Their banter and demeanor was both fresh and refreshing. To borrow a cliché, they were letting their hair down. The momentary break in the stress that had filled the first leg of our joint journey north seemed to lift the weight that each of us had borne. Even Neil.

"Lieutenant, where are you from?"

Schiavo seemed more pleased than surprised at my friend's very normal question.

"Lone Pine, California," she said.

"Gateway to Mount Whitney," Elaine said.

"You know it," Schiavo said.

"I was there with a Bureau group doing a run and climb," Elaine explained. "That route was brutal."

"Bureau?" Schiavo asked. "FBI?"

Elaine nodded.

"A Hoover gal," Schiavo said, almost chuckling. "I wanted to be you a lifetime ago. That was my dream to get out of Lone Pine. To be a fed. Not some local cop, but an honest to God agent of the FBI."

"Movies made it look fun?" I asked.

"Of course," Schiavo admitted. "But I also saw something in a book once that said one of the first female FBI agents was a former nun."

"That's true," Elaine said.

"I thought, hey, if a nun can make it, then maybe I had a shot."

"Why didn't you?" Neil asked.

"Well, first you have to have a plan to achieve that goal, and my only plan was dreaming about it," Schiavo admitted.

"You coulda done it, lieutenant," Lorenzen told her.

She nodded politely at his expression of belief.

"It turns out the plan I should have had was college and all that really responsible stuff," Schiavo said, the thin grin she wore seeming to turn inward now, as if she was mocking her own younger self. "So that didn't work out."

"You said something back on Mary Island about not even being able to dream about some of the food you saw in DC," I said. "You were poor."

She nodded almost emphatically at my reasoned supposition.

"Not a lot of high paying careers in Lone Pine," she said. "I mean, there were people there who did well. My father was not one of them."

"What did he do?" Elaine asked.

"Drank, mostly," Schiavo said, the first hint of embarrassment rising. "Then meth when the booze bored him."

"Your mother?" Elaine asked.

"Cancer when I was still a baby," Schiavo said. "She had it when she was pregnant. My grandmother told me later that my mother refused treatment because it could have harmed me while she was carrying me."

She said nothing for a moment. Neither did anyone else. Westin slept where he sat. Hart let his gaze dip away. Lorenzen, though, he looked straight at his leader, admiration in his eyes.

"Military got you out," Neil said.

Schiavo shook her head.

"No, I got me out. I ran away when I was seventeen. The day after I graduated high school."

"Why then?" Elaine asked.

Schiavo thought for a moment. It turned out to be a question she'd never really considered herself.

"I'm not sure. I think, maybe, I just saw where I was as an end, and I wasn't ready for that. I wanted to find something more."

"What did you find?" Neil asked.

"First," Schiavo began, "I found out that living on your own is hard, especially when you're still a month shy of eighteen. Second, I found that *that* was still better than what I was living with back in Lone Pine. And then..."

Lorenzen smiled. He'd heard this all before, and it still tickled him.

"And then..."

"And then I walked into a recruiting office to apply for a job," Schiavo said.

Lorenzen started to laugh now.

"You what?" Elaine asked.

"I was cold calling," Schiavo said. "You know, going into every place on the street and filling out applications. The pizza place. The dry cleaners. Places like that. I just walked into the next door and asked if I could apply for a job. I thought maybe they needed a file clerk, or something."

Lorenzen could hardly contain himself now. Across the room, I was certain I noticed Westin begin to grin with his eyes closed.

"You were just going to apply for a job with the United States Army," I said.

"I mean, they hire regular people for regular jobs, right?" Schiavo asked. "That's what I thought."

"Right," Neil said. "Lost seventeen year olds looking for work and direction, what other sort of position would they possibly have for you except file clerk?"

"See?" Schiavo joked. "He agrees with me."

Lorenzen rolled with laughter, grabbing his stomach.

"Oh, man, I love it when she tells this story," Lorenzen said.

It was our first time, and I had to admit that it was a hell of a tale. One that Schiavo could tell her grandkids one day. If that day ever came.

"Wham, bam, I'm in the army," Schiavo said, wrapping up the story of her life. "And the army sent me here."

The jovial moment slowly faded. First into small talk about our individual lives. Then into deeper discussions about the world as it was. About the blight. And about what we'd all lost.

Then, with darkness full and the storm raging, we settled in for the night. Neil and I took first watch. It began at midnight and we expected we'd be relieved and in bed by three in the morning.

We were wrong.

Eighteen

I worked the western side of the station, including the dock and the southern perimeter of the facility. Neil covered the north and east. Every ten minutes or so as we moved among the buildings, grabbing cover from the rain beneath awnings and overhangs wherever we could, my friend and I would meet up. Never at exactly the same place, nor at the same interval. Routine, in matters of security and patrol, was a weakness, not a strength. It allowed an adversary to make plans against you.

At the moment, though, our nemesis was wet and cold and relentless.

"Remember the game against Bozeman?" Neil asked as we stopped briefly in the rain shadow created by the boat shed's roof. "That night game?"

He was trolling back through memories. To a moment we'd shared in high school, on the football field, in pouring rain not unlike what we were now experiencing. We'd played the entire game in torrential, almost icy rain. Half the fans in the stadium abandoned the game before the first half was over, but there we were, both teams, cleats chewing at the muddy field, ball slipping through receivers' grips.

"That was nasty," I said.

Neil nodded. He even smiled. Something about him had changed. His frustration had dwindled to almost nothing. I knew he still wanted to get to Grace and Krista with haste, but he'd somehow come to terms with the realities of our journey.

"Grace hates the rain," Neil said. "On our way to your place, whenever it would rain, she'd want to get out of it pronto. She'd practically break down the door of the nearest house to get someplace dry."

"Walks in the rain are not in your future, I guess."

"No," he confirmed.

We said nothing for a moment, the wind blasting water from the boat shed roof into an opaque wall a few yards in front of us.

"They seem okay," I said to Neil, gesturing toward the station where Elaine was bunked down with the unit.

"Their lieutenant is all right," Neil said, almost embarrassed after saying that. "I know I've been an ass."

"You have," I said. "But you have reason to be."

Neil shook his head. He wasn't buying into my proffered excuse.

"We'd be dead on that island if they hadn't shown up," he said. "No matter how much it burns me to have to wait to get to Skagway, we wouldn't even have the chance to do that if it wasn't for Schiavo. If it wasn't for all of them."

"I wonder if we would have even made it on our own," I said.

Neil's gaze widened with the same wonder.

"We get past Mary Island, what else do we encounter ahead?"

My friend was right. We had no idea what sort of contact with the Russians might lay ahead. We knew they had been here, and were likely somewhere along the route we had to travel. The firepower the three of us had was minimal. But added to that of Schiavo's unit, now we had at least a formidable force to deal with whatever lay to the north.

"We'll get there," Neil said. "I know that n—"

He never finished the statement of certainty. The sharp *BAM* from the far side of the station cut him off. Instantly both of us brought our weapons up.

"That was loud," Neil said quietly. "I *felt* that."

I nodded. I'd felt it too, a quick, solid jolt on the soles of my boots.

"I'm going left," I said.

Neil moved right without even acknowledging my statement. He didn't need to. We both expected the other would act as we had many times before since coming together after the blight. In some ways we were equally as capable as Schiavo's unit. Our rhythms were synced in tactical situations. As civilians, this was little more than a practiced survival instinct kicking in. And, as it was now, our sensing of things that weren't quite right was heightened.

I jogged through the rain to the south side of the main building and skirted the edge. Through a window I glimpsed movement, which I knew would be Elaine and the others gearing up. What Neil and I had heard and felt would have jarred them from sleep.

Passing the window I neared the far corner of the building where I could just make out the channel's churning water. And I could see something else.

The bow of the *Sandy* was free, swinging against the dock, the source of the sound that had alerted us. Still tied at the stern, she pivoted with each series of waves and slammed again and again into the concrete and wood mooring. I reached the corner and peered around. I saw nothing beyond what I expected, just Neil at the other corner, moving out into the open.

"She came loose!" he shouted.

We both ran for the spot where the *Sandy* was tied off. From behind, Elaine and the others spilled out of the main building, geared up.

"We've gotta get that bow secured!" Acosta yelled.

I reached the edge of the dock just as Elaine did, handing her my AR as I judged the movement of the rocking deck six feet below.

"Get a rope ready," I told the others. "I'll get aboard and you toss it over."

Acosta and Westin sprinted down the dock to retrieve an extra line, Lorenzen and Enderson covering everyone, their weapons up and ready, a clear wariness about them. We were all exposed, with only the constant downpour providing some concealment where we stood. Visibility was a hundred feet at best.

I only needed a fraction of that to see my target.

BAM!

The bow smacked into the dock again as I mentally measured the jump I had to make. I counted the cycle of the boat moving with the waves. Picked an opportune instant. Then, I jumped.

Immediately upon hitting the deck my boots slipped from under me and I went down hard on my back.

"Eric!"

I rolled over fast and grabbed hold of the rail, looking up to Elaine, trying to reassure her with a quick glance. Reassuring myself was another matter entirely.

BAM!

Again the bow slammed against the solid pier, the impact breaking my grip on the rail and sending me sliding across the deck toward the wheelhouse. I reached fast for the handrail where it was mounted to the deck at the base of the steps into the wheelhouse. My hand found the stout metal and I seized onto it with a death grip, pulling myself to my knees as the *Sandy* whipped away from the dock.

"Get that line tied off!" Schiavo ordered.

Acosta and Westin lashed the line they'd found to one of the dock supports and readied to heave its coiled length down to me. I waited, riding the boat as it once again was pushed by the storming sea toward its mooring.

"Now!" I shouted.

Acosta already had his massive arms cocked and ready. He spun the beefy loop of line toward me, the length unspooling as it traveled the short distance. I grabbed at it with my free hand and took hold just as the *Sandy* was tossed yet again into the dock. Once more I was ripped from my handhold, rope in my other hand now as the waves sucked the *Sandy*'s rebounding bow back toward the channel. My body rolled against the dockside rail, rope in my hand going taut and pulling me up and almost over the side. A fresh series of waves smashed into the boat and moved her again toward the dock, releasing the tension on the line and saving me from being yanked overboard.

I took the brief chance I was given and scurried along the narrow sliver of deck alongside the wheelhouse until I was on all fours at the forward cleat, the end of the rope that had secured the *Sandy* still attached snugly around it, the other end dragging in the water over the rail. The motion of the storming sea must have caused it to snap, I thought, but there was no time to dwell on any cause. I took the end of the line in my hand and figure-eighted it around the cleat, pulling on it with all my weight to be certain it was secure. Just as the *Sandy* swung once again toward the dock I shouted up to the others above.

"Tie it off!"

I absorbed another jolt as boat met the support pillars. This time, though, it did not swing fully out into the channel. Its bow moved a few yards away, then stopped, Acosta and the others taking slack off the line as they wrapped it around a thick wooden support rising from the dock edge. As the *Sandy* was pushed again into the dock, with less force this time, they cinched up the line and tied her fully off.

"She's good!" Acosta reported.

I grabbed hold of the rail along the wheelhouse and pulled myself along until I was at the solid steel ladder mounted to one of the pier supports. With nearly raw hands and slick boots, I climbed up from the still bouncing deck and was hauled onto the dock by Neil and Elaine.

"Are you all right?" Elaine asked, helping me to stand.

I examined my palms, the cool rain feeling good upon the red welts burned into them by the rough line.

"I'm okay."

"That was a gutsy move," Schiavo said. "Maybe too gutsy."

"Someone was going to have to do it," I said.

"Lieutenant!"

It was Acosta. He'd moved past us to check that the stern line wasn't in any danger of snapping. We joined him where he knelt at the cleat welded and bolted to the dock.

"What is it?" Schiavo asked.

Acosta pointed to the rope stretching from it over the edge of the dock and down to the *Sandy*. About a foot from where it was attached a neat slice had cut almost halfway through the line, taking more than half of its strength.

"Christ..." Lorenzen said, then ran to the point where the bow line had been tied off. It was still secured there, to a cleat identical to the bow line, its limp end lying just at the edge of the dock. He picked it up and examined it.

"Cut clean," he said, looking to us. "Someone took a knife to these lines."

I took my AR back from Elaine, my gaze instinctively scanning the world beyond the falling rain.

"Get a new line on the stern," Schiavo ordered.

"Yes, Ma'am," Westin said, and climbed down to the boat as Acosta retrieved another fresh line.

"We've got a problem," Schiavo said.

"Yeah," I agreed. "We're not alone."

Part Three

Invaders

Nineteen

Morning came with the storm in full force, more wind than rain in the daylight. But it was the wind that worked against us. Wind meant waves. And waves meant a tenuous journey, one with risks that outweighed any benefit of haste at the moment. We were not leaving Ketchikan until the weather broke.

That did not mean we were sitting back, resting and relaxing. The attempt to set the *Sandy* adrift in the night had put us on an extreme state of alert. Schiavo had three of her men, Lorenzen, Enderson, and Westin, stationed outside, with one always near the boat. The rest of us remained inside, waiting for our shift watching over the only transport we had.

It wasn't certain that that was our best course of action.

"You want to do what?" Schiavo asked after I told her my idea.

"*We* want to go look for our visitor," I said.

Neil and Elaine had actually hatched the idea and shared it quietly with me. It was likely that Schiavo wouldn't see our plan as a smart use of personnel. She'd almost certainly already weighed the risk of seeking a confrontation with whoever had slipped into our perimeter during the night and decided against it. I needed to convince her otherwise.

"Visitor," she repeated, focusing on the singularity of the word. "You assume it's just one person."

"I do," I said. "They were spooked while cutting the stern line. If it was two intruders, both would have cut at the same time."

"You assume two would come out of whatever hole they crawled into," Schiavo said. "I don't. There could be more."

I had to allow that possibility. But that didn't negate the reasoning for what we were suggesting.

"I've learned," I began, gesturing to Neil and Elaine next, "we've all learned, that hunkering down isn't always the best plan. If there's a threat out there, a good offense is what we need."

She thought for a moment. Once again taking into consideration what we were saying.

"You're talking textbook tactics," she said. "Probing the enemy. Attacking into an ambush."

I wasn't certain of the military tactics she was basing her estimation on, but I did agree with the plain language. Sitting where we were would not serve us, just as it would not have served me well at my refuge when the threat presented by Major Layton was very real. There I had to take matters into my own hands. I had to act.

I had to attack.

Whether we would have to mount any major assault here, I didn't know. None of us did. We couldn't, because we were lacking information and intelligence as to just what, and who, we were up against. That was the point. We needed to get out there and locate the threat before it manifested again.

"The town is booby-trapped," Schiavo said. "Any step you take could be your last."

"And every second the weather keeps us holed up in here could be our last," Elaine pointed out. "We're sitting ducks."

Once more the lieutenant retreated into her own head. Thinking. Considering. Calculating. Deciding.

"I can't send anyone with you," she said. "I need my men to secure this station and the boat."

"We know that," I said. "We've been on our own before."

"In some hairy situations," Neil told her.

"I don't doubt it," Schiavo said.

She looked from us to where Hart and Acosta had spread themselves out on a pair of the rec room's couches, gear and weapons on the floor at their sides. Within easy reach. Everyone was ready for whatever fight came, if it did.

We wanted to take that fight to the enemy and ensure our safe departure from Ketchikan when the weather made that possible.

"When do you want to go?" Schiavo asked.

"Now," I said.

"Where?"

Elaine spread a map out on the pool table. The same map we'd marked with the locations of the booby traps.

"Through here," Elaine said, pointing to the streets where the improvised devices had been placed. "If I was trying to protect my base of operations, I'd place devices along the approach. No different than drug dealers posting lookouts."

"You think they might be in town?" Schiavo asked.

"We know they've been there to set those traps," I said. "That gives us a starting point."

For a moment Schiavo eyed the map. The town. The mountains beyond. Then she looked to us.

"If things go bad, it will take us time to get to you," she said. "And that's if we hear something to make us come."

Gunshots. Explosions. Either could signal that we needed help. Or that we were beyond it.

"Understood," I said.

Then Schiavo gave a quick nod. She was blessing our mission. We didn't have to seek it, but having her on board showed consideration to the role she'd been thrust into. It also bound us to her unit. To our common purpose.

To get out of Ketchikan alive.

Twenty

We moved through lighter rain into town and past the buildings we knew to be booby-trapped, continuing on, moving up inclined streets. Finally out of town. Into the mountains where houses were nestled close to the once green slope.

"Are you part bloodhound?" Elaine asked me.

I smiled and kept walking, focused on the way ahead. And on the asphalt roadway we were traveling along.

"Wouldn't you want the best vantage point to observe?" I replied with my own question.

"You know where we're going," she said. "Don't you?"

"I believe so," I said.

"You mind sharing what mystical power is guiding you?"

It was gentle ribbing from her. With a pinch of doubt.

"Did you notice anything on the street when we passed the last rigged building?"

I glanced back, waiting for either of my friends to chime in. Neither did.

"Mud," I told them.

"It's raining," Elaine said. "There's mud everywhere."

I shifted my direction of travel, walking along the sloppy shoulder for a moment, then tracked back onto the hard roadway. My boots left a trail of evenly spaced prints on the wet surface, the softening rain dragging the transferred mud slowly away, erasing the markings bit by bit.

"That's what I saw," I said, motioning almost covertly to the fading tracks I'd just made.

"You saw tracks?" Neil asked, quietly incredulous. "In town?"

I nodded.

"I didn't think pointing it out too openly was a good idea," I said.

Elaine and Neil both understood now. Completely.

"We're being watched," Elaine said for both of them.

"Yep," I said, trying to remain nonchalant. "I suggest we just keep following those tracks up ahead."

I saw Elaine focus ahead to precisely what I had been zeroed in on. Muddy spots on the asphalt being dissolved by the weather. Bits of embedded dirt had been trailing off the boots of the man, or woman, we'd been pursuing, leaving the equivalent of a breadcrumb trail.

"They're not doing a great job of hiding their tracks," Elaine said.

"This is not some Russian super soldier we're dealing with," I said.

"Then who?" Neil wondered.

For a few moments we walked in full silence. Listening past the *drip drip drip* of rain trickling from our hats and our gear onto the puddled roadway. Sampling the hush for anything other than the wet rustle of the weather.

"Do you think the lieutenant could be right?" Elaine asked. "About there being more than one out here?"

"It's possible," I answered.

"But you don't think so," Elaine said.

"I don't."

"I don't either," Neil added.

"That makes three of us," Elaine said.

"Good," I said. "We now have a three to one advantage and we haven't even put eyes on our target yet."

Elaine chuckled lightly. We moved in a line, leaving the residential neighborhood behind and reaching a gravel road that appeared to wind its way into a mining or quarry operation of some kind. No signage marked it, and the only building visible from where that wide trail left the paved road was, uncharacteristically, burned to its foundation.

"Interesting," Neil said.

I scanned the area, noticing a water tank just to the south. I'd glimpsed the structure from the waterfront before the clouds thickened and the rain came. A ladder hung on its side, providing easy access to its wide, flat top.

"That would give a clear view of almost everything below," I said, pointing to the tower.

Elaine nodded, then looked up the gravel road to the mountains rising beyond.

"And from up there you could see where we're standing right now," she said.

"Exactly," I said.

"There's always that chance that they were leaving that trail on purpose," Neil said.

"Either way," I said, looking up the muddy road leading past the charred building, "we know we're close."

I started moving again, staying left, close to the edge of a hill where it leveled out and blended with the road. A low wave of my hand directed Neil to the right side. Elaine, without needing any prompting, slowed a bit, bringing up the rear, glancing behind every dozen yards or so.

The open area of the mine or quarry site ended, muddy road narrowing as it snaked into the woods. No lush canopy shielded us from the rain. The weather ran down the dead trunks of what had once been living, breathing spruce and birch trees, scouring more of the grey skim that coated every blighted bit of flora. With enough time, like mountains eroded to plains, I imagined that nature would erase what the hellish microbe had left in its wake.

"I don't see any tracks," Neil said.

There was no way one could on this ground. We were walking through a layer of thin muck that swallowed all traces of who was passing. Or who had already passed. We were pursuing with blinders on now.

Until we came upon the trail.

Hardly wider than the space between two trees, it split unmistakably off from the muddy road, winding its way upward along the slope. And upon it the boot prints were unmistakable. They ran up the trail and into the grey forest, the path well worn, like a game trail.

"Rain would have obliterated those in twenty minutes," Neil said.

"They just came through here," Elaine added, tucking her MP5 high and tight against her shoulder. "Ahead of us."

Just as we'd thought, we'd been watched. It was a near perfect position to observe any approach through the old mining site. And a virtually textbook place to set even more traps. Just as a woodsman would lay snares along where his prey would travel between burrow and watering hole in the forest, our intruder had presented us with a trail that could be just as easily marked with mines. Or trip-wired grenades. Or any manner of dangerous and deadly implements.

This was where they wanted us to go. Which was precisely why we were not.

"We shift right about fifty yards and head upslope from there," I said.

Both Neil and Elaine agreed. We moved along the old dirt road, keeping quiet. Stepping over the deepest puddles so as to not splash loudly. Avoiding fallen twigs lest they snap underfoot. We needed to be ghosts in the dead woods.

Finally we started up the slope. Soggy earth slid beneath us with each step. We kept our weapons high and clear in one hand, and groped for handholds on the dead trees with the other.

A hundred yards we climbed, the rain turning to a foggy mist that masked what lay beyond twenty feet. We were in the clouds now. Cold, wet, and wary. Spread out line abreast, ten feet between each other.

"Stop," Elaine said, just above a whisper.

We halted, crouching low, everyone aware where the nearest tree or fallen log was that could be reached for cover.

"What?" I asked quietly.

Elaine squinted into the opaque world before us. Then she pointed. To a spot slightly off our direction of travel.

"I swear I heard a sniffle," she said.

In another time I might have thought she'd been fooled by the sounds of squirrels, or birds. But there were no more of those.

"How far?" Neil asked.

Elaine shrugged. There was only so much one could tell in these conditions. Any sound at all was filtered through and muffled by the thick, damp air.

I nodded and adjusted our direction toward the sound. I only made it five steps before I knew we'd made a mistake.

Dammit...

I swore within and fixed hard on what lay ahead.

Nothing. Not a single thing. The forest had been cut clear here, long before the blight had arrived, some logging operation leaving a vast swath of open space where the slope leveled out. A perfect killing field.

The moment I realized that the first burst of automatic fire split the calm day.

Rounds raked across the open ground before us and sliced into the trees at the clearing's border. No one needed to shout a warning. We all grabbed what cover we could, me behind a low mound of earth, Elaine and Neil behind a pair of toppled trees to my right.

"Stay away!"

The warning was accompanied by another burst of fire, the muzzle flashes I could glimpse revealing what appeared to be a cavern entrance some distance through the mist. It was fortified, the pulses made plain, the fire coming through slits between stacks of thick logs.

"We're pinned," Neil said, looking behind. "If we backtrack there's no cover."

Even with the ground leveling out, the apparent bunker across the clearing still rested a good ten feet higher than our position. It was shooting down upon us. Without the cover we'd been fortunate to find, we'd already be dead.

"I'll kill you all!"

More fire. Long bursts with some control. The shooter wasn't just praying and spraying. He was trying to suppress any advance on his position.

I looked to Elaine where she lay behind the toppled log a few yards to my right. Neil had crawled to a position even more to her right, seeking a position that would allow both cover and a place to return fire.

"That's not Russian," Elaine said, stating the obvious thing we all were thinking. "What the hell is going on?"

I didn't know. But if that was truly an American up the slope, or more than one, it raised some questions we couldn't answer by just hugging cover until the shooter ran out of ammunition.

"We're Americans!" Neil shouted toward the cavern entrance.

More bursts of fire were the reply. The sound of the weapon was familiar. And maybe telling.

"That's an AR or an M4," I said.

"Definitely not an AK," Neil added.

"Are you from Ketchikan?!" Elaine called out. "Did you survive the blight here?!"

"Get away!"

It was a man's voice. A young man, though the voice was edged with grit. With certainty.

"Did you try to cut our boat loose?!" I challenged the young man.

No fire came in reply to that question. And no verbal retort, either. There was just silence for a moment.

"We came up with a unit of American soldiers," I told the mystery man through the silence. "Mary Island was overrun by Russians while we were there. The soldiers took them out."

More silence. Long and lasting. I looked to Elaine.

"What are you afraid of?" she asked. "We're not going to hurt you."

"You've got that right!"

The warning came in advance of more gunfire, pinning us where we were, the young man entertaining only so much discussion from us.

"You're not soldiers!" he shouted between bursts. "I saw you last night! You weren't in uniform!"

"We're civilians!" I told him. "You've got to believe us!"

"Like hell I do."

And more fire. Rounds chewed high and low into the dead trees that surrounded us. What had been a sapling when the blight took hold snapped and toppled next to Elaine, its inch thick trunk threatening a nasty hit if it had made contact.

"Were you part of the garrison here?!" Neil asked.

No answer. Just gunfire in Neil's direction.

"We don't have too many options here," Elaine said.

I looked to the opposite side of the cover I'd found, a low mound of dirt and rock, just a quick glance around it without exposing myself for too long. The stream of fire was creating a clear zone. Punching a wide hole through the fog. I saw more clearly now the fortification he'd constructed, logs and more logs surrounding and covering the cavern entrance. It looked hastily built, but was fully serving its purpose.

"Neil," I said, sliding back behind my cover.

"What?"

"Cover fire," I said. "But aim to his right."

Neil nodded. I looked to Elaine.

"You fire dead straight at that bunker, but low."

"You're going left," she said, reading my intention.

If we could both shift his attention to incoming fire, and get his head down for even a few seconds, I might be able to get close. Maybe close enough to put an end to this.

"Give me ten seconds, then cease fire," I said.

We didn't need any friendly fire incidents once I got close to his fortification. *If* I got close.

"Ready?"

My friends looked to me and nodded. A second later, in between incoming bursts from the cavern, they opened up.

I moved as quickly as I could, my AR in hand and low as I swept left in an arcing path to the cavern, trying to come in on its flank. About halfway there the young man began firing again. But not in my direction. He was trying to suppress what was coming his way.

He hadn't seen me, and where I moved now, a good ten yards to the left, the mist was thick, swallowing me whole. I could just see the ends of the logs he'd arranged as one might sandbags. They were his cover. They would also be mine.

"You're not getting me!"

His battle cry was followed by more fire. *His* fire. My friends had silenced their weapons to clear the way for me. But this was no charging an enemy position with bayonet fixed. This was not Iwo Jima and I certainly wasn't a battle hardened Marine. The truth be told, I was scared to my core. My heart pounded, so loud I feared the sound of it thrumming in my chest would announce my approach. What moisture there had been in my mouth was gone, leaving my tongue, my lips, and everything in the vicinity as dry as the blighted desert. If this was bravery, I found it utterly indistinguishable from terror.

But what I was doing had to be done. We were pinned down. Retreating with haste might allow one of us to escape. Maybe two under the best circumstances. But not all of us. The only way for Elaine, and Neil, and me to get off this mountain alive was to get up close and neutralize the threat. To kill it...if necessary.

I didn't want to do that. Any person in their right mind would think me crazy for harboring such thoughts. For allowing such consideration toward the man trying to kill us.

The *young* man.

The young man who just might be a scared American kid.

He fired. In groups of three bursts, I counted. Each one three rounds. He was doing three groups and final quick spray before reloading with a fresh thirty round mag. As close as I was I could distinctly hear the click of the magazine release. And the wet thud of the empty slapping against the sloppy earth.

"You've got to trust us!"

It was Elaine, keeping him focused. He reloaded and unleashed another round of measured fire. I crouched and crept forward. Hugging the edge of a rock outcropping into which nature, or man, had gouged the cavern.

Nine rounds...

The close edge of the log barricade was before me. I could smell the gunpowder. Spent shells ejected from his rifle rattled against the barricade logs on the side of the cavern.

Eighteen rounds...

I brought my AR slowly into position.

"Just stop!" Elaine implored him. "We can talk this out!"

Twenty seven rounds...

"No talk!" the young man shouted and fired until he was empty.

Thirty rounds...

Go, I told myself silently.

I rose from behind the log barricade just as the expended magazine fell into the muddy ground. My focus was fully on the end of my suppressor. On what came into view just beyond it. Within two yards of me.

"Don't move!"

The order I shouted had an immediate effect on the young man. The uniformed young man. Uniformed as an American soldier. A drenched and terrified American fighting man.

"Drop the weapon," I said.

To my right I heard the slap of boots on the sloppy ground as Elaine and Neil raced toward the cavern. From the corner of my eye I could see them approach, spread out, their weapons up and ready, fingers laying just alongside the trigger guards.

The soldier looked up at me, his gaze angling next to my friends as they reached the barricade and trained their weapons over it.

"Just put it down," Elaine said.

The soldier hesitated. Frozen. The fear in his eyes more palpable than I'd seen in a very long time. This man, this boy, thought he was going to die.

"If we wanted you dead, you'd already be dead," I said. "Now put the weapon down."

He drew a breath and let the M4 slip easily from his grip.

"Stand up," I said.

He did as I'd told him. Neil and Elaine seized his arms and pulled him over the log barricade.

"We're going for a walk," I told him, lowering my AR just a little. "You first."

Our prisoner walked ahead of us as we moved back into the fog and down the mountain.

Twenty One

His name was Kenneth Avery. Private Kenneth Avery. I was
inclined to believe that. Not everyone was.

"I'm not lying," Avery said, his hands shaking atop the
table he sat at.

We'd hauled him back to the Coast Guard Station and
presented him to Schiavo just as she was about to send a
patrol out toward the sound of the firefight we'd been
engaged in.

"I'm not the infiltrator!"

"But you admit there was one," Lorenzen said.

The lieutenant stood behind her sergeant, letting him
conduct the interrogation as the rest of us watched. Because
that's what this was—an interrogation of a prisoner.

"Yes," Avery said, near tears. "How the hell do you
think they got us all?"

"They didn't get you all," Lorenzen said. "You're still
here."

Avery nodded, shame washing over him.

"I ran," he said. "Okay. I ran. I hid. And if I hadn't, I'd
be dead like the rest."

"Where are the bodies?" Lorenzen asked.

"I don't know," Avery answered, seeming ready to
weep. "I just don't know."

Then, he leaned forward, face pressed to his palms as
he sobbed. And sobbed. The emotion flowing without
restraint.

If it was emotion at all.

He'd said that a person claiming to be a refugee came down from the mountains, and that he had a wife and child up there in a cabin. They were sick, the man had supposedly told the garrison's commander, a Lieutenant Williamson. Wanting to offer what assistance he could, Williamson sent two men with the refugee to retrieve his sick family from the cabin.

Neither they nor the two soldiers returned.

As Avery told it, Williamson then took a soldier with him to search for the missing men and the family, leaving him alone to watch over the garrison's base. Alone for nearly a full day, Avery became worried, and was about to send a message over the burst transmitter reporting the situation when he heard gunfire. He geared up and headed for where he'd thought the sound originated, but spotted movement and took cover. From that position he said he'd watched at least fifteen soldiers in strange uniforms move along the road from town to the station. A while later, as the troops searched the facility, presumably for him, a boat approached and docked. After raiding the supplies at the station and loading them onto the boat, the troops lowered the flag and boarded the boat, sailing off as the sun set.

It was a hell of a story. One not unlike what 'Jeremy' had told us at Mary Island. It was a distinct possibility that they were birds of a feather. Each a member of Kuratov's elite unit. Men schooled in the ways of the west so as to slip in and exist, undetected, until they were tasked with acting. Yes, that was possible.

But I didn't think this man was that at all.

"Kenneth," I said.

Lorenzen looked to me. As did Schiavo. She'd made it clear that her sergeant was going to be the point of contact with this man we'd found. And we'd agreed to it. But they weren't seeing what I was. What I had.

Avery eased his hands away from his face and looked up at me.

"Where are you from?" I asked.

"Boulder, Colorado."

I smiled and took the knife from my belt, then a length of paracord from where it was lashed to the outside of my pack.

"What are you going to do?" Kenneth asked, nervous and afraid.

I cut a length of line and tossed it to him. He stared at where it lay on the table, then looked to me again.

"Boulder has a big climbing community," I said, recalling what a friend had told me years ago. "Isn't that true?"

The soldier looked at me, puzzled. Maybe by the normalcy of the question.

"Yeah," he confirmed.

"A friend of mine was big into climbing," I said. "Rock, mostly. A little alpine. We would play this game where he'd get drunk and have me time him tying knots. When he couldn't do a one-handed bowline in under five seconds, he'd decide it was time to put the bottle away."

Kenneth stared at me blankly. Schiavo did not.

"This is all very interesting," the lieutenant said. "But—"

"Tie me a lineman's loop," I instructed Kenneth, cutting the lieutenant off.

He looked between me and the length of cord, then fixed on Schiavo. She eyed me for a moment, and I sensed she might understand where I was going with this.

"Do what he says," Schiavo told the soldier. "If you can."

He hesitated, just briefly, then picked up the paracord and twisted it, fashioning a secure loop halfway between the ends. Finished, he looked to me, to all of us, and I reached out and took the length of paracord from him.

"This is what connected those grenades," I said, showing the piece of cordage out to Schiavo.

The lieutenant eyed the very specific loop in the line and looked to Private Avery.

"You rigged the town," she said.

"In case they came back."

"The Russians," she said.

"If that's who they were."

The lieutenant and sergeant fixed hard, critical gazes on the prisoner.

"Look, I didn't know who you were," Avery said, with emotion that wasn't yet pleading. "I still don't know. That's why I tried to cut your boat loose. I figured if I had you trapped here, I could pick you off a couple at a time just like you...like they did to my unit."

"You would have done that?" Lorenzen pressed the young man.

"In a heartbeat," Avery answered with obvious fire.

As Avery finished speaking, Westin, Enderson, and Hart returned. The corporal approached the table where the prisoner sat and dumped something from his hand upon it. Dog tags.

"Kenneth Avery," Enderson said, looking to Schiavo. "We checked his hooch. He has a good cache of arms there. Limited food. Maybe a day or two more."

"Grenades?" Schiavo asked.

"M Sixty Sevens," Enderson reported.

Exactly what had been used to set traps in the town.

"If he's a Russian infiltrator, why set traps?" I asked Schiavo. "The only people he'd expect to see are his buddies. Just like the guy on Mary Island."

Schiavo considered that, and all we'd heard from the prisoner.

"You're with my unit now, private," Schiavo said.

To that, Private Kenneth Avery shook his head.

"This is my post," Avery said. "I'm assigned here. And I'll stay here until my commander returns, or I'm relieved by authority that I know and trust."

Outside, Neil and Elaine were covering the perimeter with Acosta. Inside, Lieutenant Angela Schiavo was contending with what might be termed a small mutiny. She looked to Enderson.

"Any sign of the radio?"

"None," Enderson said.

Schiavo fixed on Avery again.

"You have any idea where your garrison's burst radio is?"

Avery shook his head.

"It was in here," he said, pointing across the room to an empty table against the wall. "Right over there. I assume they took it along with the food when they pulled out."

Lorenzen shook his head.

"If they got the scramble code out of one of the guys they grabbed..."

Schiavo knew exactly what Lorenzen was suggesting would mean.

"Kuratov could listen in on our com," she said. "And headquarters wouldn't even know it. Because I have no way to tell them!"

The sudden flourish of anger echoed sharp within the station's rec room. No one said anything. It would be Schiavo who would have to break the tension she'd just created.

"You can stay with us here until the weather clears," Schiavo told Avery. "Then we'll be out of here."

"You'll let me stay?" Avery asked, only half expecting that his insistence on such would be not just tolerated, but accepted.

"You're right," Schiavo told him. "It's your post. Your mission. I can't abandon what I've been ordered to do unless my superiors tell me to."

Avery rose slowly from the chair he'd been made to sit in. He stood at attention and brought his hand up in a sharp salute directed at Schiavo.

"There's no requirement to salute me indoors, private. Not in this situation."

Avery lowered his hand and brought it to his side, still at attention.

"I know, ma'am. I just thought you deserved it. *Especially* in this situation."

The barest smile came to Schiavo. She looked to me, no words coming right then, but everything about her look conveying a simple message to me—*thank you*.

* * *

Lieutenant Schiavo sent two of her men with Avery to his cavern hooch to retrieve his gear and belongings while she and the remainder of her troops caught some rest. Neil and Elaine and I stood watch outside, our defensive posture somewhat more relaxed than the night before.

My friend, I could see, was still having difficulty waiting. He was just expressing the frustration that came with that in a more sedate way. A way turned inward.

That had to be hell.

"What are you going to do when we get back?" I asked him.

He didn't look at me, his gaze fixed out on the darkening waters of the channel as it had been for several minutes.

"Back to Bandon?"

"Yeah," I said.

"Never let her out of my sight again," Neil answered.

I could appreciate that, though I didn't know how realistic that statement would end up being. It was a reactionary sentiment he had expressed. One totally relatable to all that had happened since returning from Cheyenne.

Then, he looked away from the churning sea and made eye contact with me. With only me. His gaze very purposely avoiding Elaine where she stood a few feet away.

"Walk with me for a minute, Fletch," my friend said.

It was a request. A polite way to ask if we could talk alone. Just the two of us.

"Sure," I said, then looked to Elaine. "Be back in a minute."

She nodded. There was no doubt that she'd heard the exchange. She understood that my friend, my oldest and dearest friend, wanted to speak to me out of earshot of anyone. Though the look about her as I turned away made me think that she was wondering if he only wanted our words to be unheard by her.

We walked to the edge of the dock. Wind waves rolled hard against it, the gusts pushing at us where we stopped. The storm was more wind than rain now. Nature's fury cut by half.

"I have no way of explaining how hard this is to say," Neil told me, looking out to the water again.

"What is it?"

"Don't ever have her with you again if there's a chance you'll see her die," my friend said, looking to me. "It's hard enough knowing I wasn't there when Grace and Krista were taken away. If I'd had to watch that happen..."

"They would have taken you, too," I reminded him.

"Dammit, Fletch!"

The outburst came so fast that I literally shuddered. I glanced behind and saw that Elaine was looking our way, but just for a moment. She turned and wandered toward the building and disappeared around the far side.

"You're just not understanding what it is you're risking," Neil said, a calm returned to his manner. "I thought about it before. That night on the boat when you asked me what I was thinking."

I recalled that. He'd considered Elaine with what I now thought could have been a measuring gaze. One that was judging, maybe for the first time, just how much she meant to me. And I to her.

"I had no idea what we'd come across on our little boat trip," Neil said, allowing a small, brief smile. "But I was thinking about how bad it could get. We'd seen terrible things, and I didn't know if you were ready to have anything happen to Elaine in front of your own eyes."

I glanced behind again, even though she wasn't there. Just for an instant I glimpsed the emptiness where she'd been, and what Neil was saying resonated. A chill, not made of the weather, slid slowly over me, from head to toe.

"I think I wanted to tell you then what I'm telling you now," Neil said, and I faced him again. "What if she'd been the one to run up on Avery's bunker and not you? And what if it had gone wrong? Can you handle that?"

I didn't have an answer for him.

"You took the risk today," Neil said. "Will she let you do that tomorrow, or the next day, or the next, if we're up against another obstacle that's trying to kill us?"

"I don't—"

"Don't say you don't know," he said, cutting me off. "Because you do know. She won't. She's a hard charger, Fletch. Just like you."

"And just like you?" I challenged him.

My friend nodded.

"This world is different than the old one," Neil said. "A bad move back then might send you to the emergency room for stitches, or maybe a cast. A bad move now..."

I knew what he was saying. There was no safety net other than what we, ourselves, could manage.

"If you can't imagine yourself watching something bad happen to her, then think about how much she means to you. It's new. Ending something now would hurt, but not as much as watching her die."

"You think I should..."

Neil shook his head.

"She's good for you," my friend said. "I see that. And you're good for her. But if it is important enough to be together, to stay together, then think very, very hard about who's going to be the first one down a dark hall. Okay? That's all I'm asking you to do."

It might have been the most heartfelt statement of concern he'd ever shared with me.

"I need her," I said.

"I know. So think about what I said. Okay?"

The wind gusted and tossed the spray of a wave over the edge of the dock. Icy droplets of water prickled cold on the skin of my cheeks.

"Okay," I said.

Neil walked away, putting a hand briefly upon my shoulder as he moved past. When he was gone I looked to the sea, as my friend had. Night was racing over the storming channel. Grey and black clouds hung over ashen islands beyond indigo water. All that I saw before me was angry, and grim, and foreboding. The world had tried to kill me. People had tried, too. But I had survived. And I wanted to keep doing so. More than anything, though, I did not want to do so alone.

I wanted to see a new world born with Elaine by my side.

Twenty Two

It stormed for five days. On the sixth we prepared the *Sandy* for departure just before dawn. Private Avery stood with us on the dock as we gathered for the last time in Ketchikan.

"If I can get communication going again I'll report your status," Schiavo told Avery.

"Thank you, ma'am," Avery said.

He wore a clean uniform. One he'd squirreled away for later use. As the lone surviving member of the Ketchikan garrison, he was clearly taking it upon himself to represent the unit he'd served with.

"I'll also report your promotion during circumstances of battle to specialist," Schiavo said. "Congratulations, Specialist Avery."

The young man went almost white for a moment, then the color came back to his face and he saluted Schiavo. She saluted back and offered her hand. Avery shook it and looked to each of us, settling his gaze on me last.

"Thank you for not...doing what you could have," he said.

"I'm glad it all worked out," I said.

Acosta already had the *Sandy* fired up, its diesel rumbling below decks as the last of us boarded. Avery untied our bow and stern lines and waved as we pulled slowly away from the Coast Guard Station's dock. We'd left a supply of MREs with him to partially replace what the Russians had taken, allowing him a good month of food to sustain him. By then we should have been able to reach Juneau, and Skagway, and report on his needing further resupply. Or extraction altogether.

"How long?" Elaine asked Acosta as we sailed past Ketchikan's airport on Gravina Island, directly across the channel from the northern part of the city.

"Thirty hours," the soldier said. "Approximately."

Behind him, Schiavo was scanning the way ahead through binoculars. It was just the four of us in the wheelhouse. The rest were mostly below, though Neil and Westin stood on deck near the stern, talking about fishing it seemed from the hand motions each was making.

"Can you do that, lieutenant?" I asked. "Just promote that kid yourself?"

Schiavo lowered the binoculars and looked to me.

"I think so," she said. "If anyone higher up wants to challenge me on it, bring it on."

She brought the binoculars back up and continued glassing the waters ahead and the shores to either side.

"Will you spell Acosta in a couple hours, Eric?" Schiavo asked.

"Absolutely," I said.

"I'll take the wheel after him," Elaine said.

"Then that's the plan," Schiavo said.

I looked to Elaine. She stood next to Acosta, her own gaze sweeping the mix of land and sea ahead, searching for threats or obstacles. She was putting herself out there. Taking the initiative. Doing her part.

Just like Neil had suggested she would.

No one was shooting at us here. Not at the moment. But my friend was right—if the time came, Elaine Morales would not hesitate to put herself into the fight.

For the first time since we'd found each other, that scared the hell out of me.

Twenty Three

Almost exactly thirty hours after departing Ketchikan, Acosta maneuvered the *Sandy* past the long pier where cruise ships would have once lined the waterfront. Sergeant Lorenzen stood next to him, binoculars raised and fixed on a small dock ahead.

"Damn..."

Lorenzen's commentary drew me to the window. I took my own compact binoculars from my pocket and zeroed in on what had elicited his response. The dock itself, about twice the size of what was needed to accommodate our vessel, was unremarkable and undisturbed. A structure just beyond it was not.

"The garrison?" Schiavo asked her number two.

"Building's gone," Lorenzen told her. "No sign of life."

Gone didn't fully describe the remains of what had been there. Roughly the size of an average house, all that was left were charred timbers and debris scattered into parking lots beyond. It was as if the place had come apart from within.

We pulled alongside the dock and tied off, everyone but Acosta on deck now, armed and geared up. When the *Sandy*'s engine was shut down, the purest, eeriest silence settled in. The quiet was almost tangible. You could feel it, like one might sense fog prickling cold at their skin while their eyes were closed.

"Is that where they were?" Neil asked.

"That's where they were supposed to be," Schiavo said.

The garrison posted in Juneau, which was supposed to number five, the same as Ketchikan's decimated unit, was nowhere to be seen. If they'd spotted us cruising up the channel it would have been prudent for them to observe and lay low. But now, as we all disembarked and spread out near the remnants of the building, using other structures and low walls for cover, anyone watching would have the perfect opportunity to make contact with us.

Or to attack.

"Check what's left," Schiavo ordered.

Lorenzen directed Westin and Enderson forward. The soldiers waded into the demolished building, scanning the debris for a few minutes before looking back to their commander and giving a thumbs down.

"No bodies," Lorenzen said.

"No anything," I added.

Schiavo let out a long, bitter breath.

"We need that radio," she said.

"What if the garrison relocated?" Elaine suggested. "If Kuratov's troops did come through here, they could have seen them coming."

"And bugged out," Lorenzen said, entertaining the thought. "If they were faced with a superior force..."

"Yeah," Schiavo said. "If. If this, if that. Everything's an 'if.'"

She was frustrated. My guess was that being cut off was wearing on her. Schiavo was obviously a capable leader, but she was facing a world that her training hadn't quite envisioned. Officers were schooled in initiative, but also in the importance of command and control. The necessity to follow orders, and to report developments to their higher authorities.

Schiavo, I could see, still hadn't grasped that, for the moment at least, *she* was the highest authority that mattered. And she was going to have to get used to that.

"Lieutenant," I said.

"What?"

"If you were able to get through to your command right now, what do you think their orders would be?"

She puzzled first, maybe at why I was even asking such a question. Then, almost calmed by the mental exercise, she seemed to calculate precisely the scenario which I was inquiring about. And the absence of reality it spoke to.

"Hypotheticals get you killed," she said.

"Correct," I said. "There's no 'if' here. There's you."

She took that in, then turned away from me and surveyed the destroyed building, looking past it to the sliver of the city visible beyond. Mountains that were once green stood grey and jagged on the far side of downtown, thin ribbons of clouds drifting past their peaks.

"Map, Private Westin."

The young soldier returned from the debris pile and slipped the map from his pack and brought it to his commander. She unfolded it and studied the city for a moment, orienting herself.

"State Capitol is due north of here," Schiavo said. "About a quarter mile at the corner of Main and Fourth. That's our rally point."

She was identifying a place to meet. But meet after doing what?

"We're going for a walk," Schiavo said, then spread the map on the hood of a car with four flat tires and laid out her plan.

Twenty Four

Juneau was a city caught between mountain and sea. It was also dead.

"Abandoned," Sergeant Lorenzen said as our group made our way along streets in the downtown area.

Three of us were with him. Elaine, me, and Westin. Neil, Enderson, and Schiavo had moved beyond the downtown area, heading to a residential cluster up the coast, just inland from the airport. It would be a five mile trudge along slick roads, and five miles back along the same for them. Our plan was for both groups to meet near the State Capitol building after our sweeps were complete, then head back to the *Sandy*, which was being watched over by Hart and Acosta.

"There's not much damage," Elaine said, scanning the storefronts. "Just like Ketchikan."

She and I hugged the left curb, occasionally shifting around cars left to rot and rust. Lorenzen and Westin kept to the right, a few yards separating each pair. Spacing maintained in the hope that any unexpected fire wouldn't take out multiple people at once.

"Who's here to riot?" Westin theorized with a question. "This isn't the big city."

"They're also well-armed," Elaine added. "Or were. People here wouldn't have put up with too much idiocy."

I suspected she was right. Aside from some broken glass and a few torched cars on side streets, the leveled building back by the dock was the worst we'd seen.

Until we rounded a corner past an auto parts store.

"Christ..."

The quiet curse that Lorenzen let slip preceded his direction to us by just a second. Following his hand motions, Westin sprinted across the street to the opposite corner, and Elaine and I jogged diagonally across the intersection to set up a strong point that could cover our rear and the direction we'd come from. But it was hard to scan only those slices of the tactical pie. What lay down the block we'd planned to travel drew our glances no matter how hard we tried to not look.

Bodies were what we saw. Crumpled at the base of a brick wall. I counted five, all shirtless and barefooted. The pants they wore matched the camo pattern of Lorenzen's uniform. And Westin's. And the other members of the unit.

It was the missing garrison. All indications pointed to that.

Lorenzen motioned for us to cover him, and a moment later he moved forward, hugging the brick wall, his weapon covering the opposite side of the street. He approached the collection of bodies and crouched close to them, examining what we'd found. Holding still. Very still. Saying nothing. It was almost as if he was praying.

Finally he waved us forward. We moved slowly. Warily. Scanning every window. Every corner. Every opening to any building.

"Damn," Westin said as he reached the horrific scene.

"Executed," Lorenzen said, rising up, pure fury in his gaze.

I looked upon the tangle of men on the cold, damp sidewalk. Their bodies had been defiled by violence. By volleys of gunfire. They'd stood as one, and fallen as one.

"How long ago do you think?" Lorenzen asked.

He'd posed the question to Elaine. I suspected that her years chasing white collar criminals for the Bureau had offered little chance to deal with things such as what we saw before us.

"I don't know," she said. "Not days and days."

It was harder in this new world to base estimates on factors that once were taken as gospel. No flies remained to lay eggs on dead bodies. No larvae would hatch. No maggots would appear. People simply died and slowly dried up, or were eaten away by wind and weather.

"They've already come and gone," Lorenzen said.

The Russians had been here. The evidence of that lay on the ground where we stood. But were they still here? The evidence we saw, and which we'd seen of their actions in Ketchikan, pointed to them being long gone. They moved like parasites. Scavenging. Supplying themselves as they moved toward some greater prize.

Skagway.

It was terrifying to think of what might happen when Kuratov reached that place. If he hadn't already.

"We have to bury them," Westin said, quiet, measured rage in his voice.

"We will," Lorenzen said. "We have to finish the sweep first and hook up with the lieutenant."

The reality of that didn't sit well with Westin.

"So we just leave them lying there?"

The sergeant faced his private, but didn't say a word. He didn't have to. Westin retreated without moving an inch.

"Same formation," Lorenzen said. "Two on each side of the block."

There was nothing more to do here. Not now. I looked to Elaine.

"I'll be lead," I said.

She nodded and I stepped past her, about to continue our patrol with Lorenzen and Westin when we heard the sound. Coughing at first. Then a voice. So soft as to be unintelligible.

"The garrison was only five?" I asked Lorenzen.

He nodded and brought his M4 up, taking aim toward the sound, its source seeming to come from a building just down the street. What had been a restaurant, according to signage that still showed above the door. The sidewalk in front was littered with glass, long windows which had spread across its façade shattered.

"Two and two," Lorenzen said.

Elaine and I crossed to the side of the street where the restaurant was located. Lorenzen and Westin crept forward past the piled bodies, slowly, weapons tracking the source of the sound. Every few steps Westin would take a look behind, scanning for an ambush. But none came. The two soldiers reached a point directly across the street from the restaurant and stopped, their weapons pointed straight through the missing front window. He motioned with one hand for Elaine and me to approach.

We moved along the wall until we were at the edge of the shattered windows, door between the two open frames. I leaned and peered inside. The space was dim, but not dark. A small amount of trash and debris was scattered about within, evidence of some scavenging long ago. Booths that had once held a lunchtime crowd were empty and dusted with the grey grit which had blown in from blighted trees. One chair was toppled. It looked little different than any of the millions of homes and businesses left abandoned across the globe.

Except for the Russian soldier lying on the counter, hand pressed against a bandage upon his stomach that was soaked red.

I reached with my free hand and motioned for Lorenzen and Westin to approach. They crossed the street with weapons up and forward. Elaine stepped around me, her MP5 trained into the restaurant so that we all now had eyes on the enemy.

"Watch our six," Lorenzen said.

"Got it," Elaine said, turning away from the building to cover the street and buildings beyond.

Neil was right. Not that I didn't know that. She was a hard charger. While entering the building here might be seen as the dangerous part of any maneuver, she was placing herself in a position where she was alone. And vulnerable. I had to fight the urge to tell her I would take the outside position, and have her go in with the trained soldiers. I had to wipe that worry from my mind.

I had to.

"Watch for traps," Lorenzen said.

Westin stepped through the broken window first, weapon aimed at the Russian, the man mumbling in his native language.

"Be careful," I said to Elaine, and she glanced briefly at me, almost confused by what I'd said.

"Go," Lorenzen said.

I had no more opportunity to express concern. I followed Westin in, Lorenzen just behind me. We scanned the way ahead for trip wires, but nothing stood out.

The Russian mumbled loudly but didn't turn his head our way. His gaze remained fixed on the ceiling above.

"Check the back," Lorenzen told Westin.

The private moved past the Russian as the sergeant and I kept our weapons on him. Less than a minute later he returned, his weapon lowered.

"Nothing," Westin said. "Back door is barred from inside."

Lorenzen brought the muzzle of his M4 up, directing it at the ceiling as he stepped close to the Russian and checked him for traps on his body, or weapons nearby.

"AK on the floor," Lorenzen said.

Westin stepped behind the counter and retrieved the weapon, checking the mag and chamber.

"Empty," Westin said, then set the rifle down on a nearby table.

"Elaine," Lorenzen called out. "Inside."

She joined us in a half circle ogling the bleeding Russian.

"He's in uniform," she said.

"Not an infiltrator," I said.

"He's one of them," Westin said with disgust. "The ones who killed those men out there. Those Americans."

"We know that, private," Lorenzen said, looking around the space as he thought for a moment. "Watch the prisoner."

Lorenzen moved across the space and stepped through the shattered frontage where windows had once protected the restaurant from the elements. I watched him step into the street and aim his M4 at the sky before squeezing off two fast shots, waiting for a few seconds, then firing two more. That done, the signal sent, he hurried back inside and joined us next to the dying Russian.

"We have to keep him alive," Lorenzen said.

"Why?" Westin asked, not challenging his superior, but allowing some disdain for the thought of assisting one who'd been party to eliminating the Juneau garrison.

"Because Enderson is miles from here and he's the only one of us who speaks Russian," Lorenzen said.

"He might know something," Elaine said, agreeing.

The Russian lay before us, his lips moving almost constantly as he stared at the ceiling, hands folded atop his bloodied midsection.

"He's saying something," I said.

Maybe it was a prayer. To save him. Or to end his suffering.

Lorenzen turned to Westin, an urgency about him.

"Go back to the boat and get Hart," the sergeant said. "Have him bring his kit."

Elaine grabbed her pack from the floor and slipped into it.

"What are you doing?" I asked her.

"No one should be alone here," she said. "I'll go and stay with Acosta at the boat so Westin can bring Hart here."

It was a logical decision. One that Lorenzen blessed with a crisp nod toward Elaine. But it also meant that she'd be out of my sight.

"Make it fast," the sergeant said.

Before Elaine headed for the exit I took hold of her hand.

"You stay safe," I told her.

She leaned close and kissed me, the expression of emotion, and the delay it caused, seeming to agitate Westin.

"Anytime," he said, impatient.

Elaine eased away and moved past Westin, the private giving me a look, both harsh and jealous, before he, too, made his way out of the building.

"You've gotta realize where the attitude comes from," Lorenzen said to me once they were gone.

"Where's that?"

"From a dead wife and a dead child he couldn't get home to before others did," the sergeant said.

How many stories like that were out there, still salting the psychic wounds of those who'd survived them?

"Where?" I asked.

"He was stationed in Japan," Lorenzen answered. "They were in Omaha. Nice and safe in middle America."

"Except they weren't," I said.

"Correct."

The Russian spoke suddenly louder, his guttural stream of words, nonsense to us, holding some greater meaning to him. He grimaced and clutched his abdomen and seemed to struggle through a half dozen breaths before whatever wave of agony had coursed through him subsided. Once more he stared at the ceiling, avoiding our gazes, and spoke almost silently.

"Hart better hurry," I said.

"Everyone better hurry," Lorenzen corrected.

Twenty Five

Westin returned with our medic in just under half an hour. Hart checked the Russian's wounds and monitored his vitals for a few minutes before starting an IV and motioning us to a corner away from the man.

"He doesn't have much time," Hart said.

"How long is not much?" Lorenzen asked.

Hart thought for a moment, looking past Westin and me to the man who was now his patient.

"He's bleeding internally and he's aspirating blood. The plasma will keep his pressure up, but not for long."

"I haven't heard any shots acknowledging your signal," I told the sergeant.

He looked to Westin.

"Either of you hear three shots while you were out there?"

"No, sergeant," Westin answered.

"Just your four when I was at the boat," Hart said.

It had been the agreed upon method of communication. Four shots in groups of two was supposed to bring the other patrol toward the sound of the gunfire, acknowledging it with three shots as they made their way. But there had been no response. The communication, it seemed, was only one way. That could mean they hadn't heard, the terrain and buildings reflecting the sharp sounds so that they were lost in the blustery wind.

Or it could mean they were unable to reply.

I forced that dark thought down and looked to the sergeant.

"If they couldn't hear it before, maybe they can now."

Lorenzen considered my suggestion, then stepped outside and into the street, firing the two groups of double taps into the air.

Hardly a second later there came three fast shots. Shots that were fired not from some distance, but close. As I watched Lorenzen react to the reply, I saw him raise his M4 into the air, holding it so his arm and the weapon formed a T.

"Here!" he shouted, and a minute later the second patrol reached us.

Neil came through the window opening and eyed the Russian as he stood next to me.

"You guys made fast work of that," I said.

"Nothing to make work of," my friend said. "The whole north end of the city, everything past twin lakes, is rubble. Burned to the ground. Just completely devastated."

My friend looked over the interior of the restaurant.

"Where's Elaine?"

"She took Hart's place watching over the boat," I explained.

Neil nodded. Accepting that. He didn't push any more of his fear on me, but I knew he was thinking it. Was feeling it.

"Specialist," Schiavo said as she entered the building after conferring with her sergeant outside.

"Ma'am," Hart said, stepping away from the patient and prisoner.

"He can talk?"

"He can," Hart said. "How much he'll understand I don't know. He took four rounds between his sternum and his navel. Tight grouping. Someone was a good shot."

Schiavo looked over her shoulder and motioned Enderson forward with a look.

"You're up," she told him. "Get his basics."

Enderson said something in Russian to the man and his gaze angled toward the private. He hesitated for a moment, then spoke, softly.

"His name is Lentov," Enderson shared. "He's a, I think it's a sergeant, or some similar rank."

Schiavo stood where she knew that Lentov could see her.

"Ask him what happened to the soldiers outside," Schiavo said.

Enderson did, listening as the Russian answered in a voice that was becoming more whisper by the minute. When the wounded man had finished, Enderson looked to us, disgust in his gaze.

"He says Kuratov ordered them executed because they shot him," Enderson said. "He found them while the Russians were searching for the garrison and all hell broke loose. The garrison surrendered when they were surrounded and Kuratov threatened to blow up the building they were barricaded in."

Schiavo absorbed that, fighting a rise of anger I could tell. We all were. The man had just described how our countrymen had been shot down after laying down their arms. I flashed back to the moment when Neil had executed the cannibals near my refuge, but that action was in response to the murder of three innocent human beings whose lives had been cut short so they could be parted out and used as food. This, what we were hearing, what we were witness to, this was not that.

This was cold blooded murder.

"Ask him about Mary Island," Schiavo instructed.

I listened as Enderson translated his lieutenant's question and as Lentov replied.

"He says Kuratov sent a small group to take the lighthouse to block the channel, or raid ships, I'm not sure," Enderson said. "He's telling it both ways."

"They could have done to anyone what Jeremy did to us," I said. "Use the light to lure them in, then take them down."

"Stationary piracy," Elaine said.

Our happening upon Mary Island had, strangely, set in motion its liberation from the Russians. That realization was incredibly odd. It was a situation, a scenario, that none of us would have anticipated as we left Bandon.

The blighted world, we had learned many times over now, was full of dark and dangerous surprises.

"Ask him where the others are," Schiavo instructed.

Enderson spoke again, and listened again, leaning closer to the Russian to catch the response he was offering.

"They left him," Enderson said. "They'd already raided Ketchikan and Juneau, so they were heading north to the next objective."

Neil's face flushed red with fury.

"Skagway?" Schiavo asked, and Enderson nodded.

"He says they had an insider in Ketchikan who'd heard from the soldiers there about a place with plentiful supplies north of there," Enderson added.

"He just worked his way up the coast," Lorenzen said.

"How long ago did they leave?" Schiavo asked. "And how did they travel?"

Once more Enderson spoke and listened.

"He thinks he's been laying here for three days," Enderson said. "They came by boat, so he thinks that's how the rest of the unit continued on."

"How many men?"

Enderson relayed the lieutenant's question.

"Eighteen without him," Enderson said.

The Russian muttered something, looking not at the ceiling anymore. His gaze was fixed fully on Schiavo.

"*Pistolet*," Lentov said, his gaze tracking down to the weapon holstered on the lieutenant's right thigh. "*Pistolet*."

One of the hands pressing against the wounds on his abdomen rose a bit, fingers extended, as if reaching toward Schiavo's sidearm.

The Russian wanted his suffering to end. He wanted to die. By his own hand.

"Let him rot," Westin said in reaction to the Russian's implied desire.

Schiavo said nothing. Not to the Russian, and not to her vocal private. She simply stared at Lentov for a moment before turning to Hart.

"How long might he lay here without attention?"

The medic thought. Searching for some exactness in the imprecise situation.

"Hours," Hart said. "Days. He's hydrated now. The bleeding is slow. But unless he gets to a trauma center, he's not going to make it."

The prognosis since Hart first saw the Russian hadn't changed, just the timing. Treatment had somewhat stabilized him. The inevitable was being delayed.

"Eric," Schiavo said, looking to me. "Do you have a throwaway piece?"

A throwaway piece. An extra handgun. Something small, easily hidden, and not important enough to care about if it was lost, or bartered away for something more valuable at the moment. It had never come to that for me, but I had been prepared for the time that it might.

"I have a small nine," I said.

"Mind if I take that off your hands?" Schiavo asked.

I didn't answer. I simply reached to the pack I'd set in a nearby booth and retrieved the weapon from within.

"One round," Schiavo said. "In the chamber. Then gear up."

I already had one in the chamber, so I dropped the magazine and put it back into my pack before slipping into it.

"Here," I said, handing the small Glock to Schiavo.

"Sergeant, keep this man covered," Schiavo said. "Everyone else outside."

We stepped through the shattered windows and watched Schiavo lay the pistol on Lentov's chest before backing away, Lorenzen covering her as she, and then he, joined us outside and moved out of any line of fire from within.

"Westin, on point."

"Yes, ma'am," the private acknowledged, leading off, the rest of us falling in behind.

The shot sounded when we were halfway down the block. Schiavo never slowed. She kept moving, weapon at the ready, a few yards behind Westin, her point man.

"Sergeant," she said.

"Ma'am," Lorenzen answered, speeding up to be nearer his commander.

"We're not spending the night. Have a detail bury the bodies and mark the location. Then get everyone back to the boat so we can get the hell out of here."

Twenty Six

We cruised out of Juneau at sundown, sailing south through the Gastineau Channel until we reached Tantallon Point and swung to the west, then north again, Douglas Island off our starboard side. No more stops lay between us and Skagway.

"Thirteen, maybe fourteen hours," Acosta said as he steered the boat from the captain's chair.

I stood with him, glassing the way ahead. Scanning for anything and everything he, or Schiavo, should know about. This was the routine, one on the wheel, and one on lookout duty, switching out with others as we progressed. Some slept. Others ate. Neil sat on the deck near the stern and cleaned his AK while there was still useful daylight.

"Then we'll know," I said.

"Know what?"

"If we're too late," I answered.

I looked back to the waters ahead. Neil had told me that there was always hope. Those words had kept me going after being shot near my refuge, and the fullness of that belief had held all the way to my friend's arrival with Grace and Krista. They had saved me, nursing me back to health. That would have never happened, though, if I hadn't had hope.

Here, now, I needed that more than ever, because everything we'd come across on our journey north pointed to an outcome that was almost impossible to fathom. Hundreds of innocents were likely in Skagway. And a unit of foreign troops, willing to kill, was almost certainly already there. They'd beaten us.

That was my worry. That was the reality that quelled the hope I wanted to have. We might reach our destination and find that the trip had been for naught. What evidence we might find there to confirm that fear I did not want to even imagine.

"Your friend wants to be ready," Schiavo commented as she came up from below.

I lowered the binoculars and glanced behind, seeing Neil reassembling his weapon after checking its internals.

"I think we may need to be," I said.

"I do, too," Schiavo said.

She stood next to Acosta and watched night settle down from above, blacking out the world ahead of us. Neil came into the wheelhouse and headed below as I switched to the thermal binoculars and scanned the world beyond the *Sandy*'s bow.

"How'd you learn to play piano?" I asked, lowering the binoculars.

Schiavo chuckled quietly and took the device from me, taking her own look at the water out there.

"Mrs. Welsh," Schiavo said. "My third grade teacher."

She kept the binoculars to her eyes as she explained.

"I was one of those kids who liked to be at school. Not the braniac kind who would stay after to do extra credit. I just didn't want to go home, and Mrs. Welsh knew that. So, she let me stay, and while other kids were reading extra books or practicing for the spelling bee, she would teach me to play the old piano we had in our room. Room eight. I still remember that, and I remember that piano, and I really remember her."

"Sounds like a wonderful woman," I said.

"She had a husband and two kids of her own, and she made time to teach the little poor girl with the drunk father how to make music."

"From what you've said, she taught you well," I said.

"It just came to me," Schiavo said. "That was my thing. Even when I wasn't around a piano to play, the next time I got to sit down at one, it all came back. It was like that was what I was supposed to do."

She lowered the binoculars and handed them back to me.

"Maybe there'll be a piano in Skagway," she said hopefully. "And when everything's wrapped up there, I can play for you and your friends. I think I'd like that."

There was a calm about her as she said what she just had. Maybe it was the hope that was beginning to elude me. Or, I wondered, was it a fatalism in her that regarded what lay at the end of our journey as an inevitability? One that would end how it ends.

That was true, I thought. We were but one thing which could influence the outcome, but influence it we could.

Influence it we must.

"I can't wait to hear you play," I told Schiavo.

Then she left the wheelhouse, heading below again. I stood watch with Acosta until we were both relieved thirty minutes later, the rotation continuing into the night, the land and the sea quiet, the trip north as peaceful as we'd hoped.

Until it wasn't.

Twenty Seven

"Something on the water ahead!"

Westin's announcement drew everyone from below decks. I was next to last into the wheelhouse, Enderson, Lorenzen, and Hart already out on deck, weapons ready. I saw Acosta standing at the front window, thermal binoculars to his eyes, zeroed in on something in the dark distance.

"It's a boat," Acosta reported. "About our size. And its hauling ass right for our bow."

"Westin, clear him to the right," Schiavo said. "I want any fire off our left."

"Yes, ma'am," Westin acknowledged, steering slightly toward the mainland.

Ahead, in the black night, I could see nothing. Not a shape, not a wake. Nothing. But if some craft was barreling toward us with purpose, that meant that they could almost certainly see us, just as we saw them. That also meant they were at least similarly equipped.

Military...

"Russians," I said.

Schiavo nodded and took the safety off her M4, sliding a window on the left side of the wheelhouse open and resting the barrel of her weapon on its frame.

"Why would they be heading south again?" Neil asked.

"Check on Mary Island," Schiavo suggested. "Reoccupy Juneau. Doesn't really matter."

"I count three warm bodies," Acosta reported, tuning his focus in a bit more. "Wait. They're adjusting course again. Collision course with our bow."

"Distance?" Schiavo asked.

"Eight hundred meters," Acosta answered. "And—"

He never got the last word out as the dark water ahead lit up with flashes and tracer rounds streaking at us. A half dozen impacts shattered the windows and sent Neil, Elaine and me diving for cover. I heard Schiavo's shooters opening up outside, the distance still extreme for their M4s.

"MG on their bow!" Acosta shouted out, describing what he was seeing.

"Get us closer, Westin!" Schiavo ordered.

There was no 'yes ma'am' reply this time, just firewalling throttles and a slight turn to the right, trying to get the charging vessel fully cleared for the battery of weapons our side could bring to bear.

"Six hundred!" Acosta reported.

Closer, but still on the outside of real world effectiveness for the standard issue rifles. Mine would be no better. Elaine's Mp5 even worse. Neil's AK, whose rounds would pack more punch, was no better in the range department.

"We need more fire out there," Neil said.

He was right. Even if just for suppressing what was being directed at us.

"I'm first," my friend said as a volley of fire tracked onto the *Sandy* again, chewing at the side of the wheelhouse.

"Go!" I shouted.

Neil rolled to the door and slipped out of the wheelhouse, shifting to the right side of the boat to reach the bow and not interfere with Schiavo's shooters.

"Neil's on the bow!" I told the lieutenant.

She didn't reply. She didn't move an inch, and hadn't since taking her position at the left side window. There she stood, exposed, opening fire now at the muzzle blasts that were our only target, rounds from the Russian machine gun ripping into the wheelhouse all around her.

Despite the gender, she had a pair of brass ones bigger than any man I'd seen take a weapon into battle.

Then I heard Neil fire. Quick bursts from his AK, the sound distinctive, a deeper crack amongst the almost wispy *ratta tat tat* from the M4s.

Acosta, too, had held his position near the spider webbed windshield, tracking the incoming boat with the thermal binoculars.

"Five hundred!"

"They're turning!" Westin said.

I slid across the wheelhouse floor to the door, Elaine right behind. We slipped out and onto deck, scrambling across the lurching surface to the port side rail. The stream of fire from the MG was raking the entire side of the boat, low and then high, water sprouting from impacts and the hull ringing like a bell with every penetration.

"If they get us below the waterline we're gonna have a long swim," Elaine said.

"Just stay down," I said.

"What?"

I could plainly hear the confusion in her voice, but I didn't answer. Instead I poked my head and weapon above the rail and took aim at the boat, squeezing off a series of rounds, trying to make each count, my aim just above the barrel spewing fire at us.

"They're slowing!"

Acosta's warning reached out onto the deck. To my right, two of the three shooters were reloading. Without warning Elaine popped up and trained her MP5 on the target, within two hundred meters now, still a Hail Mary shot for her.

"Come on..." she implored the boat closer, wanting to add her own fire to the mix.

Then, after a long burst from Neil's AK, the MG fire stopped, just a glowing barrel visible across the water.

"Keep the fire up!" Lorenzen said.

We did. A few hundred feet away now, the vessel was no longer charging, its bow hardly pushing through the calm waters. It was coasting.

"Enderson, drop a forty on it!"

The corporal followed his sergeant's order and stopped firing, lifting his M4 up a bit and loading a 40mm grenade into the fat launcher attached to the underside of the barrel. Elaine began firing now, adding to the covering fire as an almost comical *thoop* sounded from Enderson's weapon.

The results a second later were anything but cartoonish.

The wheelhouse of the approaching boat erupted in a red orange fireball, its structure peeling away like petals of some metallic flower. The craft rocked, tipping severely away from us, flames building from mid ship to bow, secondary explosions popping, grenades and ammo cooking off.

"Cease fire!" Lorenzen ordered. "Cease fire!"

Other than the rumble of the *Sandy*'s engines and the *pop pop pop* of mini explosions across the water, a quiet settled over the boat.

"Circle it," Schiavo told Westin. "Keep it on our left."

The private put the *Sandy* into an orbit around the now drifting boat. Every gun on deck maintained its aim, covering the burning vessel lest some superhuman Russian emerge from the flames with an RPG on his shoulder.

But there was none. There was no sign of anything.

Except for the body in the water.

"Check it," Schiavo said from her position at the window, coughing hard as acrid smoke from the blazing ship drifted over to the *Sandy*.

Westin slowed the boat and maneuvered it alongside the body floating face down in the water. Hart and

Enderson used a hooked pole stowed alongside the wheelhouse to snag and pull the body close. Hart reached down and seized it by the uniform collar and rolled it over.

In the light of the nearby fire we all saw that half the man's face was peeled back, one eye gone, brain exposed.

"Same uniform as the lighthouse attackers," Lorenzen said.

"And Lentov," I added.

Then, what the dead man was wearing became the least of what anyone was concerned with.

"Lieutenant's hit!"

Acosta's urgent report from within the wheelhouse drew a rush of help, Hart in the lead. Lorenzen stopped Enderson and pointed to the blazing boat.

"Keep that covered," the sergeant ordered.

Then Schiavo's second in command raced into the wheelhouse just ahead of me.

"I'm okay," the lieutenant said from where she sat on the floor, back against the wall, small pool of blood beneath her. "Am I hit? I don't think I'm hit."

I reached out and took the M4 from her lap, holding it as Hart began checking her.

"My side," Schiavo said.

Hart ripped her uniform shirt open and saw a soggy red stain on her tan undershirt. He took a scissors from his medical kit and cut the garment open, leaving only the lieutenant's bra to cover her.

"You all enjoying the show?" Schiavo asked, managing a weak smile, pain and blood loss dragging her down from consciousness.

"Hell, Acosta's got a bigger chest than you," Lorenzen fired back, assisting their medic.

"Went through," Hart said, probing both entrance and exit wounds.

"Internal damage?" Lorenzen asked.

"I don't know," Hart said.

"The Russian boat's going down," Westin said.

I looked out the window and saw exactly what the private had reported. The burning boat was slipping beneath the surface, fires quenched, a steamy mist left rolling atop the water after it disappeared.

"How you doing, lieutenant?" Lorenzen asked, trying to engage his leader.

Her head bobbed up and down. It might have been a nod. But the next moment when it came down and her chin settled against her chest it became clear that she was fading fast.

"Get her flat," Hart directed.

Lorenzen helped slide her away from the wheelhouse wall and stretched her out on the floor. Hart rolled her onto her side and applied pressure to the entrance and exit wounds with a pair of trauma bandages.

"She's still breathing," Hart said.

The rise and fall of her chest was apparent, even as she lay on her side. That was good. Little else was.

"Is there anywhere we can tie off?" Hart asked. "Working on her while we're rolling on the water is not what I want to be doing."

"Westin?"

Lorenzen's open query to the private hung there, unanswered for a moment, as Westin and Acosta checked the map they'd been using to navigate the coastal waters.

"There's actually a lodge on here," Westin said.

"It has a dock," Acosta added.

"Get us there," Lorenzen ordered, turning his attention back to Schiavo as the *Sandy*'s engine roared up to speed.

Twenty Eight

The building was rustic and set in what had been a flat meadow nestled close to the sea. We carried Schiavo up from where we'd tied the *Sandy* off to the small dock and headed for the couch in what must have been the gathering room.

"No," Hart said, pointing to a long, roughhewn dining table in an adjoining space. "There."

We placed the lieutenant on the flat surface as directed. Hart already had an IV going, clear plasma dripping into her veins as he eased the pressure bandage back and examined her wounds. He turned on his flashlight and hung it from the dark antler chandelier suspended above the table.

"Enderson, Acosta, do a sweep outside," Lorenzen ordered.

The two soldiers headed out, reluctant to leave their leader, each stealing final glances at her horizontal form as they stepped out.

"How is she?" Neil asked.

"I don't know yet," Hart said, checking her blood pressure. "Give me a minute."

We stepped back, leaving the medic to do his job.

"Can we talk?" Elaine said, her question directed very definitely to me.

"Sure."

I followed her out onto the lodge's wide porch. Adirondack chairs sat unused, the view they had once offered of the ocean and islands certainly stunning.

"What was that?" Elaine asked.

In the chaos in the wake of Schiavo being hit, I had forgotten what I'd said to Elaine, and her very obvious reaction to my expression of more than concern. I'd tried to manage her actions.

"On the boat, what was that about?"

I tried to think of a good way to share the fear that Neil had implanted in me. But there was none. At least none that she would accept without possibly decking me.

"I was just...worried."

She eyed me as if I'd just said I was from a planet two galaxies past the Milky Way.

"What do you think I am? Some fragile flower?"

"No. Can't I just feel worry? It was a crazy situation."

"Of course you can feel worry," she told me. "You just can't let that switch on the macho gene, okay? I'm in this fight, too? You do remember that?"

"I do," I said.

Then she stared at me. The verbal dressing down complete. I hoped.

"I worry about you, too," she said. "Okay?"

"I know."

She gave me a final, long look, then went back inside. I stood there for a moment wondering if what had just happened was proof that what my friend had warned me of was wrong, or that he was right. Whether it was one, or the other, Elaine had made it clear that there was a line not to cross. She was a big girl and very willing, and ready, to do her part. I'd have to learn to live with that.

If I could.

* * *

An hour after reaching the lodge, Hart had done all he could to stabilize Schiavo.

"I don't think anything vital was damaged," the medic said. "But she lost a good deal of blood. Plasma only goes so far. And I'm down to my last bag after the one I just hung for her."

"You're saying she needs a transfusion," Lorenzen said.

"Exactly," Hart confirmed. "One problem—she's AB neg."

AB negative was the rarest type. I'd read somewhere that something around one percent of the population had that type. I was O positive, just about the most common of the blood types.

"And we don't have anybody in the unit to take a tap from," Lorenzen said, again getting confirmation from the medic in the form of a nod.

"Can you rig something up to do a transfusion?" Elaine asked.

Hart thought, then half shrugged, and half nodded.

"I have all we need except a donor," Hart told Elaine.

She handed me her MP5 and started removing her jacket.

"You have one now," Elaine said.

"You're AB negative?" Hart asked.

She tossed her jacket over the back of a chair and rolled up the sleeve of her sweatshirt.

"I am," Elaine said, curious that we all seemed surprised. "I'm not kidding. I've donated before. I mean, back when there were blood drives and all that stuff."

Hart looked to me, then to his sergeant. The decision was his, it seemed. And it was easy.

"Hook her up," Lorenzen said.

* * *

None of it was by the book. The usual standards of sterilization could not be fully followed. But in two hours

Hart had taken roughly a pint out of Elaine, captured in an empty plasma bag, and was transfusing it into Schiavo, drip by drip, the precious red liquid slowly replenishing some of what the lieutenant had lost. She slept through the rest of the night, and the next day, unconscious still as darkness came, full and deep.

For the moment we were stuck. But that could not continue.

"How long until she's able to be up and out of here?" I asked.

Hart had no clear answer. No satisfyingly clear answer, that was.

"Wound like this gets you laid up in the hospital for three or four days," he explained. "Then light duty for a couple, maybe three weeks. And that's if no infection sets in."

"We can't move her?" Neil asked.

Lorenzen reacted harshly to my friend's question.

"And if we could, what good would that do?" the sergeant asked. "We drag her up north to fight a fight she can't be part of?"

"Every day we sit here is a day the Russians can do whatever they want up in Skagway," Neil said, maintaining his composure. "We have to get up there."

Lorenzen absorbed that and looked to their medic.

"Can she be moved?"

"I wouldn't advise it," Hart told Lorenzen.

"That's it, then," Lorenzen said.

Now, though, Neil couldn't hold back. Not this close to where he could reunite with Grace and Krista.

"Sitting here is getting people killed!" my friend shouted.

To his credit, Lorenzen didn't elevate the tension any more than it already had.

"I can't take wounded personnel on a potential combat mission," the sergeant said.

"Then don't," Elaine told him.

Lorenzen eyed her, piqued at her abrupt suggestion.

"Leave her here," Elaine said. "With Hart. The rest of us go on to Skagway and do what needs to be done."

Lorenzen didn't respond to what was being proposed. He remained silent, looking to where his commander lay on the table.

"How far are we from Skagway?" I asked. "Time, not miles."

Acosta had studied the route in advance from the time we'd left Mary Island. Besides the obvious brawn the young man possessed, his intellect was top notch. He retained details. Performed quick mental calculations. That he had an answer for me with little time to consider it surprised me not at all.

"Eight hours in good seas," the private answered.

I thought on that and looked to where Schiavo was resting, bandaged but alive.

"We can be up there and deal with what we find and be back the next day," I said.

"Just like that," Lorenzen said, focusing on me now. "Down by two shooters you're going to take on Kuratov and his men?"

"We do what we have to do," I said. "They're our friends up there. You can't keep us from getting to them when we're this close. Not for the sake of one person."

"I sure as hell can," Lorenzen countered.

"She'd tell you to go," I told the sergeant.

"And I'm telling you to—"

"No!"

The single word cut the sergeant off, sharp and clean. It was Schiavo, rising from the table where we'd thought she was asleep. Her body unbent slowly as she straightened, jaw clenched. She was hurting.

That didn't mean she was beaten.

"We leave tonight," she said.

She let go of the chair back she'd grabbed onto for temporary support and stood tall.

"Those people in Skagway aren't waiting anymore because of me," she said. "I'm okay."

"You're weak," Hart said.

"You need to rest," Lorenzen told her.

To that, and to the collective concern focused on her, Schiavo simply shook her head.

"Need has nothing to do with it," she said. "We're leaving. Acosta."

"Ma'am."

"You said eight hours," Schiavo recounted. "You confident with that estimate?"

He thought for a moment.

"If the seas stay like they are, we can make that."

Schiavo considered Acosta's certainty, then looked to her sergeant.

"That will put us there about dawn," Schiavo said.

Her orders given, Lorenzen reined in his resistance. But some doubts still remained.

"I wish we had a full complement of night gear," Lorenzen said. "Daylight fight against a superior force..."

"Superior in number," Schiavo said. "Not in everything."

It was a statement of confidence in her men, and in us. Six plus three equaled just half of what Kuratov had, if the dying Russian in Juneau was to be believed. Even a few less than that would leave us badly outgunned.

"We get close, see what we can see, then choose the best way to get ashore," Schiavo said. "Let's move. I want to be on the water in fifteen minutes."

There was no more discussion. Lieutenant Angela Schiavo, wounded and wise, had stated her plan. She grimaced as she reached for her pack, Westin grabbing it before she could. That she let him carry it out of the lodge and onto the boat was a pointed reminder of just how much she hurt. As much as she needed to be, she wasn't at one hundred percent, and she wouldn't be, even when we reached Skagway. If there was a fight to be had there, she would give her all.

I only hoped that, for her, it would be enough.

Twenty Nine

As Acosta had estimated, we sailed up the Taiya Inlet and approached Skagway just before first light, the new day a building mix of blue and yellow along the crests of distant peaks. The *Sandy* slowed and we scanned what we could see of the port city ahead.

Two vessels were prominent in Skagway's harbor. Both cruise ships. One, on the north side of the bay, lay mostly on its side, crushing the dock beneath it. The other stood tall and seemingly intact, tied off to the pier on the bay's southern side as if it had just arrived with a load of tourists from Vancouver.

"*Northwest Majesty*," Elaine said, reading the name off the ship's stern through the binoculars. "She doesn't look bad off at all."

"Can't say the same for the *Vensterdam*," Enderson said, making his own assessment through another set of optics. "Scorch and impact marks on the middle of the ship. Probably penetrated at the waterline on the submerged side. There were some explosions, but she didn't burn."

The *Vensterdam* was the vessel we'd seen noted in the logs at the Mary Island lighthouse. According to those it had transported more than a hundred people originally from Yuma, Arizona to Skagway. We could only hope that all those souls were offloaded before the violence which sank the ship occurred.

From a half mile outside the harbor in the dawn's light, that was what we could make out. But it was not all.

"I see people," Elaine said.

She passed the binoculars to me, and I handed them off to Neil after a quick look.

"How many are there?" Schiavo asked.

"I see a half dozen," Enderson answered.

"Any weapons? Uniforms?"

"No, Ma'am," Enderson reported.

"They're not looking this way," Neil said. "They don't see us."

Enderson lowered his binoculars and looked to his lieutenant.

"I can't see any observation post at all," the corporal said.

Schiavo processed what she was being told. I could see her weighing the right approach. With everything we knew and had been told, there should be Russians in Skagway. Along with the people we knew, and some we wouldn't. Those troops would be combat tested. They would be wary. Wanting to identify any potential threat before it drew near.

That wasn't what we were seeing here.

"Acosta."

"Yes, ma'am."

"Take us in slow, but be ready to break left for open water," Schiavo ordered. "I want shooters on deck."

Lorenzen didn't have to give any supplemental order. Westin, Hart, and Enderson readied their weapons and gear and headed out onto deck.

"I want that mountainside covered as we pull in," Schiavo directed, pointing to the eastern slope that rose up from the sea.

"We'll take forward," Neil told Schiavo.

She didn't bless his offer immediately. But she didn't ask for any explanation, either. After a moment's reflection, she nodded.

"They're your people," she said. "Be sure if you have to fire."

"We will," I said.

Elaine was first out of the wheelhouse and to the front of the boat. Neil and I joined her, the three of us crouching behind the solid bow rail as the *Sandy* crept forward.

* * *

There were no signs of any Russians. No sign of any enemy. No shooting. No resistance of any kind.

But as we neared the end of the south dock and pulled close in the shadow of the *Northwest Majesty*'s massive stern, we were unseen no more. One person, then two, then three saw us. At first they simply froze where they stood on the dock. Frightened, it seemed.

We tied off and came off of the boat. One person, the closest to us, maybe fifty feet away, began to move toward us. Then another did. And another. And another. Shouts rose from some, summoning more. And more. And more. A chain of cries announcing our presence.

People streamed out of town and up the dock toward us, moving with sluggish quickness, as if their bodies could not match the need to reach us with haste.

"Do you know these people?" Schiavo asked as the first wave neared.

I scanned the faces, making connections quickly. But not in totality.

"Most of them," I said.

"God, God, thank God," Lois Probst said as she reached us, planting her palms against my cheeks and coming to her tip toes to kiss my forehead. "Thank God you're here."

The woman lived a block over from me in Bandon. She was a blight widow, barely past fifty, her husband lost somewhere in the vast dead country while trying to get home from a meeting in Florida. I remember the mock pies she would bake, making do with canned ingredients and cracker crusts to replace the flour no longer available. In front of me now she bore the thankfulness not of the woman I'd come to know, but of a prisoner released from bondage.

"Lois, what happened?" I asked her.

"Thank God you're here," Lois repeated, my query eclipsed by the sudden rush of joy washing over her.

Washing over everyone.

All around, people were throwing their arms around those of us who'd just arrived. Elaine was trapped in a six arm bear hug by neighbors she'd known. Neil, too, was being happily accosted, though I saw him trying to push through the throngs, his gaze searching for those he'd been aching for since our return to Bandon's deserted streets.

There were strangers, too. They seemed to be congregating around Schiavo and her men even as the lieutenant tried to keep some semblance of a defensive posture. None of us knew what had happened, or what might still happen.

"A mixed military unit took them," Elaine said, slipping close to me after extricating herself from the eager embrace. "Army, Marines, Navy. They rolled into town from north and south, disarmed everyone, and ferried them from shore onto that cruise ship."

She pointed up at the hull of the *Northwest Majesty* looming over us to the left.

"Forced evacuation," I said.

"Yeah," Elaine agreed, her quiet anger echoing my own.

More and more people were pushing toward us from town, clogging the way forward and separating me from Elaine. There was no order. It wasn't panic, but it was something beyond the norm.

"Eric," Hal Robertson said, coming at me from the side. "It's great to see you!"

Hal was, of all things, a cobbler. In a world where new shoes no longer rolled off Chinese assembly lines, his nearly forgotten profession had allowed him to provide a useful service to Bandon's residents.

"Hal, we saw blood back at the meeting hall," I said to him, wanting to get some information before the building crowd overwhelmed our exchange.

The fast flourish of joy he'd expressed upon seeing me dimmed appreciably and he nodded.

"Jenny Beck," he said. "She refused to leave."

Jenny was a single mother. Or had been until she'd arrived in Bandon like many had, as refugees seeking a safe haven from the blighted and violent world. The two year old child she'd carried into town with her was near death, and succumbed to illness and starvation the day after their arrival. This was before I'd reached Bandon with Neil and Grace and Krista, so I'd learned of the sad tale second hand. I was only acquainted with Jenny in passing, as she kept very much to herself, but I knew what all others in town did—that she spent hours every single day, rain or shine, at the town cemetery, sitting at her daughter's grave, singing softly to her departed child.

I'd feared that Martin might have been the source of the blood stain we'd seen, as I couldn't imagine him agreeing to leave the place where Micah had been laid to eternal rest. The reason I had been correct about. It was with the individual that I had erred.

"The soldiers tried to talk her into going," Hal explained. "But she resisted. She fought back."

A quick flash of rage built within. Had they really shot her down right there? Were the brethren of Schiavo capable of such a thing?

It turns out, they weren't.

"She pulled out a pistol and put it to her head," Hal said. "The soldiers tried to talk her down. We tried. But she wasn't leaving her daughter. She just wasn't."

So she'd killed herself to make sure of that. It was a gut wrenching act to imagine, but one I could plainly see Jenny Beck choosing.

"We buried her next to her daughter," Hal said. "Then we were all put on this ship and brought up here."

We hadn't noticed a fresh grave in the cemetery when planting the seeds, but we wouldn't have, considering where Jenny's daughter had been laid to rest on the far side away from the paths.

So hers was the blood we'd seen. Not Martin's. That realization, though, brought another instant wondering to the surface.

Where was Martin?

I hadn't seen him among the throngs flowing at and past us.

"Hal, can you tell me where—"

The question hung there, unfinished, as Elaine's voice rose above the collective chattering.

"Grace!"

I saw Elaine pointing over the crowd, toward the dock nearest the bow of the *Northwest Majesty*. That was where I saw her face, at the same instant Neil did. He took off running, pushing his way through people we knew, and past strangers none of us had ever seen before.

"Go with him," Elaine said.

I looked to her and nodded, then sprinted after my friend, leaving Elaine, Schiavo, Hal, and the others behind. Ahead I could see Neil, and I could hear him, calling out to Grace. And I could see her face, pale but beaming, both arms waving above the mass of humanity between them.

"Grace!"

"Neil! Neil!"

I was trying my best to keep up, but no one was going to catch my friend. Or stop him. People coming the opposite way bounced off him like pinballs. He ran, and ran, and I could see that he had broken into a bit of a clearing ahead, the mass of people thinning after already streaming past. The way to Grace was clear.

But he stopped. Just stopped a few yards from her, staring.

I pushed through the last of the wave of people and realized immediately why he'd not covered the final ten feet or so to Grace and pulled her into an embrace. It was what he was seeing that prevented that. What he was seeing about her.

The small bump arcing out from her belly, open jacket allowing the loose shirt she wore to define it.

"Grace..."

My friend could only say that as he looked to her, eyes wide and wondrous. She nodded, trying to smile, and reached out to him, her body swaying. Neil rushed forward and caught her. I ran to my friend and took his pack and weapon as he picked Grace up and carried her in his arms toward town.

Thirty

Neil carried Grace through the front door of a building which had once been a small restaurant. I followed and helped him ease her into a chair, setting his weapon and gear aside.

"Is Doc Allen anywhere?"

I'd asked the question to the small group that had trailed us inside, but a familiar face, Penny Jessup, was the one who answered.

"I'll get him, Fletch," she said, and disappeared through the door just before Elaine and Schiavo came in.

"Grace," Neil said, one hand caressing her cheek, and the other planted gently atop her swelling belly. "Grace, come on. Come back, baby."

Baby...

My friend was referring to his wife. But I was thinking of the life she now carried within. The fear I'd harbored after seeing Doc Allen's note in his appointment book about 'testing' was washed away. It had been another kind of testing. One with joyous results.

"Grace," Neil said gently, urging her back to consciousness.

Westin came through the door, wide eyed and worried. Schiavo noted his presence and leaned toward him.

"Get Hart in here," she said, making a quiet but firm request for the unit's medic to get there.

"The Doc is coming," I told her, and she nodded.

"People out there are saying they haven't eaten in four days," Elaine told me.

Grace stirred, her eyes snapping open, some terror in them.

"Krista!" she screamed her daughter's name. "Krista!"

"It's all right," Neil said, trying to calm her. "You're okay."

Grace's wide gaze found Neil, locking with his. He smiled, but she didn't. Instead, tears welled, spilling silently down her cheeks.

"Where's Krista?" my friend asked his wife.

Grace fixed her glistening gaze on him, apology all about her.

"I'm sorry," she said. "I had to."

I could see in Neil's face that his heart was sinking. A grim chill washed over him, reaching across the small space that separated us to turn my insides to ice.

No...

"Otherwise she'd die like the rest of us," Grace said. "There's no food out here."

Neil puzzled visibly at what the woman he loved was saying.

"What do you mean?" Neil asked her.

She began to sob just as Doc Allen entered, slipping past the crowd gathering outside.

"Grace, what are you feeling?" the doctor asked her.

"Doc, where's Krista?" Neil asked with plain urgency.

"Let me see how Grace is first," the doctor said, putting two fingers to her wrist to check her pulse. "Grace, are you having any pain?"

She focused on Doc Allen, seizing on his question.

"No," Grace said. "No pain. I'm just..."

Doc Allen nodded and checked her pupils.

"I know, Grace," he said. "I know."

"Grace," Neil said.

She looked to him again, tears threatening.

"Where's Krista?"

For a moment she did not answer. Could not answer. Then, summoning what remained of some inner strength, she did.

"She's in the pit," Grace said, almost whimpering, then collapsed into Neil's embrace.

Doc Allen stood and my friend looked up to him from where he held his wife, confused and hurting.

"The pit?" Neil asked. "What the hell is the pit?"

Doc Allen hesitated. Like Grace a moment before, he seemed not to want to answer.

"Doc..." I gently urged him.

He swallowed and nodded and finally spoke.

"You should probably talk to the foreman."

Thirty One

Earl Cranston stood before us in a cramped construction trailer, desk and chair the only furniture, large design of something stitched together on the wall behind him. Something massive and monolithic.

"We started building it before the blight even spread out of Europe," Cranston said, lowering himself unsteadily into his ancient wooden desk chair. "It was humanity's hope."

The man let out a weak chuckle. One that belied the folly he now attached to that grand statement. He was tired and thin, skin upon his bald head almost translucent, the few wisps of hair still there hanging long to one side like the remnants of a failed comb over.

"Then six months ago we finished and these ships came in," Cranston explained, a pained sourness twisting his face. "And all the workers I'd had up and left. The Navy unloaded all the food and supplies and took almost everybody away. Just left me here with a few people and said to get ready."

Elaine looked to me when the frail man paused.

"An ark," she said. "Some sort of landlocked ark."

And this man had been the foreman of the project. It was difficult to see that sort of responsibility handled by the man who sat before us, but the wasting world had worn even the best men and women down to shells of their former selves.

"They left me here," Cranston said distantly. "Just left me."

Schiavo shook her head at the clear idiocy of the operation. It stank of bureaucracy gone mad, if there could be any other kind. Operation by committee. Someone in a bunker somewhere had set this all in motion without involving those on the front line. People like Earl Cranston.

"The cold, you know," Cranston said, his gaze wide and weary, almost shell-shocked. "The blight doesn't do well in the cold. The spread was slower in the northern climates, so..."

He looked out at us. Elaine, Schiavo, and I met his gaze. There was surrender in his eyes. Defeat. Failure.

"The cold has nothing to do with it," Elaine said.

He nodded an acknowledgment, then quickly shook his head, unwilling to let go of what his purpose had been based upon.

"No, the scientists, they have it figured out," Cranston protested, swiveling his chair to face the design on the wall behind. "This will save everyone. It will save... It would have..."

I stepped past the desk, Schiavo joining me to study the collage of blueprints.

"It's underground," Schiavo said.

"Yeah," I agreed. "And big."

"We bored it right under the slope of a mountain," Cranston said, some vaguely fond memory of the process bringing a bare grin to his face. "Just outside of town."

I pointed to the scale on one of the drawings.

"This is a thousand feet across on the short side," I said.

"Twice that on the long," she said, doing some quick mental math. "Two million square feet."

We looked to Cranston and found his blank stare angled up at us.

"They have seeds," he said. "They've been in a vault. Once everybody is sealed in they're going to grow in the greenhouses down there. There are skylights to let in the sun. Then everything will grow. And when enough grows, it can be planted outside, because the cold up here...the cold won't let...the blight can't..."

"Sunlight," Elaine said, looking to me.

"Long nights," I said, keying in to what she was suggesting. "It probably did progress more slowly up here that fall and winter."

"This confirms what we saw in Cheyenne," Elaine said.

I nodded. Schiavo noted the exchange between us.

"Am I missing something?"

I didn't answer the lieutenant. But I did look to Elaine, seeking some concurrence in what I was considering. What *we* were deciding.

"We should talk," I said to Schiavo, the implication in my manner and tone that I was seeking some privacy. "Later."

"About what?" the lieutenant asked.

"Saving humanity," Elaine said.

Schiavo let the grandiosity of that that rattle around in her thoughts for a moment. Her rumination ended, though, when a grim Sergeant Lorenzen came into the trailer and shook his head at Schiavo.

"No sign of the garrison," the sergeant said.

"The soldiers?" Cranston interjected, explaining almost matter-of-factly. "They're dead. The Russians took them out in fifteen minutes. They were firing rockets from their boat as the *Vensterdam* sailed in. That drew the soldiers' attention. Then five, six of them came out of the hills and ambushed the hell out of our boys. Killed every last one."

Cranston thought in quiet for a moment, his face suddenly pained.

"Then they made everyone gather up any supplies that weren't already in the pit," Cranston said. "They cleaned out what was left on the ships, even from the *Vensterdam.* Then they locked themselves in there with..."

"With who?" Elaine pressed.

"All the supplies and..." Cranston hesitated, then let it out. "And the children."

Krista...

"They're the insurance policy that we wouldn't try anything," Cranston explained. "As long as we left the Russians be in the pit, they would keep feeding the kids. Keep them alive down there with them."

Cranston stood suddenly and pointed to something on the blueprint collage. Three letters, SSC, at the top of one page, crossed purposely out with a stroke of black ink, a now familiar term scrawled beneath it—The Pit.

"It's the Subterranean Survivor Complex," Cranston said, trying to rub the offending gash of ink from the trio of letters. "One of my lead guys, one day he comes in here, and he does that, and writes that, and then he goes outside and blows his brains out."

Cranston stopped his attempt to erase the indelible mark.

"I think his name was Joe," Cranston said, then turned to face us again.

The man had found the edge some time ago, it seemed, and was teetering very close to it, some personal abyss ready to swallow him without warning.

"It was a mess," Cranston said, in response to no one, just some admission rising from the foggy doubt that seemed to rise and fall like some tide within. "I mean, something that big, you can't rush it. It wasn't ready. Whole sections are unusable."

"How much food is down there?" I asked the man.

Cranston scratched at his cheek as he considered my question. A red patch there, the skin warn almost beyond raw, pointed to the nervous tick having afflicted him for some time. Nails clawed slowly, methodically, until his gaze rose to meet mine.

"Years," he said. "Years. That was the plan. Everyone stays there for years while the plants grew in the greenhouses."

I looked to Schiavo, doing my own mental math.

"Years for all those people brought here," I said. "Kuratov and his men could grow old on what's in there."

"While everyone out here dies," Elaine said.

Cranston sat and quieted, the manic push and pull between insanity and reason easing for the moment.

"Sergeant..."

Lorenzen looked to his leader.

"Get all the food still on the boat and set up some kind of distribution," she instructed.

"There's got to be five, six hundred people in town," he said.

"Eight hundred," Cranston corrected. "Eight hundred and eighty two. I think. Unless someone died. Someone always dies. Like Joe."

Lorenzen eyed the odd man, but only briefly, his attention shifting back to his commander.

"We can't feed everybody," Schiavo said. "But get food to the weakest, any pregnant women, and anyone who's sick. Work with Hart and Doctor Allen to prioritize."

"Yes, ma'am," Lorenzen said, then headed out.

A trio of individuals passed him on their way in. There was a weary officiousness about them.

"Lieutenant," one of the three, a woman said.

"Schiavo," she said in introduction. "Lieutenant Angela Schiavo."

She offered her hand, and the woman looked at it for a moment before accepting the greeting and shaking it.

"Sue Reinhardt," the woman said. "Administrator of the Edmonton group."

"Good to meet—"

"What the hell are you going to do to fix this?"

The interrupter was one of the other two men, small and taut. There was a fiery distaste about him. A bitterness that bled into the room from his very presence.

"And you are?" Schiavo asked calmly.

"I'm Earl Perkins, head of the Yuma group. Now answer my damn question."

It would have been easy for Schiavo to exert some authority, much as she had done when the question of transport arose on Mary Island. But she didn't. It might have been that she'd learned from that exchange with us. Or it could have been that she realized that Perkins' fuse was already lit, and she could either wait for him to blow, or try to snuff it out.

"We're going to talk about a plan," Schiavo said. "I promise you. And we'll keep you all involved in the discussions. But we're going to need to move fast, so I hope you'll understand me needing to stay focused on my mission. Fair enough?"

Perkins didn't explode. But he didn't calm, either. His fuse seemed to stop and smolder just inches from setting him off.

"I'll expect answers," Perkins said. "Soon."

Schiavo nodded to the man, then turned to the other who'd come in with him.

"Dave Danforth from San Diego. I was appointed our leader just before we were evacuated."

Schiavo shook his hand, but didn't chance to offer the greeting to Perkins, who stood with arms folded across his narrow chest.

"I have one question that needs answering before we can figure out what to do," Schiavo told the representatives. "How many children did they take with them into the pit?"

"Thirty three," Reinhardt answered. "Every child ten and under. Boys and girls."

"Almost every parent let them go," Danforth said, a deep sadness rising. "They knew they would eat down there."

Schiavo looked to me, uncertain, then back to the representatives.

"We'll get them back," she said. "That's our first priority."

"Excuse me..."

It was Elaine, some sudden sparkle of confusion about her.

"What is it?" I asked.

She didn't answer me directly, instead focusing on the three who'd joined us in Cranston's trailer.

"You're each the leaders of your groups," she said.

"More or less," Sue Reinhardt said.

"Yes," Earl Perkins added, with certain vigor to his affirmation. "Duly elected by the Yuma Survivors Council. I didn't just fall into this."

"We all function in some leadership capacity," Danforth said, shooting a fast, icy glance Perkins' way before fixing fully on Elaine. "What is your point?"

Elaine turned to me, a serious and specific wonder about her.

"Where's Martin?"

Her curiosity reminded me instantly that we hadn't seen him yet, when, by all rights, he would have been one of the first to greet us.

"He's not here," Reinhardt said. "It was his turn."

"His turn?" I asked. "His turn to what?"

Thirty Two

Two dead tree branches had been lashed together and propped up in the middle of the dirt road, forming an X to warn any who might think of venturing past. This was the point of no return.

"Stop here," Reinhardt said, putting an arm out to hold us back. "You can't go any further."

But Schiavo did. She pushed Reinhardt's arm down and walked right up to the X, leaving Elaine and me behind with the woman who'd volunteered to guide us to this spot.

"Don't go past it," Reinhardt warned. "They could be watching right now."

Schiavo didn't cross the boundary marked by the leaning branches. She just stood there, M4 slung against her chest, and looked to the road beyond, the path disappearing as it followed a bend through the dead forest.

"Kuratov said if anyone approached the access to the pit, he'd..."

Reinhardt didn't finish. To be honest, I didn't want her to, or need her to. Just knowing that the man had made such threats against absolute innocents made it abundantly clear that we had to get Krista, and the others, out of there. Before Kuratov showed that he was more monster than man.

"Once a day at nine in the morning he said we could send one person to see that the children were still alive," Reinhardt explained. "That's where Martin is. Back there. Kuratov has his men bring all the children into one of the greenhouse areas so we can see them below. Through the skylight."

Reinhardt began to choke up.

"Then we have to leave," Reinhardt continued, forcing down the emotion that had bubbled up. "That's the only time anyone can see them. Some of them just look up into the sunlight and cry."

"Do you have someone down there?" I asked.

Reinhardt nodded, then turned away and buried her face against Elaine's shoulder.

"I'll be back," I said, leaving Elaine with Reinhardt as I joined Schiavo right near the X. "Did you hear that?"

Schiavo nodded.

"How far back there do you think it is?" she asked.

"A hundred yards or so," I said. "I'd have to look closer at the plans."

She looked away from the thinning grey woods and fixed on me.

"You know plans and construction," she said. "It's what you used to do, right?"

In the casual conversations we'd had on our journey north, we'd learned a bit about each other. That I had once owned and operated a thriving construction business had seemed like the most mundane of facts I'd shared about myself. Now it appeared it was turning out to be a most salient revelation.

"Right," I said.

Schiavo stopped for a moment and reached for the X, grabbing hold of one of the long, dead branches, gripping it for support.

"Are you okay?"

She managed a smile that was at least partially a grimace.

"I've been better," she said.

"You need rest."

"That's not a luxury I can afford right now," she said. "And those kids down there definitely can't afford to wait for me to heal up fine and dandy."

"Is that where she is?!"

I knew who was shouting the challenge before I'd even turned. When I did spin and look behind I saw Neil charging past Elaine and Reinhardt, AK in hand, not slung.

"Hold it," I said, putting my hands out to stop my friend.

"Is she in there?" Neil demanded. "Is she?!"

I planted my palms against his shoulders and gripped his jacket. Elaine came up from behind and put a hold on one arm.

"You can't go back there," Elaine said.

"Is Krista there?! Dammit, answer me!"

I eased my grip from my friend and looked him in the eye.

"She is," I told him. "With a lot of other children."

He absorbed that, a crazed and helpless look in his eyes. Then he tried to push past. Elaine and I grabbed him, with Schiavo stepping in front to block his advance.

"We're going to get them out," the lieutenant said. "But we can't do it just rushing in there."

"How do we even know she's alive?" Neil almost begged.

"She's alive."

Again, it was a voice I knew without laying eyes on the speaker. Martin approached from beyond the X. He stepped past the barrier and stood close to Neil.

"I just saw them," Martin told my friend. "Krista is there, and she's okay."

Neil let out a half sob and let his AK drop on its sling. I put a reassuring hand on my friend's shoulder and looked to Elaine.

"Why don't you take Neil and Reinhardt back to town," I said.

Elaine nodded and gently guided Neil away from the X, gathering the leader of the Edmonton group as they made their way back down the old road.

"Eric..."

Martin smiled at me. A true smile. The expression was bright and warm, while all else about the man looked beaten down. He was drained. Weakened by lack of food.

"It's so wonderful to see you," he told me.

Then the man who'd led the residents of Bandon through trials and tribulations looked to the woman, the officer, who was a stranger to him.

"I'm Martin Jay," he said, offering his hand.

"This is Lieutenant Angela Schiavo," I said, handling the introduction.

"Army?" Martin asked.

"Yes," Schiavo said, shaking his hand. "How are you?"

"I'm holding my own," Martin said. "But we have some sick people, and a few pregnant women."

Schiavo nodded, signaling she'd already made arrangements.

"You know," Martin said. "Good."

They were both leaders. Looking out for those who depended on them. And, it hurt me to realize, both understood, as I did, what fate lay ahead for the children if we did nothing.

"The day one of us doesn't show up to check on the children is the day he stops feeding them," Martin said. "Once everyone outside is dead his place is secure."

"He won't even stay in there," Schiavo said. "He won't have to. It will just be a big bunker where he keeps the food and supplies."

"And if he has that radio..." I said.

"He does," Martin said. "Two of them. One he brought with him, and one the soldiers here used."

"He'll know if reinforcements are coming to Skagway," I said.

Schiavo didn't dispute that. But she also didn't seem very interested in the speculation.

"We need one of those radios," she said. "But we need those kids away from him first."

"How many troops do you have?"

Schiavo wanted to tell Martin she'd come with a battalion. But there were no more battalions. Or companies. Or platoons. There was only what there was.

"Five plus me," Schiavo told him.

"Six," Martin said, thinking. "We've scrounged a few weapons from the area, but we've kept them out of sight. We didn't want Kuratov to know about them if he sent anyone up to check on us."

"That was smart," Schiavo said.

"So if you need more manpower, you have it," Martin offered.

"We probably will," Schiavo said. "But first we need to figure out how to get in, and how to get the children out."

Schiavo looked to me. I knew what that meant. The expertise I retained from my former profession was going to come into play.

"You've got to find us a weak point," she told me.

"Yeah," I said, the burden that came with that assignment, and the consequences of getting it wrong, clear beyond doubt to me.

"If..."

Schiavo only got that word out, then she tipped toward the crossed branches again. Before she could grope for a handhold, Martin got an arm under hers, and the other around her shoulder.

"Are you okay?"

"She's up from a bullet wound two days ago," I told Martin.

He looked to her with a quiet, incredulous admiration.

"I'm fine," she lied, realizing that a second after saying so. "I'll be fine."

She steadied herself. Martin gingerly eased his support from her.

"We'll take it easy back to town," Martin told her. "Okay?"

Schiavo didn't protest. She just began walking, our pace matched to hers, Martin close to her side, his attention more on her than the way ahead.

Part Four

The Pit

Thirty Three

I spread the secondary set of blueprints I'd taken from Cranston's trailer out on the pool table in what had once been a bustling tavern. We'd moved this more detailed inspection of the plans from the foreman's cramped office to a location in the center of town that could accommodate the whole of Schiavo's unit, Elaine and me, and a few representatives of the evacuated communities who'd been sent to observe and answer any questions about the Russians they'd encountered.

Martin stood with us, too. Gazing upon the plans with clear disdain.

"That was supposed to be our home," he said.

"It's big," Enderson commented.

He was right. I'd worked with designs and engineering schematics of projects that varied from simple apartment buildings to office complexes that covered entire city blocks. What we were looking at rendered in pale blue lines upon faded white paper dwarfed anything I'd come across.

"It's bigger than the Pentagon," Lorenzen said. "Just fifty feet underground."

I reached to the long and wide stack of paper and flipped slowly through the design, orienting myself with the layout. I'd already made some preliminary checks of the overall design, and one thing stood out. One very counterintuitive thing that worked in our favor.

"This is basically a prison," I said.

"What do you mean?" Schiavo asked, sipping from a cup of powdered energy drink Martin had insisted she have.

"It was built to keep people in," I said. "There's no provision to defend against an attack from outside. No surveillance system to watch for aggressors. I mean, it's still a fortress buried in the earth, but it's not impenetrable. Look, right here."

I put my finger to a square void depicted by thick dashed lines.

"A greenhouse skylight, correct?" I asked, looking to Martin.

"Correct," he said, pointing out others. "Right there and there, too."

"Which is the one where you look in on the children?" I asked.

"This one," Martin showed me.

"Is it always the same one?" I asked. "You haven't looked through another?"

"It's only been four days," Danforth said. "We've only been out there that many times."

"But always the same one?" I checked, and the man from San Diego nodded. "Then I'm thinking the children must be kept close by."

"Who would want to herd thirty three little ones very far?" Elaine said, agreeing.

Schiavo pointed to a number of larger spaces near the skylight in question.

"Somewhere here," she suggested logically.

"I know that area," Martin said.

We looked to him, curious. Then Danforth added his concurrence to what Martin had said.

"Me, too."

"Kuratov had us form details to transfer the food that was on the ships and in town for the workers," Martin explained, directing our attention to a specific space. "Right there, Chamber Six Six Two. That's where we put it."

"The supplies meant for everyone when the place was locked down are here," Danforth said, pointing to a chamber a good hundred yards away along intersecting corridors.

"Chamber Two Zero Zero," I said, reading from the design. "That's what Kuratov would protect, yes?"

The question was directed to Schiavo, but she looked to her sergeant.

"What do you think?"

Lorenzen studied the location briefly.

"Closer to the main entrance," he said. "They would only have to defend one point, this corridor, to deny access to the supplies from the entrance. That's where I'd place my main force."

"He puts supplies dedicated for the hostages near where they are kept," Elaine said. "I'd buy that."

"Me, too," I said.

Schiavo looked to me, sensing that an idea was brewing.

"What are you thinking, Eric? That the skylights are our point of entry?"

"Yes," I said. "They're made of a strong polycarbonate according to these specs, but it can be breached."

Schiavo finished her drink and turned to Martin.

"Among those weapons you scrounged, were there any explosives?"

"From the construction of the pit," Martin confirmed. "Yes. Some shaped charges. Block plastic explosives. Not much, but enough to get through a skylight."

Schiavo thought on the possibility for a moment, uncertain.

"We breach it, rappel down, then..."

Lorenzen nodded, buying into the doubt she was hinting at.

"Yeah, then..."

"What is it?" I asked.

"Once we're down there," Schiavo began, "then what? We initiate a firefight with the troops he has watching over the children, because he will have someone on top of them. And while we do that…"

Lorenzen pointed to the area near the access door.

"Kuratov sends his main force back," Lorenzen said. "And now we're flanked, *and* caught in a crossfire. Worst of all worlds."

What they were describing made sense. I'd found a way to get them in, but in was not a very healthy place to be in that situation.

"And if we punch through one of these other skylights closer to the main access," Schiavo said. "Then we have to split our unit. Half to deal with the main force, half to free the children."

"Even if we secured the kids," Enderson began, "we have to get them out. Thirty three kids. How? Up ropes? Through that main access door?"

Every aspect of what had to be done was complicated by the presence of the little ones. To even fathom losing just one was impossible.

"Eric…"

It was Martin speaking up. I looked to him and saw his gaze narrowed down, zeroing in on a part of the plans near where the children were suspected of being held.

"What, Martin?"

"This place was rushed, you know that, yes?"

"Cranston said something like that," I confirmed.

"When we were moving the supplies back there, I noticed some fairly substantial cracks along here."

Martin showed us where he had noticed the structural defect, along the corridor that connected the area around Chamber 662 to the section where we theorized Kuratov was keeping his main force.

"If that section is weak enough, could you bring it down with the right charge?"

Martin's question, whether he knew it or not, was, in itself, a suggestion of simple brilliance.

"There's maybe thirty feet of earth pressing down on that corridor ceiling right there," I said, smiling. "Yeah. The right charge could weaken it enough to cause a failure."

"Yes," Lorenzen said, stabbing a finger at the lines that defined the corridor in question. "That would block access for any force Kuratov sends toward the children."

"We'd only have to deal with whoever he has guarding them," Enderson said.

The plan, at least part of it, was beginning to come together now. But by the looks of it, Schiavo wasn't yet convinced.

"As soon as we breach that skylight, we announce what's happening," she said. "Can we charge and detonate that corridor before Kuratov's men get to us?"

"Or to the children," Danforth added.

Schiavo stared at the plans for a moment, planting her hands on the pool table's edge. She seemed to be tiring, something I was not alone in noticing. Martin reached to the table in front of her and took her empty cup, refilling it from a canteen.

"Here," he said, handing the beverage to her.

"Thank you," she said, managing a smile and taking a long sip before focusing on the plans again. "You that were in there, we need to know more. Everything you saw. Anything you heard. Tell us everything."

Martin began to talk, trading off sharing information and observations with Danforth. They tag teamed the data dump, occasionally answering questions from Schiavo's men. And in the rolling exchange I noticed something. Someone.

Hollis.

He'd introduced himself before we'd begun, sharing that Perkins had sent him to offer any help he could. Yet now, when he could be adding to what Martin and Danforth were telling, he stood mute. Saying nothing. Just looking at the blueprints and at other things.

Studying other things. Other people.

Schiavo and her men.

I had a good angle to catch how his eyes moved without him noticing. Every few seconds he would look one of the soldiers up and down, zeroing briefly in on their weapons. Their name patches. Rank insignia.

He was scouting them.

Then, as I paid some very direct attention to him, I saw it. Saw what I needed to bring the wariness which had come suddenly to full blown worry.

I took a small notebook from my pocket and clicked open the pen clipped to it.

"Martin, what about this?" I asked, pointing to a length of partition highlighted on the blueprints.

"That's an interior wall," Danforth answered, dredging details from his brief time in the pit. "It looked flimsy."

I nodded and wrote in my notebook, watching as Martin listened to Schiavo ask about the surface of the corridors, and whether they were slick or rough concrete. When I'd finished making the notation I gently nudged Elaine with my elbow. She first glanced where one would, to meet my gaze, but I was very purposely fixed on the blueprints. It took her just a few seconds to realize I'd wanted to get her attention covertly. Then, as I'd desired, her gaze drifted down to what I'd written in my notebook. I couldn't see her posture stiffen, but I sensed that she'd keyed in completely to what I feared.

"Do we have descent harnesses?" Elaine asked between questions from Schiavo's men.

"We have the basics with our gear," Enderson answered.

"If we have to bring the children up, we're going to need a way to secure them to ropes," Elaine said, stepping back from the pool table. "I'm going to go see if there's anything we can fashion into harnesses."

Her idea received a nod from Schiavo, who continued peppering Martin and Danforth with questions for a few more minutes before deciding she wanted to process what had been learned with her unit. They filtered out the front of the tavern, the rest lining up to follow.

That was when I acted.

"Are you going to see Perkins?" I asked Hollis as everyone neared the exit.

"Yeah," Hollis confirmed.

I glanced to the others, as if nervous about them hearing. Then I motioned toward the back door just beyond what had once been a thriving counter at the bar.

"I don't want anyone else to hear this," I said, and moved past the counter.

Hollis didn't even hesitate. He followed me to the back and stepped through the door as I opened it for him.

His head snapped right a split second later.

Thirty Four

The butt of Elaine's MP5 struck Hollis across the jaw as he stepped into the open. He crumpled to the ground against the back wall, clutching the side of his face, blood spilling past his lips.

"What the hell is—"

He never completed the question that would protest his treatment. As his gaze came up he saw Elaine, who had landed the blow, her MP5 now aimed squarely at his chest. Next to her stood Lorenzen, his M4 at the ready, but a seething look his weapon of choice for the moment. And, right beside them, Perkins stood. Staring down at the bleeding man.

"I have no idea who this man is," Perkins said.

I crouched next to 'Hollis' and held out my notebook, open to what I'd written for Elaine to read.

'Find Perkins. See if he knows Hollis. I'm bringing him out the back. Tell Schiavo.'

"Infiltrator," Elaine said.

Hollis looked from her, to the notebook again, then to me.

"Your punctuation is impeccable," he said, smiling with crimson teeth. "American."

The Russian wasn't even offering any pretense. Neither would I.

"How do you get in?" I asked.

The cocksure attitude he'd just expressed faded. He didn't answer, looking past me as Enderson brought Schiavo around from the front side of the building.

"We have ourselves a live infiltrator," Lorenzen told the lieutenant.

"Not for long if he doesn't tell us how he gets in and out of that monstrosity," I said. "Because he has to. Why else would they leave him out here? He has to report what's going on. Just like he was going to report on our arrival. Our strength. Weapons. Isn't that right, *Hollis*?"

He smiled now again, little bubbles of blood on his lips as he chuckled.

"Viktor Grishin, *Leytenánt*, six-five-nine—"

A fast slap of my gloved hand across Grishin's face halted his recitation of the particulars required under the Geneva Convention concerning the treatment to be afforded to prisoners of war. He glared up at me, a spray of blood, *his* blood, now splashed across the back wall of the building. I wondered if I would hear any protest from Schiavo, but none came.

"I am a prisoner of war!" Grishin shouted wetly.

"What war?" Schiavo asked in response.

I tapped the Russian again on his cheek, lightly now, to bring his attention back to me.

"You see, I know you can get in, and not just because you'd have to report, but because of these."

I brought a gloved finger to his chest and tapped the thick shirt there, its checkered pattern of reds and greens dotted with small, whitish objects.

Crumbs.

"Your comrades are passing you food," I said.

Grishin turned his head away, tiring of me. He was about to feel much more than annoyance toward me. Much more.

I leaned close to him and spoke softly into his ear.

"I told myself there were things I would never do. Even to survive. I'm about to break one of those promises."

The Russian turned slowly to face me from just inches away.

"Tie him up," I said.

"What are you doing?" Schiavo asked.

I stood and faced her.

"What you can't," I told her.

Elaine jerked the man up and Perkins shoved him against the wall, pulling his arms behind. It took a minute to bind him with paracord. Tight. His hands hung limp and purple behind his back when we were finished.

"Last chance before the screaming starts," I said.

Grishin said nothing, trying to maintain some stoic resolve. But I could feel his thudding heartbeat against my gloved hand where it lay on his back.

"Eric..."

I looked back to Schiavo.

"This won't take long," I said. "Why don't you and your men discuss what you need to discuss."

"HELP!" Grishin suddenly screamed. "HELP ME!"

I laughed, and the Russian quieted, his head angling back over his shoulders to look upon me.

"In English?" I said. "Really? Is that because you know your comrades would let you rot, if they could even hear you?"

Grishin's breathing quickened and he drew his head back, then slammed it against the wall. A gash opened across his forehead, blood trickling from what looked like a sick, red grin carved upon his brow. I grabbed his collar and pulled him away from the building.

"Eric, this—"

"Lieutenant," I said, laying a hard look upon her. "This is what it has to be."

Schiavo stared at the Russian for a moment, a long moment, then she looked to her sergeant.

"Get the men together and we'll hash out what we've got to do," she said.

"Yes, ma'am," Lorenzen said, flashing me a look before he walked away.

I was almost certain there was a wink embedded in it.

"Now," I said, spinning Grishin to face me, and Elaine, and Perkins. "We have some questions for you."

Elaine reached to her belt and took a knife from its sheath.

"I'm not going to tell you—"

The solid crunch of Perkins' fist connecting with Grishin's nose ended his pointless bravado before he could finish. Elaine handed me her knife and I whipped it fast up to the Russian's face.

"You're going to," I said, sliding the tip of the knife under his upper lip. "Understand?"

He tried to say 'no', and I jerked the blade up and through the soft flesh of his lip, leaving two bleeding flaps dangling beneath his nose.

"Ahhhhhhhhhhhhhhhhhhh!"

His scream was wet and came from a place I doubted he knew existed within him just a few seconds earlier.

"My friend's little girl is down there," I said. "And I will do anything to see that she comes out alive and unhurt. Because if that does not come to pass, let me remind you that what I just did to you is not fatal. You'll still be here, tied up, and I'll be coming back to you. And I won't be alone. My friend will be with me. And if you think what I just did to you was unpleasant, let me assure you that what he will inflict upon you will make you wish that I'd just gone ahead and slit your throat. So, tell me now, do you want me to remove one of your eyelids?"

At first, Grishin did not react to my question. He simply stared at me with blackened eyes, the garish hole that was his mouth trembling with stinging agony. Then, before I could say anything more, he shook his head. Just barely. Like a meek mouse.

The next question I asked he answered fully. And the next. And the next.

By the time Grishin finished telling us all that he knew, Elaine and I realized that there was another option to free the children. One whose window of opportunity was rapidly closing.

I reached to the Russian's wrist and removed his watch, then shoved him to the ground at Perkins' feet.

"Lock him up somewhere," I told the angry little man from Yuma. "If he tries anything, end him."

For the first time, I saw Perkins smile, a disturbing curl arcing his thin lips.

"Gladly," Perkins said, hauling Grishin to his feet and strong arming him away from the building.

"We have to tell Schiavo," Elaine said.

I shook my head. That would come, and, if the timing of this was to work, it would have to happen with haste. But something else would have to come first.

"We need to talk to the foreman," I said.

Thirty Five

Cranston was no longer in his office. It took twenty minutes to find him, Elaine finally tracking him down on the road to the cemetery. She brought him back to the tavern and led him to the pool table where the plans were still spread out.

"We need some information," I said, Elaine standing with me.

The feeble man looked to me, his gaze distant, a sheen of tears upon it.

"I just wanted to visit Joe," Cranston said. "We buried him."

Whatever remained of his faculties was fading quickly. We had to get some straight and precise answers out of him. And fast.

"Earl, look here," I said. "On the plan. What's this?"

His eyes tracked slowly to where I was pointing to a section of the plans deeper into the complex. Maybe a hundred feet beyond where the children were thought to be.

"Earl, what is it?" I repeated. "This square marking? Is that ductwork of some kind?"

He looked to me, confused, and shook his head.

"No. No."

"What is it, Mr. Cranston?" Elaine prodded him with gentle respect.

Cranston leaned forward, closer to the plan, his own bony finger tracing along the paper until it rested next to mine.

"Dump shaft," he said.

"Dump shaft," I repeated. "To dispose of garbage? Things like that?"

He nodded.

"Just climb up the ladder in it and pop the hatch and toss out anything you don't want," he explained with a momentary flash of lucidity.

I looked to the plans again.

"About two feet square?" I asked him.

"Twenty four by twenty four," he confirmed.

"And it only opens from the inside?"

"That's right," Cranston told me.

His fingers spread out upon the plan, both hands splayed wide, as if trying to hide what he saw before him. What he'd helped create.

"I think his name was Joe," Cranston said, slipping back into some guilt-ridden fugue state.

Elaine looked to me.

"It can work," she said.

"Yeah," I agreed. "Let's tell Schiavo."

Thirty Six

"You want to what?"

Schiavo's doubting question came just as I began explaining the plan that had coalesced after Grishin's coerced revelations.

"I go in alone," I repeated. "Through a dump shaft that only opens from the inside. It's past the location where the kids are."

"Where we *think* they are," the lieutenant reminded me.

"Right," I said.

She stood alone, facing me and Elaine in the front room of a souvenir store her unit had taken over to prep for the mission ahead. The rest of her men were out gathering the explosives we'd need, and readying a small group of civilians to provide some armed cover of the main access door.

"The infiltrator told you about this shaft?" Schiavo asked.

"He did," Elaine answered. "And Cranston confirmed it."

"It has to be opened from within?" Schiavo asked. "Won't blasting it alert Kuratov the same as when we breach the skylight?"

I shook my head.

"At six-thirty this evening, one member of Kuratov's unit will open the hatch," I said. "He'll have an MRE to pass up to Grishin, who is supposed to relay any intel on what's happening above."

Schiavo began to smile, the warm expression almost stark against her still pale complexion.

"Only Grishin won't be there," Schiavo said. "You will."

"Right," I said, tapping the suppressor attached to the muzzle of my AR. "I pop the Russian quietly, get inside, and get close to where the children should be. That should take five minutes. Make it six to be safe. At that moment your team breaches a skylight away from the one where the children are shown."

"You draw Kuratov's force even further away from the kids," Elaine said.

"Then I eliminate whoever's guarding the children, blow that weakened corridor to block any interference, and lead them to the dump shaft."

"That has a lot of moving parts," Schiavo said.

"So does a Lamborghini," I countered. "But they still work."

Schiavo thought on the plan for a moment.

"Why you?" she asked. "And why not more than one? I could slip my guys down there just as easily as you."

"No," I said. "A good number of those children know me. I'm not some stranger coming for them. That will make getting them out a quicker process. Besides, the more shooters we take down there, the more likely it is that someone makes a sound, and then we've got a firefight and all of Kuratov's men coming down on us. This has to be a stealth operation on that end. You can make as much noise as you want blowing Kuratov to hell."

"I'll be there to help you do just that," Elaine said.

She'd said she was going in. Insisted upon it. When I'd told her that I needed to handle my end alone, to be as quiet as possible, she'd shifted her focus to being part of Schiavo's entry team.

As she informed the lieutenant of her intention here, I felt that pang of fear stab at my insides. But I had to force it down. I had to.

"What about the main supplies down there?" Schiavo asked. "And the radio?"

"The children come first," I said, knowing that she would not dispute that.

Schiavo nodded. Then, she shook her head slightly, some realization rising.

"He's the boogeyman we've never seen," Schiavo said. "Kuratov. Just some legend who leaves a trail of death behind."

Not unlike Borgier. The American turned rogue French Legionnaire. Some days earlier I'd shared with Schiavo what we'd been told about the man believed to have unleashed the blight. She'd confirmed that tale as fact. Now, we had another rogue. Or a madman. Whichever turned out to be the case, it seemed plain to me that either he would die, or we would.

All of us.

"Lieutenant..."

It was Hart. He was smiling as he entered the store. An expression incongruous with the moment and what was soon to come.

Or so I thought.

"What is it?" Schiavo asked.

Hart reached into the bag slung over his left shoulder. It was from his med kit. I'd seen him pull bags of plasma from it when he still had those in his inventory. This time, though, when he eased his hand out he held a plasma bag that did not contain that life-saving liquid. Instead the contents were a dark crimson. Identical to what he'd had in a similar bag after tapping Elaine for a transfusion.

"I found another AB Neg," Hart said. "So we're going to top you off, ma'am."

Schiavo reacted blandly. As if annoyed that any consideration for her well-being was even necessary.

"Things have changed, Trey," Schiavo said to her medic, the informality she was affording him in our presence not surprising after all we'd been through together. "We're on a clock now to make this op happen."

Without saying so with any specificity, Schiavo had just blessed the plan that Elaine and I had devised. A plan she would be part of, and for which she needed to be as close to fully capable as possible.

"We have ninety minutes," I said.

Hart pulled an IV line and needle from his kit.

"I need forty five," the medic said.

Every second was of the essence, just as her health was, so Schiavo took no time to decide.

"Do it," she said.

A minute later she was flat on the floor, a needle in her arm, blood dripping into the line that delivered it to her veins. Forty minutes after that the bag went dry.

I wasn't there to witness the entire process, though. There was one stop I had to make before we ventured into the pit.

Thirty Seven

Grace lay on a couch in a house one block from the main street through Skagway. I found Neil with her, and Doc Allen.

"Fletch," my friend said when he saw me come through the front door.

He came up to me and pulled me into a hug. When we eased back from each other his smile beamed under glistening eyes.

"We're going to have a baby," he said. "Can you believe that?"

"It's wonderful, Neil."

I looked past him to Grace. In her eyes I saw wondering and fear.

"Doc says she'll be okay," Neil said. "She's just overwhelmed."

"Absolutely," I said.

My friend put a hand to my elbow and ushered me a few steps away, just out of earshot for Grace.

"What's going to happen?"

"We're going in to get them," I said. "There's a plan. I think we have a good chance."

Even that phrasing left my friend with a pained look on his face.

"It's going to be okay," I assured him. "Look, we made it here. We beat every set of odds we came up against. And we're going to keep on doing that."

Neil shifted his gaze for a moment, to a window which looked out toward the harbor, the vessels in it half visible above rooftops.

"Do you know what sank the *Vensterdam*?" he asked me.

"The Russians did."

"Doc Allen said that when that ship was pulling in the Russians fired on it from their boat. They weren't even taking fire."

"Cranston told us about that," I said.

"Fletch, if they'll do that to a shipload of helpless people..."

I knew what my friend meant. You wanted to believe that there was a code that warriors lived by. A code that had, in some small way, nearly pushed Schiavo to interrupt my violent and necessary interaction with Grishin. Not all warriors abided by a code such as that. It was certain that Kuratov did not.

"The plan is good, Neil. It is. I'm the one going in to get the children."

"You?"

I nodded.

"What about Elaine?"

I hesitated just a breath. A noticeable breath.

"She's going in with Schiavo," I told my friend.

To that he said nothing. He'd said all he could before this moment ever came.

"I've gotta go," I said, glancing past to Grace and Doc Allen. "Tell her—"

But Neil shook his head, cutting off my assurance.

"When it's done, and Krista is back in our arms, we'll know."

I understood. Anything promised now was only a collection of words. They needed fact. They needed flesh and blood to embrace so they could know, so they could believe, that the horror was over.

Thirty Eight

"You're staying," I said.

Elaine almost didn't react to what I'd said. She continued transferring unnecessary gear from her pack to the table just as Schiavo and her men were doing. Then, she froze, her gaze rising to see that I was standing right where I'd been, and that there was no hint about me that what I'd just told her was a joke.

"Excuse me?"

"You heard me," I said. "You're not going."

Just across the table I glimpsed Schiavo glancing our way as she readied her equipment. She didn't try to intervene, and she wouldn't. This was between Elaine and me.

"You're covering the entrance with the others," I said.

Elaine dialed her gaze in hard on me.

"I thought we talked about this," she said.

"We did," I said. "But I can't let you go in. I need to be focused on what has to be done. If you're there, half of me will be wondering if you're all right. Every distant shot I hear will be one that could have your name on it."

"I can handle myself," she said.

I shook my head.

"That's not the point. If it's that macho gene thing, I'm sorry. But from the deepest part of my being, I know that I would give my life for you. Except I won't be with you if that becomes necessary. And that says nothing about how capable you are. It's just the reality of what I feel for you."

Elaine took in what I'd just shared with her, seething silently. But not countering what I'd said.

"I need a good shooter at the entrance," Schiavo said, and Elaine looked sharply toward her. "All I have covering that location are weak people with scrounged weapons. I could use you there, Elaine."

There was logic to what Schiavo had just explained. And logic to what I'd said. But neither mattered to Elaine, I sensed, as she gathered up her gear and her weapon and looked between the lieutenant and me.

"Sounds like a plan," she said sharply, then left the room.

"That went well," Schiavo said.

"Thank you for giving me an out," I said.

"I didn't give you anything," Schiavo said. "The civilians covering that entrance could end up facing elite troops on the off chance the Russians decide to make a break to the outside. I sure as hell can use her there."

Schiavo continued readying her gear and checking the makeshift breaching charge with Lorenzen. This was going to be a full on assault in a confined space. And it had to be choreographed to the second. Even then, there was no guarantee of success. Or that we'd get the children out alive.

Or that any of us would live through it.

I looked to my pack. I wouldn't be lugging it with me into the pit. All I'd need would fit in pockets and the tactical vest I scrounged from the garrison's old quarters.

"You clear on the use of that charge?" Lorenzen asked.

No one was a demolitions expert. But there was enough collective knowledge to allow me some confidence in using the slender block of plastic explosive. I had a twenty second fuse with it, all that could be found among the construction supplies left when Cranston's workers had pulled out. A third of a minute. That wasn't much time to get clear of any blast that would seal off the chamber near where we believed the children were being held. But it was all that I had.

"I've got it," I said.

But the margin worried me. A lot of what was going to happen worried me. Not returning, in particular, scared me. But not only for reasons that were obvious and personal.

Once more I looked to my pack. This time, though, I lifted it from where it sat and turned to Schiavo.

"Lieutenant..."

She paused her preparations and looked to me.

"Can I have a minute? In private?"

The interruption, so soon before we were about to set out on the mission into the pit, puzzled her.

"It's important," I said.

"Okay," she said, and followed me outside.

* * *

We stood behind the store with daylight beginning to fade. I reached to my pack and retrieved the book and two vials of seeds. Elaine and Neil each held more vials in their packs.

"What is that?" Schiavo asked.

"I never told you why we went to Wyoming," I said.

Then, I did tell her. I shared our journey, and the reason for it. The purpose. Then, I handed her the prize.

"That is the cure for the blight," I said.

Schiavo took the notebook from me, handling it gingerly. Then a single vial of seeds.

"These grow," she said, half asking.

"We've seen what grew from those seeds," I told her.

"Neil and Elaine, too?"

"Yeah," I said.

"Trees? Vegetables? Everything?"

So simple, and yet so fantastical. What had once been ordinary was considered extraordinary.

"Everything," I said.

She thought for a moment, then handed the items back to me.

"You trust Martin," she said, stating a plain conclusion she'd come to.

"Completely."

"Give those to him for safe keeping. If anything..."

She didn't need to finish.

"When we're done," Schiavo began, taking a more hopeful tone, "and we have the radio, I'll report what you've got there."

That was exactly what I wanted to hear. I headed for the store's back door to finish readying my gear.

"You could have told me earlier," Schiavo said, her words stopping me. "But I understand. You keep your cards close until you have to play them."

She was wise without the pretense. Smart without the superiority. Simply spoken and self-assured. There was a lot to like about Lieutenant Angela Schiavo. And even more to respect.

"Thank you," I said.

Then we went inside together. The next time we stepped outside we'd be on our way to the pit to wrest the children from Kuratov's grip.

Thirty Nine

Schiavo's team moved north from the X barrier that blocked the dirt road. I moved east and circled past the slope that led to the pit's main entrance. The group assigned to cover that potential escape point numbered ten, including Martin and Perkins.

And Elaine.

There was no time for greetings or well wishes or final words to each other. There was only a look. Apology and love and frustration and fear volleying between us through only that visual connection.

I had no idea if I'd finally crossed some line with her that could not be ignored. This might be the end, even if we both came out of it alive. And that was all right as long as she still had a life ahead.

She looked away first. Back to the wide entrance door. I continued on, trying not to glance back. But I did. I wanted to catch as many glimpses of her as I could before everything began. And I did. Again and again. Taking in the sight of her until I crossed a small ridge and she was gone from sight.

* * *

By Grishin's watch it was six thirty on the dot when a sharp clank resonated through the hatch from below.

I stood just to the side of the square hatch covering the dump shaft, my AR ready, set on single shot, the suppressor aimed at where the opening would appear. A second later it tipped upward and a Russian soldier with rosy cheeks poked his head through. He never even knew I was there.

A single muffled shot from my AR slammed his head to the right and his body dropped from view, slender hydraulic lifters holding the hatch open. I stepped close and aimed down into the shaft. Some weak light below cast over the body of the man I'd just shot, heaped on the concrete floor, a pair of MRE pouches at his side. I counted to five, waiting for anyone else to appear. No one did. Grishin hadn't lied. Only one comrade of his came to meet him each night. That was what he'd said, and that, it appeared, was what had come to pass.

Six minutes...

That was how much time I had to get into position before Schiavo and her unit breached the farthest skylight. I wasted no more time, slinging my AR and climbing down into the dump shaft, stepping as softly as I could upon the rungs. In less than a minute I covered the fifty foot descent and planted my boots on the floor next to the dead Russian.

A single light glowed at what seemed half power in the space I'd entered. The solar arrays and fuel cells powering the facility were not operating at full capacity, a fact that didn't surprise me considering the rush job that had been done during construction on everything else, the support systems included. Even in this room I could see cracks on the ceiling and the walls. Too many, I thought. I still wasn't close to the weakened corridor that Martin had described. That, I'd hoped, had been localized. I was beginning to fear the conditions that caused it was not.

I dragged the body clear of the ladder and moved to the door. A corridor led from it, and, from memory, I knew which way I had to go, and where the turns were. I had just under five minutes to cover the distance that should only take three, but I set out with haste, wanting as much extra time as possible to deal with the threats that would certainly be waiting where the children were.

But as I made my first turn, the time table, and how I'd hoped my part of the mission would unfold, were both made impossible by what I found myself facing.

Roots, dry and knotted, hung from the structure's ceiling, their dead bark scraping my face as I pushed through. Everything I was seeing, especially in this section of the pit, screamed haste, and corner cutting. Cranston and his people had put the pedal to the metal, pushing construction crews past the point where they could execute the plans properly.

I'd seen the same result many times in my old life as a contractor and builder. The subterranean behemoth around me was crumbling, bit by bit, and had begun to even before the blight reached this northern landscape. Roots continued to grow until killed by the death reaching down from above. They cracked the substandard concrete, invading any space they could reach. Suspended now like some tangle of jungle vines they slowed my progress as I had to push through the lacework of dead vegetation.

What section was I in? I tried to remember from the plans Cranston had provided. Everything had been numbered. Rooms were labeled Chamber 639 or Chamber 138. Why they'd chosen that terminology to describe a room, a simple space, I didn't know, though, to me, it evoked images of confinement more than contentment.

As I'd told the others, this was a prison, in essence. To keep locked away those whose only act of merit was surviving.

I made my way through the thickest vines, a wall that had not been cracked or undermined appearing. There was a number on it. The remnants of some marking mostly spared from the intrusion of dead roots and the water that had once nourished them.

648...

Chamber 648. I tried to place myself by recalling the blueprints. Two corridors and a series of chambers lay somewhere beyond the clogged passageway I was in. One wall was bulged where I passed, evidence of a near complete structural failure just waiting to happen.

That was the worst possible thing I could find where I stood.

This was the way I would have to bring the children out. And beyond having to navigate them through the dead growth impeding the path toward our exit, everything around me, ceiling, walls, and floor, were liable to have already collapsed when I detonated the charge to prevent Kuratov's men from reaching this section of the pit. A sympathetic failure set off by shockwaves from the detonation was almost certain, I could see.

Everything that had been complicated to begin with had just turned near impossible.

I put that realization out of my thoughts and focused. Nothing would matter if I could not first get to the children, and then secure them, so I pressed on. The slowing lace of gnarled roots thinned the further I traveled. But something stopped me as I neared what I believed was the final corner I would have to turn before reaching the children.

Crying.

A child crying. And someone speaking to them in stilted, inflected English.

"Eat," the man said. "Is good. Eat and stop cry."

The child cried more. Other small voices tried to comfort their upset friend. Our estimation—our guess—had been right. Whether that had happened through some collective analysis on our part, or divine intervention, I didn't care. The children were here.

I glanced at Grishin's watch on my wrist. Ten seconds remained. I eased toward the corner, my AR's suppressed muzzle pointed at the ceiling.

"Eat!"

The Russian shouted the instruction. More children cried. I slid my finger onto the trigger.

Five seconds...
"Eat now!"
Three...
I breathed.
Two...
I stepped away from the wall and brought my AR to bear, lowering the muzzle and swinging it around the corner in a fluid motion.
One...
My eyes lined up on the sights atop my weapon, peripheral vision registering the presence of children and blankets and buckets to one side of my target. But dead ahead, through the sight atop my AR, a small illuminated triangle rested just below the shoulder of a Russian soldier, a solid wall beyond him.
Zero...
I adjusted my aim upward just a tick and squeezed the trigger, a sharp crack and low rumble rolling through the structure around me. The Russian never even moved. My shot, from a distance of thirty feet, punched in his right ear and exited out the left, spraying the wall with a grotesque mix that I knew would horrify the children.

They screamed and I advanced, my weapon sweeping left and right, searching for any more threats. I gave a quick wave to the weeping and terrified children, hoping to calm them.

For one the gesture worked.

"Fletch!" Krista shouted.

I cleared a space adjoining the chamber which held the children. It was a room, not large, but it was jammed with cases and cases of MREs. Another opening led to a bathroom, its toilet hopelessly clogged, the stench it spread into the area as a whole just registering.

"Fletch, it's you!"

Krista bolted up and ran at me as gunfire erupted in the distance. A measure between two points that was warped by corridors and turns and sounds reflecting off walls made of cheap concrete. But they were distinct enough. American and Russian weapons. Dull thuds of grenades.

Schiavo's unit was engaged in battle.

"Fletch, you're here!"

Krista threw her arms around me. I took a moment from the task at hand and hugged her with one arm.

"It's okay, sweetie," I assured her. "We're going to get out of here. All of us."

The fire in the distance grew more frantic. And louder. The battle was shifting this way, a sign that was both positive and frightening. Kuratov's men were retreating. But they were retreating in this direction.

"Krista, get back with the other children, okay?"

She backed away, the joy that had overwhelmed her fading away.

"What is it, Fletch?"

I had to think. And fast. There was no way I could get this many frightened children to the dump shaft before Kuratov's men reached us. Many were in shock. The escape part of the plan, of my plan, simply wasn't going to work.

And now the folly of what I'd insisted upon became clear. I was one man. There could be a dozen or more charging in my direction at this very moment. While the decision to enter alone made sense if everything had gone as planned, the odds of that happening should have been clear enough to make me reconsider my insistence on that point. And now I was going to pay for it.

As were the children.

Unless...

Unless I could prevent the Russians from reaching this part of the pit. My thoughts flashed back to the weakened structure. I'd planned on setting a charge in the corridor fifty feet beyond the Chamber 662. I could still do that, I knew. It would collapse that passage, but also the escape route. We would be cut off. Entombed.

But we would be alive.

Those outside would know that. They would move heaven and earth to dig the children out.

And that was that. My decision came that fast. It was the only way.

"Krista, everyone, listen to me," I said.

More than half of the children, mostly the youngest, cried and whimpered uncontrollably. But several of the older ones, Krista included, focused on me, forcing their fear and tears down for the moment.

"I want you to get all the little ones back into that corner," I said, as gunfire drew closer and closer. "You have to get—"

In an instant, seeing only the expression on Krista's face change, I knew that I'd made a terrible calculation. Yes, I'd killed the Russian guarding the children. It turned out, though, another had now come.

"Move away from the children," the voice said behind me, in deeply accented English. "We wouldn't want them to get hurt."

Tears welled in Krista's eyes. The man must have run ahead of Kuratov's retreating force to get his comrade, or to bring the children forward as hostages. Whatever his reason for being here was, it didn't matter. He had the drop on me.

"I do not want to hurt the children," the man said, a hint of that warrior's code I'd feared was lost still present in this soldier.

My AR was slung. My hands were away from my body. Any move toward my rifle, or the Springfield on my hip, would be my last.

I stepped to the side, keeping my hands in the open, rotating slowly until I was facing the Russian. Behind him, the battle was growing louder. Shouts could be heard. Commands in Russian. Cries of pain.

"Goodbye," the Russian said, his AK leveled at my chest.

My last thought right then was not one of disappointment. Or regret. It was of Elaine. I pictured her, and held that image, waiting for the weapon aimed at me to spit its fire and death.

"Uurghhh."

The sound gurgled from the Russian and his eyes bulged, body trembling suddenly, the AK slipping from his grip and falling to the floor. He jerked once, then twice, and dropped vertically, like a marionette whose strings had been snipped. When his body hit the floor and tipped toward me I saw the handle of a combat knife protruding from the base of his skull.

And I saw Elaine standing a few inches behind where the Russian had been ready to kill me just seconds before.

"Christ..."

It was all I could manage to say. She stepped toward me and reached to my face. Her hand was smeared with blood, but I didn't care one bit when she put it to my cheek and left it there for a brief second.

"We'll never get them out through that mess," Elaine said.

She'd obviously decided, at some point, to ignore my plea. Following me into the pit she'd made her way through the same tangled roots and weakened corridors. Obstacles of impossibility.

"Can we hold them off?" she asked. "Just the two of us?"

I shook my head and handed her my AR.

"You stay with the children," I said, taking the small block of plastic explosives and the short fuse from a pouch on my vest. "I'm going to take that corridor down."

Ricochets sounded in the near distance. The very near distance.

"Cover that passageway," I told Elaine.

"You'll never reach the corridor," she said. "They've already reached it. Can't you hear that?"

I leaned in fast and kissed her, then pulled back.

"I don't have time to explain," I said. "Just keep the kids in the back corner and fire down that corridor. Keep them pinned away from here. I need one minute. Then take cover."

"But—"

I never heard what she said, if she completed the statement at all. I ran around the corner and down the passageway I'd come through, fixing the fuse into the powerful charge as I moved. In thirty seconds I'd reached the section where the walls and ceiling were threatening to crumble. Just a stiff breath would send them tumbling.

I had more than that.

I set the charge at the base of the bulging wall and popped the igniter on the fuse. The stiff yellow cord sizzled. Sparks spread from its end as the fire that would detonate the blasting cap crept swiftly down toward the explosive block.

Then, I ran, bulling my way through the roots, moving away from where Elaine and the children were. I could never reach that space in twenty seconds. All I could do was get as far away from the weakened area as possible and find a solid corner.

And pray.

I never found that corner. Coming through an open doorway into a chamber less than fifty feet from the charge I was slammed through the air and into a wall as the blast wave from the explosion hit me. My body fell to the floor and I pulled my arms and legs into a tight ball, hoping to absorb the collapse that was happening all around me, weak light going out as the structure fell in on itself.

And on me.

Forty

I could barely move. Two slabs had splintered from the ceiling and come down, striking the floor and toppling into me as clouds of pulverized concrete swirled, choking and blinding me momentarily. Nothing felt broken. No bones seemed to be crushed. It was simply that most of my lower half was pinned in the corner of the space I'd hoped would protect me from the blast.

From my vest I managed to retrieve a small flashlight. Its beam clicked on to reveal just what I faced.

Jagged sections of what had been the structure of the chamber lay just a few feet over my head, smaller chunks angled across my lower half. I shifted the beam to examine the area around me, what there was of it. A void about the size of a compact car's interior surrounded me. No light penetrated through any cracks. No sound. And, I feared, no air.

I was buried alive.

The explosion had done what I'd hoped in this spot. I could only hope that a sympathetic collapse had spread to the weakened corridor where Kuratov's men were. There was the possibility that Schiavo's unit might be close enough to suffer the effects as well, but the choice I'd made was to try and save the children. The chamber that held them appeared solid from the brief time I'd spent in it. No obvious cracks. No intrusion by dead vegetation. No water seepage. With any luck the children, and Elaine, would be alive and well, awaiting rescue.

My fate, I knew, was likely different from theirs.

No one knew where I was. I'd dashed off through twisting hallways to a room I'd never intended to set foot in. And that room, which had collapsed around me, along with much of the structure nearby, was now my tomb.

The situation was bleak.

But it was not hopeless.

There's always hope...

Yes, there was. I could not dig my way out. The size and weight of what had fallen around me was beyond my ability to move. But I could do something. Until the last breath left me.

I reached to the floor next to me and grabbed a length of rebar that had snapped during the collapse. Shed of its concrete cloak, I lifted the steel rod and slammed it onto the surface of a slab. The strike resonated sharply, echoing metallically in the confines of the space. Whether it would be heard beyond that, I had no idea.

But I had hope.

Again I drew the rod back and hit the slab. And again. And again.

* * *

My flashlight was dying. A glance at Grishin's watch, which had survived the collapse with little more than a scratch on its glass, showed me that I'd been down here for eight hours. For seven of those I'd slammed the piece of rebar over and over against the concrete slab. But my strength was gone. I was spent.

The air was growing hot, and moist. It tasted almost sick with each breath I took. Dust caked my lips. The inside of my mouth was painfully dry. But other than the reality that I was slowly suffocating, my body had come through the event remarkably well. Even my legs, immobilized beneath a pair of concrete slabs, were not damaged. I could move them slightly. They hadn't been crushed.

The fact was, I was going to make a decent looking corpse.

I laughed at that thought, then coughed. Even as my body was weakened and succumbing to a dwindling air supply, my mind remained mostly sharp. Over the hours I'd drummed against the slab in hopes of eliciting my rescue I had thought about the overall situation. I'd imagined being outside. With the others. I'd let my mind craft the how and the when of our departure from Skagway.

And, of course, I'd thought of Elaine.

She had gotten out. She had to. That was the only outcome that made any cosmic sense. We'd sacrificed to save the children. They, and she, deserved to see the sun and breathe the air.

I was going to miss her.

Clunk...

The sound was just off to my right and slightly above. Just the remnants of the collapsed structure shifting. Sounds like that had jolted me several times since my burial Early on I'd been buoyed by the sharp snaps and pops. Rescue, I'd thought. Salvation.

Nothing followed but more occasional smacks and groans as concrete and steel slipped and ground against one another.

Clunk... Clunk...

Again the sound came. I looked toward it.

"Hello," I said, my voice weak and wispy.

Clunk...

Was that still shifting? Maybe the remainder of the chamber about to come down upon me and end things quickly?

Clunk...

Fletch...

Clunk...

"Neil..."

I spoke my friend's name after hearing him call to me. Was it an illusion? Some dying dream?

Fletch...

"Fletch!"

If it was a dream, it was more real than any I'd ever known.

"Neil..."

My voice cracked, too soft to hear. I looked to the rebar that lay next to me. What strength I had left I used to pick it up, and to lift it, and to strike it down upon the slab with every ounce of force I could muster. Then, it fell from my grip.

I had nothing left.

"Fletch! Fletch! Is that you?!"

Rocks tumbled. Gritty dust rained down. A crack opened above. The beam of a flashlight sliced through the narrow opening.

And air rushed in.

"Neil..."

"We hear you, Fletch!"

I breathed. And breathed. And watched as the world above opened to me once again, bit by bit.

Part Five

Departures

Forty One

I was pulled from darkness into more darkness.

But it was darkness that I knew. Darkness that I craved. A night sky dancing with the light of dead and distant stars.

"Fletch, can you hear me?"

I opened my eyes and nodded at my friend as he leaned over me. He was smiling. Actually smiling. Whatever joy he might feel at finding me would not be expressed if...

"They're okay?" I asked, coughing out the last word.

"They are," my friend told me. "We dug them out four hours ago. They're all okay. Every last one."

"And..."

Another coughing fit choked off what I wanted to ask. That turned out not to matter one bit.

"She's fine," Neil said. "Elaine is just fine."

I managed to catch my breath and spit the grit from my mouth as someone handed me a canteen of water. Hands lifted me and guided me out of the hole they'd excavated with their bare hands and small tools. I sat on the stump of a felled tree and tried to gather my thoughts.

"She saved me," I told my friend.

"I know," he said. "I know."

It wasn't an admission that his worry had been wrong, but it did speak to some realization that, as much as he feared what I might face with her in a dire situation, being *with* her in such a situation might very well be the best of both worlds.

"Where is she?"

"Just up the road with Martin and the lieutenant."

"Schiavo is okay?"

Neil nodded, though there was less than full joy in the gesture.

"And her guys?"

My friend shook his head.

"Acosta," Neil told me.

Acosta. A bear of a young man. He'd survived the blight, the years after, and fell here, in a place he could not have imagined he'd be fighting.

"In the collapse?" I asked.

I was almost afraid to know, but I had to. If he'd fallen at my hand, in the collapse I'd initiated, however necessary, there was little doubt that knowledge would haunt me for some time.

"No," Neil told me. "He went down in the firefight. They took Kuratov by complete surprise."

That part of the plan, even with the loss, had worked. But my hastily improvised part?

"How many did they get?" I asked.

"Little more than half," Neil told me. "You got the rest. Brought the roof right down on them. They're buried in there."

"We got them all?"

My friend nodded, grinning at my incredulity. He reached out and helped me to my feet.

"I think there's someone who'd like to see you," Neil said.

A short walk through the dead woods and up the road proved him right. Very right.

Elaine broke away from Martin and Schiavo and walked toward me, flashlight of the rescuers guiding the way. I stopped when she reached me. She put her hands on my face, gently, as if testing that I was really here.

"We need a vacation," Elaine said.

"I can't say I disagree with you."

She slid her arms around my neck and held me tight. I was sore. I'd been battered and blasted. Parts of me hurt that I didn't even know existed. But I wasn't going to let her go. Not for this. Not for anything.

Forty Two

We buried Acosta in the cemetery just outside of town.

He was accorded what military honors Schiavo, and all those he'd had a hand in saving, could manage. Men from Yuma fashioned a coffin out of wood scavenged from a building whose structure would likely not survive another winter. Someone found a trumpet. Someone else used it to play taps. Schiavo spoke. His comrades fired a volley of rounds in salute. Then he was lowered into the hole dug by hand and dirt was shoveled in.

And that was that. Another death. This one, at least, not anonymous, like so many had been since the blight. Private Fernando Acosta was not a forgotten corpse left to be ground to dust by wind and weather on the prairie somewhere. He was known. He was loved. And he would be missed.

"Any response to your communication yet?" I asked, walking alongside Schiavo, my hand holding Elaine's as we made our way with the others back toward town.

One of the radios had been found. Kuratov had stashed it with the food and supplies near where the initial assault on the pit had begun. Whether it had come from Ketchikan, or belonged to the garrison from Skagway, wasn't apparent, and, frankly, didn't matter—that it worked and allowed Westin to initiate satellite communications once again was.

"The next satellite pass is in an hour or so," Schiavo said, looking to Westin. "Is that right?"

"Eighty minutes," Westin said.

"We should have some idea around then what the plans are for this place," Schiavo said, her gaze sweeping over the hundreds who'd made the short trek to pay their respects to her fallen soldier. "And for these people."

The White Signal was still blasting across the land, choking opportunities for normal communications. Westin had explained during a quiet moment on our journey north that the signal originated in a satellite and was, due to the destruction of ground-based infrastructure and controllers, difficult to manage. Now that Schiavo had sent a message to her headquarters, one updating the status of Skagway and the existence of a potential cure for the blight, it was hoped that the incessant and monotonous broadcast would be shut off in the near future.

"In terms of what to do with everyone," I began, "I might have a thought on that. On how to get them out of here."

"You might?" Schiavo asked. "What kind of transportation do you have in mind?"

I raised my free hand and pointed over the roofs of the town ahead, to the white bridge of the *Northwest Majesty* looming against the blue sky.

"She came in on fumes according to the crew," Schiavo said.

A skeleton crew of sixteen, all volunteers from the cruise line that had operated the vessel before it was requisitioned by the government, were mixed in among the survivors they'd brought north. The *Vensterdam*'s surviving crew, numbering just eight, had been similarly cast into the mix of humanity forcibly brought to Skagway.

"What about the other ship?" I asked.

"The *Vensterdam*?" Schiavo asked.

"Yeah," I said.

"Fuel," Elaine said, coming quickly up to speed.

"While I was laying in that hole yesterday, I was sort of gaming how I would get us out of here," I said. "If the only thing keeping the *Northwest Majesty* stationary is lack of fuel, we give her a transfusion from the *Vensterdam*. Same process has worked before."

"Clever," Schiavo said, smiling at my allusion to the fill up she'd received courtesy of Elaine.

"It's a chance," I said, dragging my suggestion back toward the realities it might face. "The *Vensterdam*'s been on her side flooded for a while."

"I didn't see any fuel slick when we pulled in to the harbor," Schiavo said.

"If her fuel tanks aren't ruptured..."

The lieutenant nodded at Elaine's hopeful musing.

"Then you may have a ride out of here," Schiavo said, then thought for a moment. "If it's possible, it would be a big job. I'm going to have my hands full with other matters. Do you know anyone who could shepherd the project?"

"I do," I said. "And so do you—Martin."

"He held Bandon together," Elaine said. "Even had it thriving, as much as that was possible."

"He knows how to get things done," I added. "And, he knows how to get people to get things done."

Schiavo considered who we were proposing. She'd already met Martin, and I suspected already had a sense that he was a capable leader. From the concern he'd shown her while in her weakened state, I knew she also considered him a decent human being.

"Can you see if he'll take it on?" she asked me. "I need to go wait for that reply."

"Sure," I said.

Schiavo and her men, short by one now, split off as we entered the town and headed to the store they'd taken over. Elaine and I walked on, together, still holding hands. She glanced over her shoulder at the weapons slung on our backs.

"You think this will always be necessary?" she asked me, nodding to the firepower we toted. "Armed at funerals, at weddings, while gardening."

"You're planning on gardening?" I asked, feigning shock.

"If we find green when we get back home, I'm gonna be a backyard farmer."

I could see that. And I could see myself right alongside her, hands plunged into the wonderful soil. But I understood the question she'd posed. The wondering that had risen. I had no problem being armed in my day to day life, and hadn't even before the blight wiped away the social structures meant to prevent most crime and thuggery. What Elaine was talking about was beyond that. She was referring to the readiness posture most had adopted as sort of present day minutemen.

"I don't know," I said. "I don't know how many random threats are still out there. My guess is fewer and fewer every day."

"We can hope," she said.

People like Moto from Cheyenne. He'd been vaporized so that we might survive. But others like him, in places across the globe, how likely was it that they could hang on much longer to cause the mayhem and pain that they reveled in?

"Once they're gone," I began, "it's like we have a clean slate. To do everything over again without having to invent the wheel, discover fire, map the world."

"You almost sound like you think this was all a good thing."

I shook my head at Elaine's suggestion.

"No, what happened happened. Whether what comes next is good, or better, than what we had...that depends on us. On all of us."

She squeezed my hand tightly and leaned against my shoulder as we walked.

"Despite your obvious flaws, I kinda sorta love you," she said.

"Well, despite my obvious flaws, I absolutely certainly love you."

We could have said more to each other right then, but we'd said all that really, truly mattered, so we walked in silence into town to the stop we wanted to make together.

Forty Three

Grace sat in a chair at the front of the house looking out the window, her gaze glued on Krista where the little girl played hopscotch on the sidewalk with a friend she'd made from San Diego.

"I'm surprised you can let her be more than five feet from you," I said.

Neil, half sitting on the arm of the chair, as close to his wife as he could be without actually resting on her lap, couldn't disagree with what I'd playfully observed.

"She needs to be as normal as she can," Neil said. "Do normal things."

"In an abnormal world," Grace interjected, looking away from her daughter outside to where Elaine and I sat on the couch, a muted, thankful joy in her gaze. "I want to thank you two so much. I want to thank everybody."

"Grace, what else would we do?"

It was my way of deflecting the appreciation she was expressing. But I understood that she needed to say it, and needed us to know the totality of what we'd done for her. And for Neil. Not to mention Krista.

"Neil, you," Elaine said. "You'd do the same."

Grace and Neil both looked quickly out the window as Krista squealed, their hearts skipping beats until they realized that the sound came from the girl's celebratory shriek after landing her marker in the desired square.

"Breathe again," Elaine told them.

"You're going to have to get used to the whole breathing thing, buddy," I said.

He puzzled at me, but Grace didn't. She shifted his hand from where it rested on her arm to the small bulge of her belly.

"Hey there, coach," Grace said to him. "*Birthing* coach."

"Oh, brother," Neil said. "I haven't had a chance to think about that part."

"Right," Elaine chided him playfully. "Because *that's* the difficult part."

More shrieks of childish happiness rose from outside. Grace looked again, no urgency now, but some subtle concern rising.

"Did she see...things down there, Fletch?"

I knew what Grace was asking. I didn't know the best way to answer. But I had to offer something that was both truthful, and consoling.

"Grace," I said, and she looked to me. "Listen to her. That's what matters. Not what anyone saw. Just listen to that laugh. Okay? She's here. She's alive. And she's yours."

It took a moment, but she smiled.

"Thank you, Fletch."

I stood and walked to where she sat, planting a kiss on her cheek.

"Elaine and I have to get going," I said. "We have to run a mission for the lieutenant."

"A mission?" Neil asked. "What kind of mission."

"Recruiting," I told him.

* * *

Martin was supervising the removal of the accessible supplies from the pit when Elaine and I approached.

"You've got this humming," Elaine said.

"So far," he said, dragging a sleeve across his brow. "We've got fifty working this shift. Chris Hill thinks he can get that forklift the construction crews left behind working. If so, this will move a lot quicker."

He'd taken on this task without being asked. Just jumped in knowing that the hundreds who had filled Skagway would need to eat for as long as they were here.

"Reinhardt is handling rationing and distribution," Martin told us. "Danforth has his people working on water. The purification unit here was damaged in the fight. We'll get it all figured out."

"And Perkins?" I asked.

"Bitching about something, probably," Martin said.

Cases of MREs flowed out of the pit's main entrance in a bucket brigade formed by dozens of volunteers. Heavy blue barrels containing dry goods were rolled up the incline by two and three people at a time. This job was getting done. And it would have to get done without Martin.

"You're needed elsewhere, my friend," I said to him.

It took just a few minutes to explain the idea to him. He listened, intrigued, gears working in his mind. Already he was silently identifying pitfalls the effort might face.

"It's no sure thing," he said when I'd finished. "But—"

Corporal Enderson's sudden arrival, jogging through the dead woods toward us, cut Martin's comment short.

"What is it?" I asked.

Enderson took just a second to catch his breath. When he had, the expression he flashed spoke volumes before he ever said a word.

"Lieutenant just got off the radio," the corporal said, beaming.

"Your HQ replied?" Elaine asked.

Enderson nodded, grinning now.

"She wants you," he said, looking to Martin. "And you, Eric. At the store in five. Got it?"

I nodded.

"What's going on?" Martin pressed the young soldier.

But Enderson didn't let on. He simply let the joy about him show.

"In five," he repeated, then he turned and jogged off the way he'd come.

"Well that was interesting," Elaine said.

"Can you stay here for a bit and help keep this running?" Martin asked Elaine.

"Of course."

Then Martin looked to me and pulled the gloves from his hands, setting them atop a stack of boxes.

"We've been summoned," Martin said to me. "Let's not keep the lady waiting."

Forty Four

Schiavo stood before us. Lieutenant Angela Schiavo. Acting in the official capacity which had been thrust upon her. And which she now openly embraced, with joy and the barest hint of emotion.

"We're taking you all back home," she said.

Martin looked to me, tired relief in his eyes. It was just the two of us representing Bandon at the briefing Schiavo had called after receiving a reply from her superiors. Two each from the other three enclaves that had been forcibly evacuated were in attendance as well, and would certainly report back to their friends and families the welcome news.

"I'm authorized to apologize on behalf of the President of the United States," Schiavo told us. "This should never have happened."

Still, this announcement did not set back the clock. Not everything could be fixed by an expression of regret and a one way ticket home.

"What about those who died?" Perkins asked. "What good does an apology do them?"

He had a hundred and twelve people looking to him for answers. People who'd been dragged across the desert from Yuma and shoved onto a commandeered freighter. They'd left the Arizona border town with a hundred and fifty. Thirty eight of his friends and neighbors had been lost in the Russian attack on the *Vensterdam* as it neared Skagway. Souls that never should have been put in that kind of jeopardy in the first place.

"They're in a better place," Reinhardt said, her words drawing a harsh look from Perkins.

"Bullshit," Perkins said.

Schiavo focused on the man challenging her. The joy she'd felt just a moment before was gone. What rose in its place was the calm certainty of a warrior. One who'd been tested in battles her superiors couldn't have envisioned a scant few years ago.

"The Yuma group will be dropped off near Santa Barbara," Schiavo told Perkins. "From there you'll be taken by Army transport helicopters back to your community."

Perkins looked away and shook his head. He'd lost more than he should have. More than any of the groups had.

"The Bandon folks will be dropped first on the way south," Schiavo continued. "San Diego last. And the Edmonton group will be taken home by a contingent of Marines that will be arriving soon by air. A quick refueling stop in Fort Nelson and you'll be home in time to start up hockey season."

Reinhardt laughed lightly, the expression of joy more than welcome.

"So you're dumping us right back into the hell you kidnapped us from," Perkins challenged Schiavo. "That and some apology by proxy is supposed to suffice?"

The man seethed. Openly. The veins in his neck bulged. His teeth bared. Were there not a room of people who would intervene, I was fairly certain he would have attacked Schiavo at that moment. Defusing the moment, the emotion, seemed an impossible task.

I was wrong.

"You won't be dropped off and forgotten," Schiavo told Perkins, looking to each and every one of the representatives next. "You will be regularly supplied."

"Supplied?" Reinhardt asked. "What does that mean?"

Schiavo almost chuckled.

"More than even I would have thought possible," the lieutenant said. "I've been informed that stockpiles of many of the things we've all become accustomed to are ready to be delivered. MREs, canned staples. I've also been told that there was a concerted effort to maintain large herds of livestock in secure facilities. Most have survived, and every community will be getting an allotment of animals to allow breeding and, eventually—"

"Steaks," Martin said, smiling.

Schiavo smiled back at Martin, the expression of joy more than just reflected. It seemed shared. Between the two of them.

"We can hope," Schiavo said.

The rage that had risen in Perkins settled as he took in what the lieutenant was sharing.

"There are animals," Perkins said, having some difficulty believing what he was hearing. "Animals?"

"Yes," Schiavo confirmed. "And, apparently, a way to feed them. I don't know how. The message I received was from Washington, and it had some detail, but I'm sure there's a lot still to learn. But, the bottom line is, when you reach home, you're not going to be left to fend for yourselves. We're going to help."

The mood in the room was subdued. But not sad. It was the kind of sudden quiet that came when a great dread had passed.

"Just how will the people going by sea be moved?" Danforth asked.

"Well, if an idea that Eric here had pans out, you'll all be enjoying a Spartan cruise south on the *Northwest Majesty*. If, for some reason that isn't possible, Navy transports will handle the move. I'm hoping it's the former, because the Navy can't get here for another sixty days."

"If the cruise ship can be used?" Danforth asked.

Schiavo didn't have any real idea. There were dozens of moving parts to the operation. But someone had already begun imagining those parts working together in harmony.

"Two weeks," Martin said. "I think we can get done what needs to be done in that time. I'll talk to the ship's crew and try to nail down a more concrete timeline."

Two weeks. Fourteen days. And we'd be on our way.

"I think, unless there are any questions, your people might want to know what's going to be happening," Schiavo said, looking to Reinhardt as a low, rhythmic rumble began to rise in the distance. "Sounds like the ride for the Edmonton group is just about here."

A quick exchange of hugs and offers of appreciation ended the gathering, those in attendance filtering out in quick succession.

"You handled that well, Lieutenant," Martin told Schiavo once Perkins had left the room.

"You're not going to fix his world," I said. "No one can."

"I know," Schiavo said, flashing an almost uncomfortable half smile at us.

"What is it, Lieutenant?" I asked her.

"Apparently it's Captain, now," she said. "That was part of the message."

"Congratulations," I said. "Right?"

She nodded and sat in the chair that had once supported a clerk at the store's register.

"I'm not sure what a promotion means these days," she said. "I'd have a company with that rank in the old world. I have six men."

She paused, realizing she'd made a mistake.

"Five," she corrected herself.

And they were men. One and all. And they respected the hell out of their leader. They would die for her, or kill for her. That I knew. That I'd seen firsthand.

The sound of the aircraft approaching rose, an odd *whup whup whup* that seemed more helicopter than plane. Schiavo noticed my curiosity.

"Ospreys," she said. "Big tilt rotor things. Flies like a plane, lands like a chopper. They always look like a child's toy to me."

"How soon will Reinhardt's people be leaving?" Martin asked.

"First light," the captain said. "They'll be the first to see their home again."

Schiavo quieted, some hint of dark realization in her pause.

"I never will," she said, looking to Martin and me. "See home again."

I might, I knew. If I ever decided to venture inland from Bandon to explore what had become of Missoula. But that possibility was fraught with the realities of what I might find. And what I did not want to find. I feared the place I'd called home would exist only in memory for the remainder of my days.

"Well, then I hope you find someplace to call home," I said to Schiavo.

She accepted that wish I'd offered with a quick nod and a smile, but said nothing, her attention shifting to Lorenzen as he came through the front door.

"Didn't the message say four birds were coming in?" the sergeant asked.

"Yeah."

"There are five," Lorenzen said. "They're setting down on the airport apron right now."

"Are they bringing any troops?" I asked.

"Yes," the sergeant answered. "They'll offload Marines to secure Skagway and points south."

"Five, eh?" Schiavo wondered aloud. "I should probably go check with the pilots on the discrepancy. If you'll excuse me..."

"Of course," I said.

"We're going home," Martin said as he watched Schiavo leave. "Home."

"I know," I said.

It had always been our plan, our goal, to bring those who had been taken back to Bandon. But with no idea how that eventuality would transpire, the reality of it, when flavored with all that we'd been through, with all that we'd overcome, was all the more sweet.

"Do you think..."

I didn't finish the question that had risen. Instead I found myself fixed on Martin. He stood where he was, still looking at where Schiavo had been. If this was junior high, this might have been an appropriate moment to pass him a note asking if he liked her.

But this was far from that very innocent time. This was the real world. The new world. A place where subtlety did a disservice to things that could be as fleeting as they were wondrous.

"She's a good leader," I said to Martin, and he nodded, still looking off to the door. "A nice person, too."

"It seems that way," he said, swallowing hard, some self-consciousness rising as he finally looked my way. "I'm going to go let everyone know about the plans."

I smiled and nodded at his avoidance.

"Okay, Martin," I said.

He left the room where the news had been delivered, and when he was gone I realized that I stood alone in the hollow silence. The solitude, which some people sought, especially in the old world, unnerved me now. I wanted to be with others. I wanted to feel life around me.

I left the room and walked out into the world that echoed with screams of joy. The news that we were all going home had begun to spread.

Forty Five

I came out of the briefing to crystal daylight showing through great billowing masses of white clouds. The blue sky beyond them was as brilliant and pristine as the Montana skies I missed. Beneath them, in the distance, I could see the squat grey bodies of the Ospreys just landed at the airport, engine housings at the end of each wing tipped so that their slowly spinning rotors were horizontal to the ground. Marines were offloading in single lines, fully equipped, at least three dozen in total it seemed.

But they did not come off of the last aircraft which had arrived. It sat slightly away from the four others, rotors not spinning down, but rather idling. As if its stay was to be brief.

"Everyone is going nuts," Elaine said, coming up behind. "Nothing's getting done down at the pit for the next few hours."

"To be expected, I guess."

We stood and watched the Marines march slowly from the airport toward town. Schiavo met them about half way and seemed to be conferring with the unit's commander after he stepped out of the column.

"Still a lot of work to be done," Elaine said.

"Yeah," I agreed, my gaze again finding the lone Osprey sitting away from the others.

"What is it?"

"That last aircraft over there," I said, pointing. "Did you see anybody come off of it?"

Elaine shook her head.

"I think it landed a couple minutes before the others," she told me. "One flew over the pit ahead of the others. Maybe whoever was onboard was already off by the time you came out."

"Yeah," I said.

Elaine puzzled at my fixation on the lonely aircraft.

"Is something wrong?"

"No," I said. "No. It's just odd."

It was. To me. But for the life of me, I couldn't put my finger on why.

"Hey," Elaine said. "Look down there."

I did. Right where she was gesturing. Spontaneous celebrations had broken out on the main street through Skagway.

"This is a good thing," she said. "Let's go join in. Enjoy the moment."

I smiled. But I had another idea.

"You go," I said. "I'm not sure Neil and Grace have heard yet."

Elaine accepted my alternate plan. She gave me a quick kiss and headed down toward the revelry. I watched the Marines enter town, and I watched the fifth Osprey for a moment more before I started walking to where Neil was staying.

* * *

My friend stood on the front porch of the house staring out toward the town and the harbor beyond, sounds of joy reaching even this far.

"You're missing one hell of a party," I said as I joined him on the porch.

"Sounds like it," he said, looking to me. "Someone from San Diego ran by shouting like the town crier."

"So you heard."

My friend nodded, his confirmation subdued. More than that, actually. It was almost as if some doubt had risen within.

"Home," he said.

"Yeah."

Across the rooftops of what passed for Skagway's downtown, the engine and rotor noise of an Osprey grew louder. Just one. The aircraft rose into the air, higher and higher, its rotors tilting forward. It gained speed and banked, in full airplane configuration now, and flew over the town, threading its way through the peaks to northeast.

It was the lone Osprey that had seized my interest, gone now. Why it had come with the rest a mystery for now.

"How is Grace?" I asked, glancing toward the house.

Neil watched the aircraft for a few seconds more until it was completely out of sight beyond the sharply sloped mountains.

"Resting," he said, smiling as he faced me now. "Doc Allen wants her lying down every few hours."

My friend looked preoccupied. Worried, even. There seemed to be little of the relief or joy that he'd expressed since we'd freed Krista. I supposed he was entitled to swings in his mood with all that was on his plate. A wife carrying a child he'd not known of until reuniting with her. A step daughter, as loved as any flesh and blood offspring, in danger but now safe. The journey home still to come, with memories of the perilous trek we'd made here fresh in his thoughts.

"She's going to be fine," I told my friend.

He accepted that assurance with a tepid nod.

"You okay?"

"Life is funny, Fletch," he said to me. "Even in this world. We had a place in Bandon. A home."

"We still do," I reminded him.

"Yeah," he agreed, but with vague concurrence.

"We're going to get there, Neil. Schiavo said we're going to be supplied. They have actual livestock they'll be bringing to us sometime after we're back."

He seemed to brighten a bit at hearing that. By a degree or two.

"Real food, Fletch. That will be...something."

I began to wonder if my friend was suffering something not very different than what was affecting Grace. Stress, fatigue, worry. It had come like an avalanche and receded like a tsunami racing back to sea.

"You need a rest, Neil."

To this he nodded, the gesture true.

"I am tired."

"Go spend some time with Grace," I said. "If you need a break later, Elaine and I will watch Krista for a while."

My friend smiled at the offer. At my concern.

"You're my best friend, Fletch."

"Right back atcha," I said.

Neil gave me a quick, friendly pat on the shoulder, then went inside to be with his wife and daughter. I left the house and walked back into town and joined the celebration.

Forty Six

We sat on the dock, the four of us, relaxing while Krista played with a pair of girls nearby, and while three dozen men and women worked on the far side of the bay, as they had for a full week now, attaching pumps and fat hoses to the half-submerged *Vensterdam*. With some luck, and an equal amount of effort, the transfer of fuel from the grounded cruise ship might begin to her brethren within days. And then, with a bit more luck, and some divine grace thrown in for good measure, the *Northwest Majesty*'s engines would rumble to life again and we'd be on our way to Bandon.

On our way home.

I did think of it as that now. In the time before we'd set out from there in search of the almost mythical tomato plant, the town, and those who called it home, had begun to seem too much a place stuck in neutral. A place hoping for the best without taking steps to ensure its long term viability as a sanctuary for survivors.

But that had changed. That doubt I harbored had been ground down on our journey to Cheyenne, on our trek to and from a living hell. Bandon now did not seem like home—it was home. My home. And Elaine's. For as long as she'd have me.

I wanted to return there, with her, with all who'd been spirited away. I wanted to stay there. I wanted a life there. Because I believed we now had a chance to turn things around. If not for the whole human race, then at least for what part of it had found safe harbor in the seaside town.

"You cannot be thinking serious thoughts," Neil said, catching me off guard.

"What?"

He tipped a swallow of beer back and smiled, his hand laced with Grace's. They sat close, in patio chairs pushed together, his gaze probing me. Knowing that I'd drifted off into some musing of a serious nature.

"It's all good, Fletch," he said, no slur in his words, but a warm glint in his eyes from the building buzz. "No more worries. We top off the tanks in this bad boy and head for home."

"*We*?" Grace pressed him. "We, especially *you*, aren't on that wreck over there covered in grease and oil so the tanks can be topped off."

"It's a collective effort," Neil said, accepting her ribbing with good nature. "Whose idea was it?"

My friend extended his finger toward me and raised his beer.

"Fletch," Neil said. "The man of the hour, the week, the year. The man with the plan."

Elaine leaned close and kissed me on the cheek, soft, warm, and quick.

"He's not wrong," she said.

One of the first teams aboard the *Vensterdam* had located which fuel tanks hadn't been punctured and polluted with seawater. A team that followed them in had stumbled upon fifty cases of beer, far past its 'sell by' date, but with a dip in the harbor's water to chill the bottles, our small group was enjoying its first 'cold one' in a long, long time. And maybe the last for the foreseeable future.

"I'm not sure which I'm happier about," I said. "That they found useable fuel, or these longnecks."

I sipped at mine, still on the first bottle. Neil was well into his fourth.

"What were you thinking about?" Grace asked, her beverage a straight up glass of tea that one of the men from San Diego had brewed in a huge batch. "Just a minute ago."

I'd thought we'd slipped past my friend catching me in thought. But the reprieve had only been momentary.

"I was thinking about home," I said. "That's it."

A dull ache spiked suddenly on my chest, right where a chunk of concrete had bounced off of me during the pit's collapse. The tactical vest I'd worn then had provided enough of a buffer to save me from any broken ribs, but not a serious bruising. I reached to the spot and rubbed hard against the pain that came in intermittent waves.

"Your chest?" Grace asked, noting my discomfort.

It was the nurse in her zeroing in on symptoms.

"Not a heart attack," I assured her. "Just something to remind me of being buried alive."

As I massaged my sore flesh I felt something else that was a reminder. A talisman that took me back to Mary Island. Something in my shirt pocket. I reached in and retrieved the small round of reddish metal.

"What's that?" Grace asked.

I held the plain medallion between my thumb and finger and stared at it.

"Kuratov gave one of these to each of his men," I said.

"One of Schiavo's men took that off a dead Russian on Mary Island and gave it to Eric," Elaine explained.

Grace's expression soured at what she'd just heard.

"You're going to keep it?" she asked.

I held the keepsake. I felt it. Then, I wanted it no more.

"No."

I flicked it over the edge of the dock and into the harbor. It disappeared silently and unseen into the cold, dark water.

"Not a place I want to remember," I said.

Neil leaned forward in his chair, a sappy, buzzed smile on his face.

"In high school, this guy never threw anything away," my friend shared. "He had gym socks from his freshman year still in his locker when we graduated."

The mocking laughter that sprang from that revelation was deserved, I knew.

"Hey, I'm not the only one hanging onto things that have no use anymore," I said. "Am I, Special Agent Elaine Morales?"

"Oh, please," Elaine protested. "My FBI credentials are not equivalent to old gym socks."

"You think that's over the top?" Grace asked, nudging Neil with an elbow. "Show them what's in your cargo pocket. Go on."

My friend fumbled with the button on the pocket that sat mid-thigh on his pants. After a few inebriated seconds, Grace leaned over and retrieved what she'd only hinted at.

"His passport," she said, holding up just that. "Mr. State Department world traveler still carries it with him. Everywhere. Like he's expecting some customs agent to pull him aside and ask for his papers."

"Some of those customs guys are pretty scary," Neil said.

Elaine reached out and took the passport, flipping through the pages, eyeing all the entry and exit stamps from points around the globe.

"Oh, to be able to travel as you did," Elaine commented.

Grace stood right then and took Neil by the hand, easing him up from where he'd sat. She took the nearly empty bottle from him and set it down on the dock.

"Mr. World Traveler here needs to walk some of his celebration off," Grace said, pulling him along.

Neil reached unsteadily back toward his passport, missing the stiff document by at least a foot.

"You live vicariously through that for a while, Elaine," Grace said. "A more sober representative of our government will get it from you later. Keep an eye on Krista for a bit?"

"Of course," I said.

Grace led Neil up the dock and toward town.

"He's letting loose," I said. "He needs to."

"He's definitely feeling little pain," Elaine said, handing my friend's passport over to me as she, too, stood. "I need to hit the little girls' room. Be right back."

She crossed the dock to a shed where some portable facilities had been brought back to working order. Left alone I watched Krista play, and saw the first stages of supplying the *Northwest Majesty* begin, workers stacking pallets of supplies retrieved from the pit near the ship's loading ramp. Sitting there, taking it all in, the sights and sounds and feel of the day's waning hours, I opened my friend's passport and flipped through it, marveling at the places he'd been.

Russia. Japan. Ukraine. England. Egypt. South Africa. China. Thailand. And on, and on. Country after country that his midlevel position at the State Department had afforded him the opportunities to visit.

Except...

Except there were some countries not listed. No entry and exit stamps for places he should have gone. For one place I knew he had gone.

Brazil.

It was where he had traveled with a US team to consult on the blight. Where he'd learned enough information to convince him that warning me was a prudent, if illegal, thing to do.

"Brazil," I said aloud, confused.

Certainly a country suffering through the early stages of the blight would have tracked who entered and exited their domain with extra vigilance. Wouldn't they?

But there was more. There was not one stamp in his passport from any country south of the border. No Mexico.

No Central America. No South America. None. Yet, as he'd told it, he was a state department liaison between the Brazilians and American agricultural officials. Why would that job fall to him, someone with no apparent expertise in that part of the world? Wasn't that the point of being a liaison? To be the expert on the place you were traveling to?

I looked back through the stamps in his passport, just to make certain I hadn't missed something obvious. But I hadn't.

"You okay?"

I looked up. It was Elaine, back from her bathroom run.

"You look like someone just stole your puppy," she said, then sat down next to me.

I closed the passport and handed it to her.

"You can give that to Grace when you see her," I said.

Elaine opened the front cover and again perused the places my friend had been, her attention fixed on thoughts of those faraway lands. Lands that were now dead places on a once green world.

Neil...

I didn't know what to think about what I'd seen. And I didn't know what to do. Broaching the discrepancy between his documentation and the narrative he'd shared with me might be the simplest thing to do. But was it the right thing to do?

Grace, while not fragile, had begun her pregnancy under trying circumstances. If there was some reason why Neil had concocted a story about visiting Brazil as the blight began its spread, I had no way of knowing if its revelation would bring an unnecessary strain upon Grace. And upon them. She needed him. Krista needed him. And he needed them.

And what was there to gain if I did confront him with what I saw as evidence of a lie he'd told me? A rather large and important fabrication. Would any good come of it? Was it even important right now, as we prepared to leave Skagway for home?

No. It wasn't. I knew that. When we'd returned, and had a chance to adjust once again to life in Bandon, life as a community of survivors, then, maybe, in a casual way I could ask my friend about it. For now...

"It's going to be a nice night," I said, reaching to the chair next to me and taking Elaine's hand in mine.

"Yeah," she said. "It is."

We sat there and let the day dwindle away. Watching Krista play. Letting the world spin on.

Forty Seven

In five days, two less than what Martin had estimated, we boarded the *Northwest Majesty* and maneuvered cautiously out of Skagway's harbor, down the Taiya Inlet, and past Baranof Island and Port Alexander to open water. There would be no creeping along the inside passage, down narrow channels between the mainland and rugged islands.

Our voyage home would be on the ocean. On the Pacific. That word translated roughly to 'peaceful'.

Not every day that followed, though, could be described as such.

Forty Eight

Two days after leaving Skagway I stood at the starboard rail as the *Northwest Majesty* sailed through calm seas, the vast Pacific to the west, islands and the mainland to the east. The ocean faced me, and I it. Across it there were almost certainly people like me, like us, who had hung on. Who had survived. Maybe some who were thriving. Men, women, and children who'd been through similar hells to those we'd faced and come out more than alive.

I wanted to believe that.

The hells we'd been through were behind us now. That, too, I wanted to believe. As farfetched as it might have seemed not too long ago, I was beginning to consider that there might be some semblance of a government left. One that, after stumbling through foolish and tragic mistakes, was gaining its footing in this new world. It, like the rest of the nation, had been whittled down to the minimal amount of moving parts necessary to maintain some functionality. The organs of the state had been starved to something closer to what the founding fathers had envisioned. Institutions lean and focused on the necessary.

It had only taken the near destruction of the nation, and the human race as a whole, to bring about that possibility.

That, though, was a distant consideration at the moment. If anything, this was a new beginning not only for governments, but for those they served. For people like those of us aboard the *Northwest Majesty*.

It had taken a week while the fuel was transferred to prepare the once luxurious cruise ship for departure. In shifts it was cleaned, debris removed, though there was no major damage to it. The *Vensterdam* had suffered the totality of the Russian assault. The *Northwest Majesty*'s systems were mostly intact, and repairs made those that weren't at least serviceable for the six hundred or so who would board her.

Provisioning took up the final days in Skagway. Pallets of MREs and canned stable foodstuffs were loaded. Enough to feed those aboard during the journey home, and to leave with each group who departed to supplement what they would, hopefully, have waiting upon their return. In Bandon we'd left a healthy amount, enough for months. Enough to carry the whole of the town's population through the end of the year and toward spring. With what we'd be bringing back with us, we could make it through the next fall.

There was the hope, though, that there would be more waiting for us. Things to harvest when the time came. Things green and alive and wonderful.

That was the hope. In fact, I believed, in the long run, it was our only hope.

But that desire had to be paired with what I knew. With certain realities. How could relationships, lifelong friendships, continue unless predicated on some new understanding? Or on accepted avoidance? Could I erase what had happened and just hold with better memories? Football games and double dates. Ditching school and hunting trips. Superbowl bets and too many laughs to count.

Could I?

Should I?

The apparent lie Neil had told me, as hard as I'd tried to force it out of my thoughts, refused to exist in that state of denial. Whenever I saw him aboard, walking with Grace, or playing tag with Krista in one of the empty ballrooms, it rose again, hanging there in the negative space between us like some sickness. I didn't let on that I had any doubts about the story he'd shared, but, in all honesty, I tried to avoid those moments where we would end up alone together. Doing so was easy enough most of the time. He and Grace were treating the voyage as a sort of last getaway before the realities of a new family member began to draw near.

But in those few instances where I did stand with my friend, away from others, the thing that was nothing and everything all at once gnawed at me inside. And when it did I found myself shifting any discussion that arose to the old, and the familiar. To reminiscences of our youth. Of the place where we'd come to know and trust each other.

It was a place, a time, a feeling I feared I'd lost forever.

"What are you thinking?"

I turned away from the rail and saw Elaine just behind me. She stood in a spot where, in another time, in the old world, vacationers would be strolling about, on their way back from one of the ship's restaurants, or on their way to one of the nightly shows which certainly played in those happy times.

"I'm not sure."

She stepped closer. Then close.

"People who stare at the ocean are usually thinking of somewhere they want to be."

It took me a moment to trace my thoughts, and then I realized she was right.

"Missoula," I said. "A long time ago."

"Why?" she asked, genuinely curious.

I could've answered with a simplistic explanation that I wanted what had been then to be now. That, though, wouldn't scratch the surface as to the why. It would keep the reason, which was born of doubt, an impossible uncertainty, close. Just for me.

But I was more than just me now. I was part of *us*. I couldn't keep what was tearing at me to myself anymore.

"Neil lied to me," I told Elaine.

She shifted position and stood next to me at the rail now, listening. Wanting to know.

"When he was buzzed back on the dock we got a look at his passport. We were looking at the stamps after Grace took him for a walk to sober up."

"I remember," Elaine said.

"I told you before how he warned me about the blight," I reminded her, and immediately the look about her changed to one of coming realization.

"He went to Brazil," she said, recalling what I'd shared. "He was part of an advisory group or something. Working on the blight."

"There were no stamps in that passport from anywhere south of the US," I said.

She puzzled visibly over the inconsistency.

"Maybe it was just a mistake," she said. "He might have had to replace the passport."

"Most of those stamps were from years before the blight hit," I countered.

She thought on that for a moment.

"I don't know, Eric. I wish I had some explanation."

"Yeah. Me, too."

"You obviously haven't talked to him about it," she said. "Is this really important enough to tie you up in knots?"

"No. No, it's not. This is the first thing resembling relaxation any of us have had in..."

"I get it," she said.

"There'll be time," I said. "Once we're back in Bandon and settled in. It can wait."

That's what I told her. But it wasn't the reality I was projecting.

"You need a break," Elaine said. "From everything."

"That's why I booked us this cruise," I told her, trying to lighten the moment.

In her eyes I could see that I was failing miserably.

"Look, I get that you can't just let go of what he said completely. But can you put it aside for a while? For me?"

I imagined I could. If what had transpired was vexing only me at the moment, I could, as Elaine requested, put it aside. Especially for her.

"I can do that," I said.

"Good," she said, and took my hand. "Come with me."

Forty Nine

Of all the necessities that had been stripped from the *Northwest Majesty* during her appropriation by the government for use as transport, the tailor and dress shop aboard remained relatively well appointed. Few in the post blight world had seen any need for evening gowns and tuxedos.

Elaine, though, was one of those who did.

"Overdressed really doesn't begin to convey how I feel."

That was what I said to Elaine as we walked hand in hand across the ship's atrium, past faux greenery still vibrant, our attire more fitting to a night of fine dining and dancing than to some post-apocalyptic journey home. She'd found a tuxedo that fit my trimmer than usual frame almost perfectly, and a long dress that hugged her form in ways that made me forget the why of our being where we were and allowed me to just cherish how absolutely beautiful she was.

As we passed a gleaming panel of glass I took in my reflection.

"Lipstick on a pig," I said.

Elaine nudged me playfully.

"What are you saying about my taste in men?"

We continued on, others aboard glancing our way with approving looks. As we descended a shallow flight of stairs toward the lounge I heard music. Not canned tunes piped through speakers, but real, simple, beautiful music. A piano.

Coming into the lounge I saw the source of it.

Angela Schiavo sat at the piano which was a fixture in any ship's lounge, her fingers tapping the keys with light precision. She was not in uniform, but attired as a civilian in scrounged clothes, jeans and a blouse, that softened her appearance and highlighted the simple beauty about her. Sitting next to her on the instrument's cozy bench, alternating between watching her play and just watching her, Martin seemed to very much agree with my assessment. To put it plainly, he looked smitten.

"I hope you're okay with the music I arranged," Elaine said.

Schiavo and her team were accompanying us on the voyage home. On everyone's voyage home. With the first stop being to transfer us to shore, they would continue on, to Santa Barbara to disembark the Yuma group, and then onto San Diego with the group which had survived in that city. From that point, there was no indication where she and her men would be sent.

This was very likely one of the last times we would have to spend with her.

"Shall we?" I asked, stepping onto the small dance floor and offering my hand to Elaine.

"Yes," she said, her acceptance both formal and touching.

Then we danced. We looked into each other's eyes and moved to the music. There was no precision to our steps. My attempt at leading approximated as much, but it wasn't about the obvious things we were doing. Not about the swaying and the posture and the proper hold.

It was about being. Just being. With her. In this place. On our way home. To a better place and future.

That was the thought I held onto. Both of us did. So fiercely did Elaine and I embrace that disconnect from the blighted world that neither of us noticed that the music had stopped.

"We have a problem."

Elaine and I froze mid-step. It was Schiavo. She'd come onto the floor, Martin with her. Beyond them, Westin stood next to the piano, his M4 in hand.

"What's wrong?" I asked.

"Someone's missing," she said.

Fifty

"The Marine garrison in Skagway entered the pit after we left to retrieve the bodies and any buried supplies," Schiavo said, standing next to the radio where it had been installed on the bridge. "There were seventeen."

I looked to Elaine.

"Kuratov had eighteen," she said. "Including himself."

Right then Neil entered the spacious bridge and stood next to Lorenzen.

"Westin said something's wrong," my friend said, and Schiavo brought him up to speed quickly.

"We were all relying on witness counts, captain," Lorenzen reminded her. "That number was based on what we were told. Could've been wrong."

"Off by one," I said.

Schiavo nodded, staring absently at the diagram of the ship she'd had the first officer pull for her. The long rolls of paper blueprints were spread out upon the navigation station table. Every compartment was depicted. Every cabin, every closet, every engineering space.

"Could be," she said.

"But you don't believe that," Elaine said, reading the captain's demeanor and body language.

"No," Schiavo said. "I don't."

"You think he got aboard," Neil said. "Kuratov."

"I do," Schiavo confirmed.

"Any real evidence that it's him and not one of his men?" Elaine asked.

Schiavo shook her head.

"Call it a gut feeling," she said.

It was a feeling I tended to agree with.

"If I'm one of his men and I crawl out of that hole, I surrender," I said. "My leader promised me survival, and what did he deliver? I know I can have a full belly if I hand myself over. If I try to go covert..."

"Then you're going to be treated like a spy," Schiavo said, finishing what I'd laid out.

"Kuratov doesn't have that option," Lorenzen said. "Not after executing prisoners and holding children hostage."

"He's a dead man if we find him," Elaine said.

"When we find him," Neil corrected her.

There was bravado in the exchange. But truth as well. Kuratov, if he was aboard, could be desperate. But he was certainly dangerous.

"There were dozens of people loading the ship before we left," I said, remembering the controlled chaos on the dock. "He could have grabbed a case of MREs and walked up that ramp in the midst of it all."

"No one would have noticed," Lorenzen said. "All anyone was thinking about was getting home."

That was true. Everyone wanted to get home. To leave Skagway and set sail for places familiar and longed for. In that haste, though, had we skipped one very vital step in making sure our voyage would be successful?

"The big bad wolf was dead," Schiavo said. "Except, maybe he wasn't."

* * *

There were hundreds of spaces in which Kuratov could hide. Thousands, possibly. Passenger cabins, crew cabins, closets, engineering spaces, ducts, shops, restaurants, dry storage lockers, lifeboats.

"We split up," Schiavo said after gathering her team and the few of us who could support them.

None of the seven listening to Schiavo thought that was anything close to a wonderful idea.

"I don't like it either," she admitted. "If we double up, that's four teams. It could take days to check everywhere."

"We could enlist some help," Elaine said, back in her pseudo tactical gear after changing from the evening gown. "We have people from Bandon who manned perimeters and have been in some serious skirmishes."

"That's exactly what I don't want," Schiavo said, looking to me. "Stealth. Quiet. This requires that, too. If this turns into a panicked free for all, he'll just hunker down. We need to catch him when he moves. When he breathes. When he coughs. Hell, when he farts. It's move and listen. Move and watch. We take our time. That's how I say we handle this."

For as much as the plan was unpalatable, her theory seemed close to spot on. Kuratov would have to leave some sign of his presence. Some trail. Being observant might very well be the best approach.

Armed and observant.

"All right," Schiavo said. "We have eight warm bodies."

"Nine."

The correction came as that late addition to our group approached.

"Martin..."

Schiavo eyed him, puzzled and pleased. He carried a silver Winchester pump, a bandolier of 12 gauge shells slung over one shoulder. That he'd joined us in the ship's empty theater was surprising. That he knew what was happening was not. Schiavo, to maintain good relations with the three communities on the voyage south, had informed Martin, Danforth, and Perkins of the possible threat to be dealt with. She'd asked them to keep the information confidential, while suggesting that they come up with some reason to have their people stay in groups.

"We don't really need volunteers," Schiavo told him.

"I need to do my part," he said, nodding toward the captain next. "And you're still not healed."

She half glared at him, half smiled.

"If that's not true, just say so, and I'll be on my way," Martin told her.

Both Doc Allen and Hart had strongly suggested that Schiavo take the opportunity to rest during the downtime the voyage south would provide. Prowling through the ship on a hunt for some Russian super soldier was not that.

"I wouldn't mind you having some backup, captain," Hart said.

"Thank you for your input, specialist," Schiavo said to her medic.

Schiavo knew this was a losing battle. She could order Martin to stay behind, and could put herself out there, alone, weakened by her recent vising from a Russian machine gun round. If she did that, though, she'd be exhibiting not toughness in front of her men, but recklessness.

"You're with me, it looks like," Schiavo acquiesced, turning to the plans again. "Now, let's split this up."

* * *

As I completed just over half of my search of the crew area four levels below the main deck, I was beginning to doubt some of what we'd assumed.

What was Kuratov's plan? What was he thinking? What end did he see for himself? And for us?

I asked myself those questions as I slowed in a maintenance passageway. If Kuratov had snuck aboard and hidden himself somewhere, he had done so with some purpose. To simply hitch a ride south to the lower forty eight seemed unlikely. What would he do once there?

Would he be able to disembark as easily as he'd slipped aboard?

Was escape his only motive?

"No," I said softly to the deserted corridor. "He wants something."

But what?

I thought on that. What would a man like Kuratov desire? An *officer* like Kuratov. A *defeated* officer like Kuratov.

Satisfaction.

Or, as it was known to most, revenge.

Possibly he was aboard at this very moment setting in motion some plan to sink the *Northwest Majesty*. To send all who were aboard to some watery grave. Could he do that?

Unlikely, I thought. He would almost certainly need a cache of explosives to scuttle the huge ship, something he could not have snuck aboard, and which we, while provisioning the vessel, had not brought with us.

Those obstacles, though, did not completely inform my dismissal of that possibility. To simply eliminate everyone seemed more an act of war than a search for retribution. So if not the whole, then what part of it? What individual cog of the machine that had brought him down did Kuratov want to seek his vengeance against?

"No..."

I knew. In a flash, I knew. If he'd snuck aboard with those loading supplies on the ship, that meant he would have spent several days in hiding. Using the escape and evasion training he had certainly mastered. In and around town. On the ship. Watching. Listening. And what would he have heard?

He would have heard her name. He would have seen the handshakes and hugs offered to her.

To Captain Angela Schiavo.

I turned and backtracked the way I'd come, turning right and shoving the door to the crew stairwell open, bounding down three steps at a time. Down one deck. Then two. Until I reached bottom and a door that warned against entry. Engineering, the space beyond was marked. Through the barrier before me I could not just hear the thrumming of the massive engines, I could feel them. My whole body seemed to vibrate from the soles of my feet upward.

This was where Schiavo had tasked herself with searching. Beyond this door. And I had no way of knowing if she was in there alone, or if the boogeyman had already found her.

She wouldn't be alone, though. Martin would be with her. That bettered the odds if she was being stalked, but by how much. Kuratov was, according to all that I'd learned from Schiavo and her men, a ruthless, cunning, highly capable killer.

But he was also desperate. And, I was thinking, either weak or ill. For all his supposed prowess, his unit, after ravaging both Ketchikan and Juneau, and eliminating the Skagway garrison, had been bested by a smaller force led by a freshly minted commander with little combat training. Was it possible that he, or many of his men, had been wounded in that battle to take the northernmost point of their campaign?

Something, I suspected, had degraded his ability, and his unit's ability. Whatever it was, it might hint at a fatalistic streak now emboldening the man. That could either harden his resolve, or weaken his faculties.

As I pushed the door to the engineering space open, I was hoping it was the latter.

The noise within was deafening. I came almost immediately upon two crewmen, part of a complement of workers that was beyond skeleton. In an assignment that likely required dozens, the pair I encountered were holding their own. They pointed to my unprotected ears as I entered and handed me a pair of earplugs. I inserted the hearing protection and moved past. They eyed me with curiosity, not suspicion as I moved into the space.

Huge turbines spun at dizzying speeds nearby. I worked my way along a narrow catwalk that hung off their supporting structure. Ahead I saw nothing in the brightly lit space. No hint of life. No Kuratov. No Schiavo or Martin, either.

Continuing on, I came to another thick door, one that let me out of the incredibly loud power plant space and into an adjoining area where long banks of electronic controls and displays dominated one entire wall. Another crewman was stationed in here, his hearing protection more modest in the quieter work area.

"What are you doing in here?" the young and serious man asked.

He was from the Philippines, I thought, as were much of the crew which had stayed on after their vessel had been requisitioned by the Navy.

"Have you seen anyone come through here?" I asked, shouting a bit, if only to hear myself through the surprisingly effective ear plugs.

The worker gave no answer, just pointed, to another door at the far end of the space. I nodded a thank you and continued on, both relieved and puzzled that I was finding nothing. To locate Kuratov so soon was far from a certain outcome, but if he was truly aboard he would have to know by now that a search was underway, and he would have to conclude that he was the subject of it. The time to make his move was dwindling. In his mind, he might feel compelled to act.

But he had not taken any action in here.

I pushed through the next door, the noise abated here enough that I pulled the earplugs. As soon as I did I heard the footsteps. Two sets.

The next door just ahead opened and Schiavo and Martin came through.

"Eric," Schiavo said, surprised. "You finished your section?"

I shook my head, suddenly feeling like an idiot.

"We cleared all the way forward on this deck," Martin said.

"That's good," I said, plainly wanting to kick myself.

"What is it?" Schiavo asked, approaching as she noted my frustration.

I explained my theory that Kuratov might be targeting her specifically. She didn't dismiss it outright, but didn't abide by its logic either.

"You might be giving him too much credit," Schiavo said. "I've been thinking that he's not really all there right now."

"Too easy a time taking him by surprise," I said. "I was thinking the same thing."

"I mean, I'm sure he's furious, but what's he going to do?" she asked.

"What's he even capable of?" Martin added.

I wasn't feeling as foolish anymore. But I also wasn't feeling great about our ability to find the man if he was just aboard, hiding in a dark corner.

"What do you want to do?" I asked Schiavo.

She thought for a moment.

"Once everybody's done and we meet on the bridge, we'll just go into waiting mode."

"Are you sure?" Martin asked.

"We'll let the crew know to report anything out of the ordinary," Schiavo said. "We can stay ready. And stay in pairs at least. That's probably the best we can do. Just stay sharp."

I nodded. She was right.

"I'll go finish my deck then find Elaine," I said.

"We'll see you on the bridge," Martin said.

* * *

It took me just under forty five minutes to complete the sweep of the crew area I'd already started. I found nothing. No signs at all of any unexpected presence. Then I headed for the bridge.

I never made it there. Westin and Enderson were coming my way on the main deck.

"Something up?"

"Going to check out a report of an MRE pouch in a cleaning closet," Enderson said.

That could be a hot lead, I knew. What reason would there be for that discarded item to be in a closed space? None that were innocent, I thought.

"You want some backup?" I asked.

"Sarge and the Captain are already on the way," Enderson told me.

"Did you see Elaine on the bridge?"

"I think she was heading back to your cabin," Westin told me. "The Captain cut her and Martin loose when this report came in."

Elaine was heading back to the cabin. On her own.

"Thanks," I said.

Before they could say anything more I was moving toward the stairs. Our cabin was six decks up. I ran up the wide, switchbacking staircase, then sprinted down the hall toward our cabin.

Fifty One

Three steps into the cabin I shared with Elaine I froze. The door had just clicked shut behind. Across the space the balcony slider was open, cool air tossing the curtains about. And right in front of me, on the foot of the bed we'd made after rising in the morning, there lay a small round of metal, reddish in color. It was one of the simple, plain medallions that Kuratov gave to his men. I'd discarded the one given to me on Mary Island, tossing it into Skagway's harbor days before we'd departed. This was not mine. This one came from somewhere else.

From someone.

Click...

I had hardly turned a few degrees toward the sound behind when the hard side of a folded hand struck me on right temple. A dull shockwave spread across my head and spilled down through my body as if I was a hollow vessel. Every ounce of energy I'd possessed was instantly gone. My legs collapsed and my body tipped forward, bouncing off the edge of the bed and thudding to the floor, the world above me dark and spinning, flickers of light drizzling in from the edge of my vision. Light that formed a full body halo around the figure coming down at me.

"Eric Fletcher," the voice said, the accent dripping with guttural Slavic inflection as it continued in stilted English. "You now know hell."

It was Kuratov. Aleksy Kuratov. The boogeyman in our waking nightmares. And he was here, hovering over me, hands stripping my weapons away even as I mounted a dazed attempt to resist. The beefy Russian simply swatted my hands away and spun me onto my stomach once I was disarmed. My jacket was yanked down past my elbows and the man expertly twisted the fabric to bind my arms together. He drew a foot back and drove a painful kick into my ribs, then flipped me again so that I lay face up.

Then he lowered himself so that he was sitting on my chest. He bent forward, looking into my eyes from just a few inches away.

"Eric Fletcher," Aleksy Kuratov said, a sickening stench on his breath.

My vision was almost fully back, the daze I'd been knocked into dissipating.

"You are him?"

He knew my name. And he held some interest in me. Why, I had no idea.

My confusion lasted just for a moment.

"Gershin say it was you," Kuratov said, ogling me with eyes that were sallow and glassy. "He say it was your idea."

Gershin...

"You are Eric Fletcher."

He'd gotten to Gershin where he was being held in the old constable's office. Through a window in the single cell. Just large enough to provide communication from inside to outside.

I was right, I knew. I'd just had the target wrong. Kuratov wanted vengeance, but not against the person who'd led the assault. He wanted satisfaction from the one who'd conceived it.

Me.

"I cut your face like you cut Gershin's face," Kuratov said, producing a small but menacing knife to bolster his threat. "Cut your tongue out, your nose off, then your eyes."

He steadied himself with one hand on the end of the bed and brought the knife over my face, aiming its blade down at my mouth.

"Then, when you are monster, I throw you overboard," he said, laughing wetly next. "And then I wait for your woman to come to cabin."

Elaine...

She wasn't here, and, based upon what Kuratov had just let on, she hadn't been. Why, I didn't know. But I was grateful. For the moment.

"She will know me," Kuratov said, leering, a gurgle at the back of his voice. "Then I will cut like you."

He held the power over me. But I couldn't let that be. I had to change the dynamic. Still coming out of the fog he'd knocked into me, I had to think, and act, quickly. Before Elaine did show up.

"You lost," I said.

Kuratov's smile twisted.

"We beat your men at Mary Island, and we slaughtered them in Skagway."

"Keep talking, American. It will make more the sweet when I tear your tongue out."

One thing I knew from the almost intimate proximity Kuratov had allowed between us was that I'd been right. He was not well. The sickly smell of his breath, and the wet hoarseness of his voice spoke to some infection. The heat bleeding off the man as he leaned over me screamed fever. And the way he was supporting himself with one hand against the end of the bed. He was favoring one side, and protecting the other. Shielding it.

Just as Schiavo had after being shot.

Kuratov was wounded, on his left side. His energy was low. His mind numbed. Only his exceptional training and will had allowed him to take me down so easily. Had he been functioning at full capacity, I was certain that my time on this earth would be severely limited.

It might still be, but I was not going without a fight. And, even then, if I had to go, I wanted to take him with me.

"Your men were weak," I said. "Untrained Americans beat them."

The twisted smile folded in on itself until his mouth turned to something almost animalistic, teeth bared under curled lips. His anger was building to fury.

"By American *women*," I said, twisting the metaphorical knife.

Using his fury he drew the knife back, readying to plunge it into my face. That was the moment, at the instant his arm was highest, that I drove my right knee upward, as hard and as fast as I could, slamming it into his ribcage on the left side.

"Ahhhhhhhhhhhhhhhh!"

He screamed and stabbed downward with the knife, his body spasming in pain. The blade missed my face, and my head, skimming off the edge of the mattress just beyond. I rolled as he coughed, spitting blood, and scrambled to my feet, arms still bound awkwardly behind.

"Arrgghhh," Kuratov grunted, pulling himself up with one hand, the knife firmly gripped in the other.

I backed toward the open balcony door. Kuratov stepped clear of the bed and tossed the knife aside, reaching with his good hand behind his back. To me that meant he had a gun there. And once he had that in hand, my part in this lopsided duel would be over.

As his hand came back from out of view I charged at him, lowering my shoulder. The pistol, small and black, came up, his aim adjusting to my lowered profile. He squeezed a round off. The shot cracked sharp and painful at the nonexistent range between us. I felt a hot spear of fire drag across my back and heard the glass balcony door explode behind. Before he could correct his aim and fire a follow up shot, my shoulder slammed into his midsection, throwing him back against the wall separating the bathroom from the cabin. I felt a rush of air as the breath was knocked out of him.

But he wasn't down, or out. He tossed an elbow against my head, missing and connecting with my neck. For an instant my vision flashed white, and when it cleared I saw the pistol again swinging my way. Another shot, at this range, and he could not miss.

I dove this time, hurling my body toward his injured side, and as I did I felt something slip behind my back. The makeshift bindings he'd quickly crafted had loosened on my right arm. Driving my shoulder into him again, the sleeves which had locked my hands and arms together came fully loose and I reached for the pistol. He fired again, this shot not grazing me this time, but missing wide, burying itself in the room's dresser in a shower of splintered wood.

With one hand I grabbed the wrist of his gun hand and, with the other, I powered a fist into his injured side, a wet splash covering my hand with blood as it made contact. But as I pulled back to strike again, Kuratov swept his left leg fast across mine, knocking my feet from under me. I lost my grip on his gun hand and tumbled backward to the floor, landing between the bed and the dresser.

And that was it.

Kuratov straightened, his body in agony as he stepped away from the bathroom wall and stood just beyond my feet, the cabin door behind him. There was no move I could make in this position. No strike to stop him from where I lay. My only hope was that the sound of the shots would have been noticed, bringing an armed response and keeping Elaine from suffering the fate I was about to.

"American," Kuratov said, gasping, blood trickling from his mouth. "Loser."

He brought the pistol up. I watched it rise, and as I did I saw something. Just behind him. At the very bottom of the cabin door where light bled in from the hall beyond. Through the slender space where I saw two dark spots. Shadows that blocked the light.

Someone was standing right outside the door.

"FIRE!"

I shouted the command at the top of my lungs, an instant of confusion at my outburst flashing on Kuratov's face just before the wooden door behind him exploded inward, a hole the size of a dinner plate appearing in it. The front of the Russian's dark shirt turned instantly darker as it was shredded by tiny projectiles punching through his midsection. Before his body folded in half and collapsed, spine and ribs shattered, a pulpy spray erupted from the exit wound that the double ought buckshot had made, covering me and the balcony curtains with bits of the Russian's insides.

I scooted back, away from Kuratov, his dead hand still holding the small pistol, a gush of blood spreading under his unnaturally bent form. Just behind, the cabin door, nearly obliterated by the shotgun blast, swung slowly inward, bent hinges screaming. As it came to a stop against the wall I saw a familiar face just outside, shiny Winchester pump smoking in his hands.

"Are you all right?" Martin asked, stepping into the cabin, his shotty trained on Kuratov's lifeless body.

With some effort I came to a sitting position against the dresser, then lifted myself up.

"How did you..."

I was grateful but confused as to how Martin had ended up outside my cabin at just the right moment to save my life. He reached out and helped me up, guiding me past the dead Russian to a spot near the door. In the hall I could hear voices rising in the near distance and a rush of footsteps racing our way.

"Elaine wanted to check on Grace and Krista after Angela...after Captain Schiavo was finished with us. I walked her there. She wanted to let you know where she was, so I said I'd find you and bring you by."

Enderson and Westin had been wrong. Thankfully so. Elaine hadn't been returning to our cabin. If anything this day was to be ascribed to divine intervention, I would think it that.

"You're bleeding," Martin said. "Your back."

"A graze," I said. "I think."

He helped me out into the hallway as Schiavo and her men neared. Westin and Lorenzen stepped past, M4s up and ready as they stepped into the cabin.

"Looks like a minor wound," Martin told Hart as he approached and opened his med kit.

I looked to Martin, pure gratitude in my gaze.

"Saying thank you isn't enough," I said.

"I'm glad I heard you," Martin told me. "I was going to kick the door. That would have been too late."

Lorenzen came out and looked to Schiavo.

"It's Kuratov," the sergeant reported. "Dead."

Schiavo took a moment to process the sudden and violent end to something we hadn't expected when beginning our journey home. After a moment she looked to the man who'd saved the day. And my life.

"That was a gutsy move, Martin."

He didn't dispute her characterization of his blind shot. But he also wasn't eager to elicit any accolades.

"Let's keep this between us," he said. "All right? I just helped out where I could. Fair enough?"

He was humble. And he was human. It seemed that all Martin Jay wanted at that moment was to move on. To continue home. In peace.

"Fair enough," Schiavo agreed.

"A pretty good graze," Hart said after checking my back.

"Get him a fresh cabin and get him bandaged up," Schiavo said.

* * *

Ten minutes later I was in that new cabin, one deck up, our belongings transferred by Enderson and Westin just as Elaine arrived, rushing in after learning of what had happened.

"Are you okay?" she asked me, only ten percent frantic.

"No hard hugs for a few days," Hart suggested. "I'll have Doc Allen give my patch job a proper look in a bit."

Elaine put her arms gingerly around my neck and held me, firm but not tight.

"You okay now?" Schiavo asked from the doorway as Hart packed his med kit and stepped past her.

I nodded.

"Good work," she said, then reached in and pulled the door shut.

Elaine eased back and let her gaze play all over my face. Over every inch of it. Every wrinkle. Every dark stain of dried blood.

"I'm going to run some water and get a cloth and clean you up," she said. "Then I'm going to lock that door and keep you in here with me until we're home."

"We'll have to eat," I reminded her.

"We'll order room service," she said.

"Might be a long wait."

"That's fine with me," she said, then kissed me softly as the cool ocean breeze spilled into our cabin.

Fifty Two

The crew used a trio of lifeboats to shuttle us to shore in a process that took three hours. At the end of that time only Martin, Elaine, and I remained aboard the *Northwest Majesty*. Schiavo stood by as our personal gear was loaded on the last boat for the final trip.

"To say this was pleasant would be wrong," Schiavo said. "But I'm glad we came through it together."

Elaine gave her a hug, then I did the same, her own arms circling me with gentle consideration for my slight wound.

Then she looked to Martin.

"It was a real pleasure to meet you, Martin."

"The pleasure was mine, Angela. Entirely mine."

In another time, in the world as it was, a promise might be made to visit once again. But this was not that world, nor that time. Separations were almost exclusively permanent in this emptied out civilization we'd been cast into.

"I'll miss you," Martin said.

I could see that Captain Angela Schiavo wanted to say the same. Wanted to do more than offer words. But the position she held, and the reality of the situation, dictated that the end which was dealt to her, and to Martin, should not be prolonged.

"Goodbye all," Schiavo said. "I wish you the best."

We boarded the lifeboat and it was lowered one more time into the slightly choppy waters a half mile off

Bandon's coastline. Its pilot sped us toward the harbor we'd departed from, the three of us looking back toward the ship that had carried us home. Dozens of those who still had days to go before reaching their own towns lined the rail on the upper decks and waved. Elaine and I put our hands in the air and returned the goodbye gestures.

Martin did not. He did nothing but stare through the open side door at the spot we'd been lowered from. The spot where Schiavo, where Angela, stood staring right back at him as we moved farther and farther away.

* * *

Ten minutes later we stood on the dock in Bandon's harbor and watched the lifeboat skim across the water back toward the *Northwest Majesty*. Soon she would sail southward and be gone from this place, from our presence, for good.

Martin turned away from the ocean and looked to the entirety of Bandon's population, all standing along the dock and the parking lot near the harbor. He paused for a moment, then looked to me, and to Neil, and to Elaine, before facing those he'd tried to shepherd through difficult times. Now, he hoped, there was some good to be found.

"According to our friends who traveled to Cheyenne," Martin began, "There might be something worth seeing up at the cemetery."

Some hopeful, expectant glances volleyed about amongst the crowd, but no one moved. Then, after a moment, the mass of people began to step aside, parting, leaving a pathway open for Martin to move. To lead them where we all wanted to go.

Fifty Three

Martin walked just ahead of us, chosen to be the first, four hundred and eight pairs of eyes looking past him. Scanning the way ahead up the trail to the cemetery. Just before he reached the low crest that blocked its view from the shore he stopped. Frozen in his tracks. His gaze angling down to the dirt path at his feet.

It was not only dirt. Something else was there. Sprouting up through the grey topsoil. Groping toward freedom and air and sunlight. Something green.

A weed.

Martin crouched and reached to the small miracle and touched it gently. A breath caught in his throat as emotion surged. He looked behind, to those who'd followed him along the path. His eyes glistened as his gaze met mine.

He rose and continued on, the mass of people behind walking around the lovely green weed, eyeing it with wonder. With hope.

"It worked," Neil said just behind me, an expression of welcome surprise about him. "It actually worked."

I didn't want to echo his sentiment. Not yet. But when we reached the crest of the path and looked fully upon the cemetery grounds, I knew. I knew that he was right. I knew that we'd succeeded.

Green...

It was lovely and real. There was grass and there were plants and there were trees. Flowers bloomed low, their colorful petals opened to soak in the sun.

"This is impossible," Elaine said as our fellow residents rushed past. "It's too fast."

"The good professor turned the blight on itself," Neil said. "He engineered its ability to destroy quickly into growth that happens just as quickly."

We'd considered that before. But the theory seemed more than proven here. There was no other explanation. Trees we'd planted a month before as seeds were now hip high. And, beyond that, there were more of them.

"We didn't plant anything over there," Elaine said, pointing toward the road that bordered the cemetery to the east.

We hadn't. Yet the carpet of grass that had sprouted from the few seeds we'd plunged into the earth between the headstones had crept that way. Life had spread. And was continuing to do so. Seeds spawned by the new plants had been carried on ocean breezes across the landscape.

Martin crossed the greening expanse, next to trees that seemed too perfect to be real. He let his hand rub across fat green leaves and brought his fingers to his nose to sample the scent.

"Apple," he said, looking to where Elaine and I trailed him a few feet behind. "I remember that smell."

A lot of sense memories were being stimulated, I suspected. Smell. Sight. And soon, hopefully, taste.

Martin continued on. I knew where he was going.

"Let's give him some time," I told Elaine.

She stopped next to me and we stood and watched Martin cross the newly green earth to where Micah was buried. He stood there, looking down upon his son's grave, and he began to weep.

"Let's go," I said.

Elaine and I rejoined the others across the cemetery, Neil coming toward us from the crowd.

"I was talking to Hal Robertson," my friend said. "He thinks the troops that disarmed everyone stored the weapons in the old Ford dealership. We'll have to check it out and organize a redistribution."

I thought for a moment on what he'd shared.

"In a day or two," I said, my response both tired and distant.

Neil picked up on my odd demeanor, but he didn't push the issue. He simply accepted my suggestion with a nod and turned, heading off to where Grace and Krista waited.

"You okay?" Elaine asked me.

I looked to her and I wanted to smile, but, at that very moment, I couldn't.

"Let's go," I told her.

She took my hand and we walked through the crowd and out of the cemetery, heading home.

Fifty Four

I woke to the feel of Elaine against my back, her left arm draped over me. Holding me close.

"Good morning," she said, her breath sweet and soft against the nape of my neck.

"What time is it?"

I rolled toward her, onto my back, and she propped herself up on one elbow, face hovering just above mine.

"Six, maybe six thirty," she guessed.

Guesses were all we had at the moment. No one had gone out to the spot on the Coquille where the hydro generator had once been driven by the steady current. A current which sometimes pushed as much debris through the submerged turbine as water. In our absence it had likely been clogged by bits of old, rotting wood that tumbled hourly into the waterway upstream. The backup solar panels were doing nothing of the sort, it appeared. Some damage to the lines that brought their harvested energy to town was probable. It would take time, a day or two, I imagined, before the juice would flow again to the implements of life. Implements that had survived the blight far better than their owners or creators. Refrigerators. Lamps. Saws. Drills. Pumps. Fans. Clocks.

We'd be back where we were, but not where we all wanted to be. That would take far longer. I'd be dust by then.

Some things, though, the intangibles, might never be the same. Connections. Relationships.

Friendships.

"Go talk to him," Elaine said, reading me, much like the friend she was referencing had the entire time we'd known each other.

"We just got back," I said.

"So you want to stew over this for a couple days? A few weeks? A month or two?"

I didn't, but that would be the likely avenue I'd choose. The path of resistance to looking my friend in the eye and confronting him with the lie he'd told me. The lie that informed so much of the experiences he'd shared from the moment he came to my business nearly two years earlier to warn me of the coming blight.

"He could have a good explanation," Elaine told me, though the hint of doubt about her as she gave the possibility voice did nothing to bolster any belief in it.

"I can't imagine one."

"All you're doing is imagining," she said. "Stop that and get the truth from him."

It was a simple enough direction. One that made sense. Except for the fact that having to pry for facts and reality from my friend was an alien endeavor. There was no way he could have lied to me about his presence in South America before the blight exploded northward, but he had. The lack of any stamps in his passport backed that belief.

"Go already," Elaine urged me.

"It's early," I said, trying to delay the inevitable.

She fixed a look on me. One that called out the BS I was shoveling better that any words could.

"Okay," I finally said, swinging my legs over the side of the bed. "I'll go."

I wasn't looking forward to any of what was about to come, but I couldn't avoid it. Not if our friendship meant anything to me. And it did.

It meant the world.

Fifty Five

The door was closed and the curtains were drawn. The new day was being shut out, morning denied entry to the home of my friend, his wife, and their little girl. All was quiet at the quaint house beyond the wide porch. Very quiet.

Too quiet.

I knocked, the screen door rattling with every tap of my fist upon it. Soon a press of the doorbell button would once again raise a tinny chime within. A porch light might still glow in the early wisps of daylight. But not now. At this moment, as I stood on my friend's porch, the house was as dead as it had been in our absence.

Something was wrong.

I pulled the screen door open and tried the knob beyond. It turned, the latch clicking as I pushed the front door inward.

"Neil..."

Silence. That was what greeted me.

"Grace..."

An unsettling stillness filled the front room. I stepped in, letting the screen door slap shut behind. Nothing appeared out of place. No furniture was disturbed. No items toppled. But something was there. Something that should not be.

Neil's AK. It lay on the coffee table, magazine attached. I stepped close and looked down upon the weapon. Its safety was on.

My hand shifted to the Springfield on my hip, hand resting atop the pistol, at the ready.

But ready for what?

"Neil, are you back there?"

I looked down the hallway as I asked the question in the emptiness. The bedroom doors were open, one on the left, and one on the right. The bathroom door, too, was not closed.

"Neil, I'm coming back there, okay?"

I expected no answer, and received none. My words were out of an abundance of caution. I didn't want to surprise my friend or his family if they were back there, unable to respond. Restrained. Even hurt.

Please, no...

The floorboards creaked lightly as I entered the hallway. I passed the bathroom first, its simple confines empty. Towels were draped neatly over a rack.

I moved on. To the next door. Krista's room on the right. I peered around the edge of the door jamb and saw the room empty, the bed unmade. It had been slept in. No clothes were strewn about. No mess other than that pink comforter peeled back and hanging over the edge of the mattress.

"Neil..."

I spoke my friend's name again simply because I wanted to hear his voice in return. I was wishing for that very thing. Worry was filling me now, and it crept into my throat, nearly choking me, bile-like. Impatience overpowered my sense of caution and I rushed to the next door, the final door, and looked into the room beyond. Neil and Grace's bedroom.

There was no one there. The covers on the bed were similarly dragged to one side, as if they'd been roused in a hurry. I stepped into the room and moved about the space. There was no sign of a struggle. No blood. No broken lamps or furniture.

"What the hell..."

I moved back through the house, through every room, opened every closet. Then I crossed the back yard to the garage and looked within, only to find nothing.

Nothing.

I almost cupped my hands around my mouth and shouted out my friend's name through the makeshift megaphone. Almost.

Only the odd, soft sound from the east stopped me.

It rose like a whisper. As if huge feathers were being whipped through the air. Loud enough to notice, yet hushed to the point that anyone still slumbering would not be jolted from sleep.

I scanned the sky over the neighborhood rooftops in the direction of the sound, which began to take on a rhythmic quality. Like a soft fluttering. A heartbeat with no low register. Wind pulsing.

Whoo... Whoo... Whoo... Whoo...

It almost sounded like...

"A helicopter," I said to myself.

It did sound like that, but with the volume dialed down to almost nothing. The recognition of what I was hearing, or thought I was hearing, registered both concern and wonder. I'd had experiences with rotorcraft that were both deadly, and welcome. One had tried to turn Neil and me to Swiss cheese at my Montana refuge. Another, of a slightly different kind, had very unexpectedly saved our asses on Mary Island.

If this was another visitor come by air, it might mirror either event I'd previously been party to. Or it might have come for reasons entirely different.

I left the back yard and moved onto the street, straining to catch a glimpse of the craft, its form still obscured by the low peaks of houses and the taller points of dead pines beyond. But the throb of its rotor was coming from the east. That much I could tell. And that made me wonder if Neil had somehow heard it, earlier than I had. Had he roused Grace and Krista to investigate?

No. I discarded that possibility almost immediately. He would not have taken them toward some unknown to investigate. And he would not have left his rifle at home if he'd gone on his own. With only the Springfield on my hip I felt half naked, but I'd only left the house to go to Neil's home. Lugging additional firepower hadn't seemed like a necessity at that point.

I hoped that it would not be now.

A door opened near the end of the block, Mrs. Amelia Shand, all eighty years of her, stepping onto the porch in her robe, narrowed gaze finding me as I passed.

"What is that noise, Eric?"

If the years had dulled any senses the aging widow possessed, hearing was not among them.

"I'm going to have a look, Mrs. Shand. Don't worry."

She nodded, annoyed at the early morning disturbance, and stepped back into her house. I moved past her residence, and the last two on the block, then started across a field that had long ago been covered with tall grass and flourishes of wildflowers when the spring rolled around. It would again, I was starting to believe. Soon, I hoped.

For now, though, it was dirt. An expanse of dried earth that I crossed to reach the dead woods beyond. I worked my way through the barren trees and over snapped logs and tangled branches. A clearing lay ahead. I knew this from numerous walks I'd taken and patrols I'd been part of after first arriving in Bandon. Through the grey trunks rising from the equally monochrome earth I could just glimpse that open area, the size of two football fields. More woods lay beyond, and the remains of a brushy hill hemmed the clearing in to the south. All in all, the wide space had once been a place where deer grazed, and where the adventurous rode dirt bikes.

Now, though, it was very plainly a landing field. The slate grey helicopter cruising toward it left no mistake about that.

With a whisper the craft sailed over the crumbling woods in the near distance, the wash of its spinning rotors snapping the tops from dead pine and fir trees as it passed over them. Low. Hardly a few yards between it and the barren peak of the once proud woods.

A helicopter. Different from any I'd ever seen.

No...

I corrected myself. I had seen it. Seen something like it. In the days and weeks after the raid that eliminated Osama Bin Laden in the middle of a Pakistani city, images of the once secret craft were splashed across news programs. It was a stealth version of the venerable Blackhawk helicopter, workhorse of the military. This one bore none of the rounded contours of its ancestor, though, sharp angles and geometric slabs forming its skin, tail rotor encased in an equally odd housing.

It settled onto the flat meadow as I came out of the woods. Its side door slid open and two men in dark military uniforms hopped out, suppressed ARs in hand, weapons sweeping the area and zeroing in on me. I made no move from my position thirty yards from the craft, and, more puzzling than their appearance from the sky, the troopers made no move toward me. From the corner of my eye I saw the reason why. They were waiting for what they'd come for. For who they'd come for.

Neil.

He jogged across the field with Grace and Krista at his side, each carrying just a small bag. Moving quickly until they were all at the helicopter. A crew chief within helped them climb in and began securing belts that would hold them in the simple seats.

That was when Neil glanced out the open door and saw me.

He hopped from the helicopter's cabin and put a hand to the arm of one of the soldiers. The trooper lowered his rifle, the other following his lead. My friend walked past them. Toward me. Meeting me where I stood in the dusty field, rotor wash spinning a whirlwind of parched earth around us.

"Neil, what the hell is going on?"

He looked at me for a moment. A stretch of silence that was so uncharacteristic for the man I knew. The man I'd known. My friend did not mince words with me. He never had.

But here, standing in the maelstrom of man-made wind, he seemed, if not at a loss, at least restrained in what he wanted to say. Or what he could say.

"Fletch, someone tells a story. Then someone repeats it. Then someone else does the same. By the tenth person, black is white and white is black."

"Neil, I don't understand."

"I know," he said. "I wish I could change that, but I can't."

I looked past him through the dirty haze. Grace and Krista were now belted into seats within the stealthy chopper. The former's gaze was fixed out the open door at me, a mix of regret and hope about her. She was sorry, but necessarily so. As if what was transpiring, though enigmatic, was not optionally avoided.

"Fletch..."

I faced my friend again. There was so much to say. Too many questions to ask. But, I suspected, there would be few, if any, answers offered. And, even worse, no time in which any explanation could be given.

"We have to go," he told me.

"Where? Why?"

I had to ask. Almost demand to know. None of what I was seeing made sense. And nothing that my friend was doing or saying gave me any insight, or any comfort, whatsoever.

"They wanted me to leave in Skagway, but I wouldn't. I wanted to get home. I thought it would be okay once we were here. That everything would work. But...I was wrong."

In Skagway? Was that what the fifth Osprey had been there for? To take my friend and his family away, as this sleek helicopter was about to do now, right in front of me?

"I'm sorry, Fletch."

He turned to walk away and I grabbed him by the arm. The two troopers advanced toward me through the dust. Once again my friend signaled for them to ease up. And once again they complied. They followed his direction. His command.

He was someone to them.

"Fletch, you have to let go. You have to let *me* go."

"Neil, how am I supposed to do that? After..."

After all that had happened. All that we'd been through. Suffered through. Overcome. I didn't have to voice those particulars. He knew.

"You're just going to leave?"

I thought I saw the beginning of a nod. But it never fully formed. Instead my friend gripped my arm now, and drew me close.

"Get out, Fletch," Neil said, keeping his back very purposely to the troopers. "Find a hole and bury yourself while there's still time."

I puzzled obviously at my friend's warning.

"What are you talking about?" I pressed him.

Neil chanced a glance behind and the troopers inched closer. He looked back to me, a deep, ominous worry in his eyes.

"Black is white," he reminded me. "White is black."

"Neil..."

He let go of my arm and eased his from my grip.

"You can't trust anyone," my friend said. "*Anyone.*"

My mind raced, chasing explanations as to what had happened to put my friend in this state. This state of vague warnings and some secretive plan to flee with his family, leaving all else behind. Me included.

"You don't have much time," he said.

I wanted to reach out and grab him again. Grab him and throw him to the ground and pummel him until some sense returned and he told me, without any crypticism, just what the hell was going on. But the firepower and muscle standing just yards away would make that a foolish act on my part. Maybe even a fatal one.

"That's it?" I pressed my friend. "You're just going? Leaving me here with no explanation?"

A warning horn sounded from the helicopter.

"We've gotta move!" one of the troopers shouted to Neil. "Now!"

My friend nodded and looked to me, a finality to the connection. As if he was severing all that we had ever been with a parting glance.

"I tried, Fletch," Neil said. "I really did."

"Tried what, Neil?"

All about him saddened right then. His face turned grim. Apologetic.

"To save everyone," my friend replied. "I couldn't."

Save? From what? The questions were bursting in my head like blinding fireworks, popping off painfully close.

"I have to save who I can, Fletch."

He gestured with a sideways nod toward the chopper. To Krista, and to Grace, and their unborn child.

"I'm sorry," Neil said, his last words to me.

Then he turned away and jogged back toward the troopers, passing between them and climbing into the helicopter next to Grace and Krista. The armed duo kept their weapons low, but their eyes stayed focused on me as they backed toward the chopper, joining the others inside. The side door slid shut, leaving just a small window

through which I could see inside. Neil looked out, meeting
my gaze as the rotor spun up, wind blasting across the dirty
field, a muffled *whop whop whop* rolling across the
landscape as the chopper rose into the air, floating upward,
finally banking right, its nose diving as it sped east toward
the rising sun.

He was gone. My friend was gone.

And I was left to wonder why.

Part Six

Voices

Fifty Six

Much happened in the following months as summer spilled into fall, and fall into winter.

The fruit trees that were waist high when we returned from Skagway now reached higher than Bandon's tallest person, Greta Beane, a former national volleyball standout who towered gracefully over the townspeople at six feet and six inches. They sprouted fruit by Thanksgiving and, in defiance of what had been some natural seasonal order, produced even as the chill of the season took hold. Similarly, the vegetables, both root and stalk, flourished, adding to the plain and preserved foodstuffs all had become accustomed to. Grass seeds that we'd planted prior to heading north in search of our friends had sprouted and spread, carpeting the fields beyond the cemetery with a green that was natural and gorgeous and cool underfoot.

The seeds we'd brought home from Cheyenne, seeds which had been crafted through trial and error while the master of the process was slowly starving to death, had germinated and thrived at the accelerated speed we'd expected after seeing the growth in the Wyoming greenhouse, and confirmed upon our return to Bandon. There had always been that fear that, out of a controlled environment, we'd find that they would mature at a normal pace, denying us of any usable bounty for many months, if not years. Or, worse still, that no growth would happen at all. The blight, we knew, had not gone away. It surrounded us still. It infected the soil. The air.

But it had been beaten. At least here. This land, our land, was turning green again. The fields were alive, if silent. Hills once grey and barren were sprouting wildflowers and weeds from generational seeds carried on the ocean breezes, offspring of the first plants. And the cycle had begun. Life, which had been absent in this form for more than two years, had returned.

Then, a week before Christmas, the boat came.

It was large and squat and grey, approaching from the north to anchor a mile offshore. Navy was my first thought. Nearly everyone's first thought. The real Navy. *Our* Navy.

A trio of Air Cushion Vehicles, what were commonly referred to as hovercraft, spilled out of its open stern well and ran toward the beaches south of town, dragging roostertails of sea spray behind. Most of Bandon's residents gathered on the coast road to meet the vessels. Arms were plentiful. But no one harbored any illusions of resistance against what was charging toward land.

Then again, no one expected that this was any sort of hostile act requiring a coordinated defense. What we were witnessing, we believed, was the fulfillment of a promise.

Schiavo hadn't been blowing smoke after all.

"LSD Forty Seven," Doc Allen said, lowering the binoculars through which he'd been surveying the operation unfolding offshore. "Landing Ship Dock."

"Dock Landing Ship," Ken Petrie corrected from behind. "That's the *Rushmore*."

Ken had spent thirty years in the Navy and had retired to Bandon hoping to spend his best years fishing and hunting. That was a year before the blight. Now he was helping to identify the vessel that might very well be bringing us still more hope of both surviving, and thriving.

"Those are LCACs heading our way," Ken added, adding more specificity to the identity of the watercraft. "Landing Craft Air Cushion."

The first LCAC hit the beach and scooted across the damp sand. It slowed and stopped a dozen yards from the road, its billowing side skirts collapsing as the engines throttled down, sand blasting from beneath, the solid hull settling gently to earth. Upon it we could see vehicles. Trucks. No true uniformity to their color, but a certain beefiness to them that screamed military grade. Their engines rumbled to life, black smoke belching from vertical exhausts, diesel engines spinning up.

But before any vehicle moved toward the unfolding bow ramp, a figure descended. A familiar face.

Schiavo.

I glanced toward Martin where he stood a few yards away and saw a small, true smile build upon his face as she approached.

"Captain," Martin said in greeting, offering his hand.

Schiavo, in a mottled grey camouflage uniform, took his hand in hers and shook it. Then she held on. Or he did. It was only for an instant longer than necessary, but that it happened made me smile.

Schiavo looked to me, and to Elaine, then let her gaze sweep slowly over the rest of the town's residents who had come in greeting. Who had come with hope.

"We have some things for you," Schiavo said.

Someone cheered. Then applause built. The clapping rippled through the crowd as trucks began to roll off of the LCACs and onto the sand, forming a line that drove onto the road and convoyed slowly into town.

"I recall you said you had functioning freezers," Schiavo said.

"We do," Martin confirmed.

"Good, because we have frozen turkey," Schiavo said. "And chicken. And beef. Fish. Vegetables. Even some ice cream."

The assembled crowd behind me first murmured what they were hearing between the applause. Then they shouted it to each other. Real food, not something out of a pouch or can, had been delivered. The cheer that erupted and rolled toward Schiavo upon that new reality setting in almost drown out the sound of the final trucks rolling off the last LCAC.

Then we all went silent when we saw what was borne on the backs of each of those vehicles.

"That's a cow," six year old Evelyn Mercer said, correctly identifying the beast contained on one of the trucks.

But it wasn't just one cow. It was seven. Plus an equal number of steer. And there were goats. And pigs. And cages of chickens. Ducks. Some other birds and other land animals that I was too quietly giddy to identify.

"Aerial survey a month ago showed the fields around Bandon were greening up nicely," Schiavo reported.

We'd heard an aircraft around that time, I recalled. Flying south to north just inland from the coast, at maybe ten thousand feet altitude. Its presence had startled some, and caused worry in others, but almost as soon as it had arrived, it was gone.

"They'll support grazing soon," the captain continued. "But we brought you some machinery that will process the blighted trees and vegetation into feed that will keep the herd and flocks viable until the fields are fully established."

As she finished, the LCACs, empty now, buttoned up and revved their powerplants, rising up on the beach, sand billowing as they turned and rode their cushions of air back onto the water toward the *Rushmore*.

"They have another five loads each to bring in for you," Schiavo said. "And some help. A doctor."

Eyes angled toward Doc Allen. His aged eyes welled as his wife hugged him from the side, a warm and thankful smile building as he fixed on Schiavo.

"Does this mean my social security will start paying again?" he asked with genuine humor.

"I'll see what I can do," Schiavo said, focusing on the crowd again. "A small unit will also offload with the supplies. Just six strong. They'll be staying as a sort of garrison. To help. To protect. Though I doubt they'll be much need of that."

"We've managed that pretty good ourselves," Oren Kelly reminded her from the crowd.

"No doubt about that," Schiavo said. "Their commanding officer will only act in consultation with your leadership."

Then she looked to Martin. Straight at him. And again she smiled within the officiousness of what she was reporting.

"I believe you'll all get along well with her."

Martin's head cocked just a bit with understanding.

"You..."

Schiavo nodded.

"And my guys," Schiavo said. "Well, guys plus one."

Martin soaked in the news. He'd lost so much. Given up so much. All so the town, his town, our town, could survive. If some small measure of happiness could be his with Captain Angela Schiavo putting down some semblance of roots here, that was the least he deserved.

"The plan is for resupply visits every two to three months," Schiavo said, then she turned to me and Elaine. "Those seeds you recovered, and the process outlined in the notebook, well..."

"They replicated it," Elaine said. "Your people did what the professor did and it worked, didn't it?"

Schiavo breathed, relieved to be able to bring us the news directly.

"Yes," she said. "There's now a sustainable way to produce blight resistant seeds and plants. Anywhere we want."

For some reason, this news struck a joyous nerve within Elaine. She turned toward me and leaned her face against my shoulder. Tears welled and she smiled.

"It's over," Elaine said. "The blight is over."

"Nothing left for it to kill," Schiavo confirmed. "Anything that grows now is immune."

Martin almost couldn't believe it.

"Over," he said, the word spoken mostly with breath, as one might a quiet prayer.

Schiavo looked past me, to the crowd beyond, searching. For someone. I knew who.

"Your friend," she said. "Where is he? And his family?"

I should have been the one to tell her. To share the tale and the details that only I knew. But it was Elaine that explained what had transpired.

"A stealth Blackhawk?" Schiavo asked, mildly incredulous.

"Yeah," I confirmed.

"You saw that with your own eyes?" she pressed. "That's what picked them up?"

I nodded. She looked away for a moment, thoughts seeming to swarm her suddenly.

"What is it?" Elaine asked.

Schiavo looked back to me, to us.

"Let's talk after my unit hits shore."

Fifty Seven

We set up tables and chairs in the meeting hall, approximating the look of a conference room. Mostly the tables were so we had a place to set our coffee cups as we settled in to listen to Captain Schiavo.

"When everything went to pieces, there was a time when no one knew who was in charge," she said, addressing Martin, Elaine, and me.

We sat on one side of the table, Schiavo at the end, the entirety of her unit opposite us. Lorenzen, Enderson, Westin, and Hart. And a new face. Quincy. Specialist Sheryl Quincy. To look at her it was hard to imagine that she was a replacement for Acosta. He was bulk and fury in battle. This petite soldier seemed so far from that physicality that it was almost jarring.

But if Schiavo had brought her, had chosen her, I had to give credence to that, and suppress any chauvinistic impulses I had that were judging the newcomer based upon appearances alone.

"For a while there were competing governments issuing orders," Schiavo went on, looking to Elaine and me with purpose. "Your man who had authorization to launch that missile in Wyoming...the okay came from one of the rival governments. Not the real one."

I turned to Elaine. We said nothing, but I could sense that she was feeling exactly what I was—gratitude. A thankfulness that we'd convinced Ben, Colonel Ben Michaels, to use the nuke to save our own skins. In doing so we'd preserved the seeds and, maybe, helped save the world. But we'd also inadvertently prevented an American city, Duluth, from being vaporized.

"Over the last six months everything got folded back into place," Schiavo said. "The factions coalesced around the president. The one who actually got the job because people voted for him. That's where my orders come from. From the real commander in chief through his designated military commanders."

She paused there. Not nervous, but almost on edge. Maybe even angry to the slightest degree.

"Eric, what you described, the troops and the bird you saw, that was not authorized by the president," Schiavo said. "Or anyone in his government."

She didn't say outright what she was conveying. But it was plain enough.

"There's still another faction operating," I said.

"Yes," she said. "One that's well equipped, according to what you saw. Gear and transport like that isn't just left around for the taking."

"That means entire units have gone over to this faction," Elaine said.

Schiavo nodded.

"We were wondering why the White Signal was still broadcasting," Schiavo said.

"This other faction," Elaine said. "They have the satellite, don't they?"

Schiavo nodded, just a hint of grim concern in the admission.

"I already passed on what you told me through a burst transmission. If there are any orders because of that situation, I'll let you know. Right away. Fair enough?"

I nodded. So did Elaine. Martin, though, gave no indication of reply. He'd said not a word since we'd sat down with our coffee to hear the captain out.

"Martin..."

I spoke his name to draw his attention. But he did not look to me when he finally spoke. It was to Schiavo that he set his gaze.

"Captain, you should know," he began, "that I don't intend..."

He hesitated there. Elaine glanced my way, concerned.

"Martin, what is it?" I asked.

Now he turned, facing me from where he sat, Elaine between us.

"No one ever elected me to anything," he said. "I just fell into this role because of Micah. There's no reason I should be sitting at this table any more than anyone else in this town. Certainly not more than you."

I wasn't sure where he was going with this stream of spoken consciousness. That he'd been Bandon's leader, elected or otherwise, was something all had accepted. Because of Micah, or not, he'd nonetheless exhibited a way with the reins of power. Sometimes he had wielded it with force through subordinates, as when we'd first landed in Bandon in search of an enigmatic locale we knew only through equally cryptic radio broadcasts. But he'd also shown a depth of understanding on that very same night. In the hours that followed our arrival when he introduced us to his son. To the savant who was, for all intents and purposes, the Eagle One we'd been searching for.

Bandon was Martin's home. But Micah was his life. His reason for being. For surviving. When the boy, his boy, died peacefully in his sleep, I'd sensed that a large part of who Martin Jay was evaporated into the ether. His position as the de facto leader of the four hundred plus people who called Bandon home had been predicated mostly on what the child had provided for the community, and in the short span between Micah's passing and our departure for Wyoming, Martin's sense of purpose had seemed to dim. Now, as he spoke to us in the meeting hall where hundreds had once gathered to hear him discuss town business, only a few hung on his words. To him, I thought, it was the few who mattered most.

"I'm done," Martin said. "I'm not in charge anymore."

"Martin..."

Elaine was quietly surprised. Maybe shocked to a degree. I suspected any of Bandon's residents who heard what we just had would react similarly.

"I never wanted this," he said. "I've been proud to do what I have, and I've tried to do what I thought was best, but now..."

He didn't finish. His gaze simply shifted toward the one who'd called us all to this meeting.

Schiavo met his look. Her eyes glistened slightly. Martin smiled and slid his chair back, standing for a moment. Not moving. He cleared his throat, some emotion threatening to overwhelm.

Then, he left us. Walked out of the meeting house, just Martin Jay, citizen of Bandon, Oregon.

Elaine stared at the table for a moment before looking up.

"Now what?" she asked.

From the end of the table an answer came. A suggestion that was the most logical way forward.

"Sounds like an election is in order," Specialist Sheryl Quincy said.

Schiavo let the flourish of emotion she'd allowed fade, then looked to the newest member of her unit. Quincy immediately feared she'd stepped out of line by expressing a course of action before her commander could weigh in.

"My thoughts exactly, Specialist," Schiavo said.

Fifty Eight

An odd normalcy began to settle over the town of Bandon following the *Rushmore*'s arrival and departure.

For Christmas we had ham. Thawed and smoked by an eager group of men from the street bordering the park. Those who wanted to were invited to a community dinner in the meeting hall. Those who desired a more traditional feast with those closest to them came and picked up plentiful portions, along with the vegetable and potato side dishes, and returned to their homes to celebrate in a more intimate fashion.

More came together to ring in the New Year. Someone had found an old supply of fireworks and we rang in the stroke of midnight watching rockets burst over the Pacific, drizzling blue and red and green sparkles upon the black water.

One of the town's children, Lexi Overstreet, a girl of eight, proclaimed loudly over the staccato noise of the celebration that this was the best New Years *ever!*

For some reason that appraisal buoyed me. It was simple and joyous and unsullied by what she, and everyone, had been through over the past months and years.

The fields beyond town had been fenced to contain the cows, and cattle, and sheep, and myriad of other livestock the *Rushmore* had delivered. Residents with ranching experience stepped up to the plate and tended to the herds. Chickens, which had numbered in the low hundreds when brought ashore, had more than doubled in number. Eggs were plentiful, and, when the hen population was stabilized, fresh fowl would be available to all on an ongoing basis.

An election had been held, not long after Martin announced, to us first and to the entire town the next day, that he was ceding any authority that had been granted him. He'd simply said that he wanted to attempt having some sort of normal life. There were worries that he could not be replaced. But, in the end, when the town coalesced around a single candidate, unanimity replaced any concern.

Everett Allen had been chosen for the position of Bandon's new Mayor. Doc Allen. He'd accepted the responsibility, joking that he needed something to do now that there was a Navy doctor to handle the majority of the town's medical needs. His wife, he'd also explained, couldn't stand him under foot all the time at home, so keeping busy with the business of Bandon was his only way to keep from scuttling a fifty year marriage.

The person most happy, though, about Doc Allen taking the municipal reins was Martin Jay.

I'd feared that in the absence of some structure to his existence he would be forced to face the loss he'd suffered without distraction. Without the buffer of responsibility to focus his thoughts and actions elsewhere.

That did not happen.

What I'd first noticed hints of in Skagway, some nascent connection between Martin and Captain Schiavo, had developed even further on the voyage back home aboard the *Northwest Majesty*. Once he'd distanced himself from the day to day leadership of the town, I began to see them together more and more. He always maintained a respectful distance from her when she was on duty, but in those times when she switched from urban camo to blue jeans and a blouse, they seemed to enjoy each other's company more and more. It seemed clear to me, and to

Elaine, to everyone who spent any time around them, in fact, that a relationship was blossoming.

That was confirmed to me on a rainy day in January when Martin knocked on my door. On our door.

"Martin," Elaine said, opening the door to find our friend standing in the shelter of our porch.

Our porch...

Elaine had moved in with me. In the new world, even one that seemed to be creeping toward a normalcy that bore small resemblances to the old world, moving in required little more than shifting several duffels of clothing and personal items, along with a few favored pieces of furniture, from her house to mine. At first it had felt odd, sharing this space, my space, with another. And it still did, though the reasoning behind it had changed.

Neil and Grace had sealed their union. They'd been married, in a ceremony before those that cared for them. Those that knew them. Even with my friend's absence weighing heavy still, and an anger toward him that I could not yet process away, the path he had chosen had always seemed the right one. The proper one.

Elaine, though, was hesitant. When I'd broached the subject of marriage, a construct that, even in this most tumultuous time, was based upon ideals I held dear, she'd seemed only mildly tolerant of the possibility *someday*.

I loved her. And I knew she loved me. But I also knew I could not force the issue with her. She'd suffered loss in the unknowns surrounding her brother's fate. And, as odd as it seemed, what my friend had warned me about—not putting myself in a position to witness something terrible happening to Elaine—might be at least part of what was influencing her reluctance to make our relationship permanent in a traditional sense.

So when Martin came to our house dripping from the downpour, I had no idea that the request he was about to make would change my life. And Elaine's.

"I'm going to ask Angela to marry me," Martin said as he sat in the living room with Elaine and me.

"Martin," Elaine said, standing to lean across the coffee table and give him a quick hug. "That is so, so wonderful."

"It is, Martin," I echoed.

Elaine sat next to me again and put her hand atop mine, gripping it firmly.

"I think she'll say yes," Martin said.

"She will," Elaine said, calmly giddy. "I know she will."

Girl talk. That was what came to mind. The thoughts that the fairer sex share only with each other. Elaine had spent enough time with Angela to have some sense of where her feelings toward Martin stood. The certainty she expressed about his proposal being accepted convinced me of that.

Martin and I, on the other hand, usually talked about fishing when we spent any time together.

"The reason I'm telling you this is..."

He hesitated there, trying to choose his words, it seemed.

"Would Micah have liked her?"

His question was posed with true, heartbreaking emotion.

"I know he's not here, but I can't imagine myself with anyone that he wouldn't have...loved."

It was more than touching what he was feeling. Not doubt, but a desire for confirmation that his son, by proxy, would approve of the woman who was very clearly making him happy. That he considered Elaine and me to be those who might serve as the conscience of his departed son made me, and her, I was certain, feel honored.

"Martin," I said, and he looked to me. "If you and Angela hadn't found each other, I think Micah would have found her for you."

Elaine squeezed my hand and looked to me, the barest skim of emotion in her gaze.

"Thank you, Eric," Martin said. "Thank you, Elaine. Both of you. I really don't know what I..."

He stopped there. That road led to melancholy. To bitter memory. And he wanted none of that now. Not here. Not with this decision made.

"I'm glad you're my friends," Martin said.

* * *

We lay in bed with the window open and rain pattering on the greening earth outside.

"Do you think they'll have kids?"

Elaine asked the question with her head resting on my chest, the both of us gazing past the fluttering curtains at the trickles of water spilling off the eaves.

"That's a tough one," I said.

Martin was in his early forties. Angela her mid-thirties. Age was no barrier. But other factors would obviously influence any decision in that arena.

"I want a child," Elaine said.

For an instant what she'd said didn't register. Then, as if there'd been a thunderclap from the storm, it did, and my head angled slowly toward her. She looked up at me and rose up on her elbows, face hovering over mine.

"Is that a crazy thing to want in this world?" she asked me.

"No," I said. "It's not. It's absolutely sane. On every level."

She looked at me, surprised at the quiet fervor of my acceptance of her desire.

"Without new life, we go away," I told her. "Humankind."

"So it's just a question of biology," she said, half grinning.

"No," I assured her. "It's more than that. It's..."

I couldn't say it. Elaine sensed what I wanted to say, and why it was difficult to do so.

"It's a statement of hope," she said for me.

Hope...

I could have let thoughts of my friend rise right then, possibly to overwhelm what was happening between Elaine and me. But I didn't. Neil Moore was not the exclusive purveyor of hope. Of a belief in tomorrow. And his absence didn't diminish the importance of it.

"Yes it is," I said.

There was something else that was a statement of hope. Or that would be.

"Excuse me," I said.

I slipped out of bed. Elaine sat halfway up and pulled the comforter up to cover herself against the night's soothing chill. She watched me go to the closet and reach to a shelf within, retrieving a small pouch. With the tiny fabric bag in hand I returned to the bed and sat on the edge next to her.

"Hold out your hand," I said.

She puzzled at my cryptic manner, then eased a hand from beneath the covers and extended it, palm up. I held the bag over it and tipped it upside down, letting the contents spill out.

A ring.

Her gaze fixed on the simple band and the even simpler stone set into it.

"I went looking through the shops in Skagway before we left," I said.

Her face was blank with surprise. As if some wholly unexpected event had occurred, either disaster or miracle.

"Now, that can be just a ring," I said. "A gift. Something you wear. Or..."

"Or..."

Her prompting warmed the already true smile upon my face.

"Or it can be *the* ring," I told her. "The one that really means something."

She looked again to the simple piece of jewelry, still resting in her palm.

"Which kind of ring do you want it to be?" I asked her.

Slowly, she began to smile. Then her gaze rose to meet mine.

"I want a child, too," I said. "Children, actually. And I want them with you. I want us to be a real us. Do you understand?"

For a moment she just looked at me, the hard, almost harsh woman I'd known her as when first arriving in Bandon a distant, impossibly inaccurate memory now. She was strong and smart and vulnerable and tough and beautiful. She was everything to me.

"Eric..."

"Yes?"

"Will you ask the damn question already?"

So I did. And she said yes. I slipped the simple ring carried home from Alaska onto the third finger of her left hand. Then I kissed her, and I held her, and we lay in each other's arms, listening to the fresh rain fall as we drifted off to sleep.

Fifty Nine

We sat in the park, the four of us. Martin, Angela, Elaine, and me. On benches near the field where plastic turf had once spread its manufactured greenness across the space. That was gone, dirt left in its place. An expanse of still infected earth surrounded by yellow tape. Earth that bore the tiniest of green sprouts. Blades of grass, real grass, that were feeling the winter sun upon them.

"I can smell it," Angela said, the civvies she wore a very purposeful reminder that, for the moment, she was not Captain Schiavo. "That grass smell. Can you?"

We all sampled the air, noses twitching to inhale what was carried on the soft breeze.

"I smell it," Elaine said.

"It's been so long since I smelled that," Angela said.

Martin looked to me and gave a facial shrug.

"Must be a girl thing," he said. "I smell steak."

Elaine and Angela smirked at the comment, but Martin was right. Someone was grilling up beef, maybe a street over from the park. An offering to the meat gods in honor of the coming spring. I looked into the wind, toward where the scent originated, and I kept looking. Away from the conversation. Away from my friends.

"You're quiet," Martin said.

I turned to him now. I was quiet. It was a silence not born of sadness, but of realization.

"What is it?" Elaine asked, putting her hand gently on the back of mine.

I smiled before I spoke. Because it was a happy thought that had seized me, even if it was wrapped in so much worry and discord.

"She'd be due about now," I said, and those with me knew who I was talking about.

"Grace," Elaine said.

We'd hardly spoken about her, or Krista, or Neil in the months since they'd left. For a while after that event, beginning with the stealth chopper rising into the sky and disappearing over the dead woods to the east, I'd obsessed about my friend's departure. His inexplicable and enigmatic flight from me, and from a place I'd thought, that I'd truly believed, he saw as his home. A depression gripped me. I wondered if there was something I should have seen. Something I should have known. I punished myself for not reading more into the lie he'd told. A lie I still had no full understanding of, but which, I suspected, played a part in the why of his leaving.

My friend, I now knew, hadn't just been keeping secrets. He'd been cultivating them.

"I hope Krista gets a brother," Martin said. "That's what I hope."

"She'd love a little guy," Elaine agreed. "So would Grace."

Angela offered no comment. I suspected she felt incapable of making any relevant observation on the state of my friend's family. Her interaction with him, and them, had been brief, and mostly official. Only on the transit back to Bandon had she interacted in an informal manner with those we now spoke of, but even those moments had been brief.

"He'd love a son," I finally chimed in. "His dad would have been a terrific grandfather. What that kid would have gotten from that man..."

And there I stopped. I didn't want to dredge a loss some distance in the past and sully it with what Neil had done. His father, a man I respected greatly, had died, cancer eating him up as the blight exploded. That was what Neil had told me, at least.

I shook my head, openly.

"You can't keep doing this to yourself," Elaine told me.

Spring weddings were ahead for us. Martin and Angela in late March, and Elaine and me in early April. That was a joy that lay ahead for us. I wanted to focus on that. I needed to. I knew that.

But knowing it did not make putting my friend and his family out of my mind easy by any measure.

"Sorry," I said to her, and to the others. "I just find myself questioning everything he's told me since..."

I'd tried to move beyond the constant doubt. Some days I was successful in doing that. Most, though, some recollection crept into my thoughts and, again, I would weigh what Neil had said against what he had ended up doing. And when I found reason for suspicion in his statements, a sense of failure on my part would flourish, if only briefly. But every instance of that grated on me. Inside. I had been fooled, been made a fool of, by the very person I'd always, *always*, believed had my best interests in mind when he acted.

"Why did the chicken cross the road?" Martin asked out of the blue.

I looked at him and had to smile.

"Why?"

"To get away from your depressing ass," he said, offering what had to be the most perfect punchline ever crafted for the clichéd joke.

Angela looked to me and tried not to laugh. She failed, the giddy reaction bursting from her. Elaine joined in. Then Martin. With laughter rolling from the trio of my friends, I could resist no further, and doubled over, the cathartic release almost overwhelming me.

We laughed, and laughed, lost so deeply in the absurd humor of the moment that we almost missed Corporal Enderson racing across the park, small radio in hand. His expression was not frantic, but confused.

"Cap'n," he called out as he neared and stopped.

Schiavo quieted and stood from where she sat next to Martin. He, too, rose, eyeing the youngish soldier with a hint of concern. Elaine glanced to me, the same vague worry sparking in her gaze, the joy that had filled us for a few moments wiped away.

"What is it, Mo?" Angela asked, addressing him informally in some attempt to ease his obvious tension.

It didn't work.

"The White Signal," Enderson said. "It just stopped."

"Stopped?"

"Yes, ma'am."

Schiavo eyed the radio in his grip.

"Let me have a listen, corporal" she said.

She was Schiavo now. Captain Angela Schiavo. She'd reverted to the formality expected in any interaction when civilians were present.

But Enderson didn't follow her instruction. Not immediately.

"It stopped," the corporal repeated. "But something else started right up."

"A new transmission?" Elaine asked.

Enderson nodded, an uncertainty about the gesture. As though he was unsure just what it was he was confirming.

"Let me see that."

Schiavo held her hand out and the soldier put the radio in it. She focused on the display, electronic bars rising and falling, indication of a transmission in absence of the volume being turned up.

"What did you hear?" Martin asked.

Enderson thought for a moment, his gaze lost, then he shook his head.

"You all should listen for yourselves," the corporal said.

I rose, Elaine following, joining Martin where he stood close to Schiavo and Enderson. The captain reached to the volume knob and advanced it slowly.

A faint voice crackled within the static. Repeating a single word again and again.

"Ranger. Ranger. Ranger."

Then it would quiet. A few seconds later the word would be spoken again. In the same sequence. The same tone.

"Ranger. Ranger. Ranger."

A familiar tone.

Enderson looked to me. Then Martin did. Then Schiavo. Finally Elaine added her gaze to those fixed upon me. Eyes watching for my reaction. Friends hurting, for me, at what we were all hearing on the radio. At who.

"That's Neil's voice," Elaine said.

"Ranger. Ranger. Ranger."

I nodded. Then I reached to Schiavo and took the radio from her and shut it off, silencing my friend's voice.

Thank You

I hope you enjoyed *The Pit*. Please look for other books in *The Bugging Out Series*.

About The Author

Noah Mann lives in the West and has been involved in personal survival and disaster preparedness for more than two decades. He has extensive training in firearms, as well as urban and wilderness Search & Rescue operations, including tracking and the application of technology in victim searches.

Made in the USA
Middletown, DE
23 July 2017